THE AMULET
OF ELEMENTS

THE AMULET
OF ELEMENTS

Rose Marie Machario

Cover art: Randy Humphrey
Cover art in this book copyright © 2019 Randy Humphrey &
Seventh Star Press, LLC.

Editor: Holly Marie Phillippe
Published by Seventh Star Press, LLC.

ISBN Number: 978-1-948042-79-6

Seventh Star Press
www.seventhstarpress.com
info@seventhstarpress.com

Publisher's Note:
The *Amulet of Elements* is a work of fiction. All names, characters,
and places are the product of the author's imagination, used in
fictitious manner. Any resemblances to actual persons, places,
locales, events, etc. are purely coincidental.

Printed in the United States of America

First Edition

DEDICATION

For my children who inspired me to write this book. To my family and friends who helped me along the way, never allowing me give up. To my dad who will never get to read my words.

A special thanks to Stephen and Holly for believing in my story, and who brought me into the Seventh Star Press family. To Ashley Burt who created the real-life replica of the Amulet. To Les Murphy who helped bring my vision for the cover to reality with his original concept art. To Randy Humphrey who designed the cover art that you want to get lost in.

This book is also dedicated to everyone out there who has ever doubted their creative worth. Never give up, and always dream big...

Once upon a time, in a world where evil ruled and magic was practiced openly. This story is unlike any fairy tale ever told, because it is not a fairy tale at all. It is a true story about a princess and a prophecy...

CHAPTER 1

Princess Ellyria Rose could not understand why she was seemingly held prisoner in her own castle. Her only true friend was her oversized, solid-black wolf, Isis, gifted to her at birth. Isis was her best friend and guardian; she never left her side. Often times, the pair could be seen splashing about in the fountain that stood in the royal courtyard. The stone carved to perfection, the fountain was statuesque in appearance with a rainbow of orchids and lilies surrounding it. Inside the main fountain base were fine details of what appeared to be a giant flower stretching toward the heavens from its circular pedestal. The water was not very deep, so it was perfect for splashing about and cooling off in the summer sun. The fountain was a magical place for Princess Ellyria, it was her soul's pleasance.

Everyday life for her consisted of lessons and the etiquette of becoming a lady, which was quite boring to Princess Ellyria. Reading was her only escape into worlds far beyond her wildest dreams. She longed to experience adventures like the characters in her favorite books. In the many books that she had read, women were always depicted as the fairer sex. They needed shelter, protection, were unable to stand on their own two feet, and always portrayed as damsels in distress. Sometimes she felt that way about herself, for she did not possess the skills of a knight, nor the brains of an alchemist, certainly not the leadership qualities of a king, and she could not train a dragon if her life depended on it. Which was why she envied her four older brothers, it seemed to her that they had it so much easier than she simply because they were men. While her brothers were off being heroes, she was never allowed to go along because her nanny said it was unladylike. She felt it was unfair for her to be left behind, in what felt like a prison without walls with only her needlepoint and studies. More than anything, she wanted to be more like her older brothers, because they had the most noble of duties and made their parents proud.

"I wish I had been born a male instead. I would have my choice of noble duties," she said as she stared at her reflection in the mirror. Princess Ellyria wanted to have her own purpose, and to be able to live her own dreams, alas it seemed she could reach for the stars only in her imagination. Her brothers all had a purpose, and were living out their dreams, so why could she not? They were the heroes of this story, and she was just the damsel in distress. Of course, she would not trade her brothers for anything in the world. She was now closer to them than she had ever been and she loved them as much as they loved her. Yet, she still yearned for adventures of her own and could not shake the feeling that she was missing out on her own life.

She brought herself back to the task at hand and gazed upon her reflection once more. It would not be too long now before her mother arrived to see if she was ready. She began putting the final touches on her hair and makeup when her mother walked in.

"I see you are just about finished, my dear," her mother said.

"Yes, mother."

"All of the guests have finally arrived. They are here just for you, you know."

"Yes, I know." Princess Ellyria's response sounded weak, even to her.

"What is the matter, darling?"

"Nothing, I am fine. Just a little nervous is all." It was hard to shield her emotions from her mother.

When Princess Ellyria was growing up, all she ever knew was her family. Now she was about to be thrown out there for all to see, or perhaps even scrutinize. What if she could not live up to everyone's expectations of her? Still, she knew she should put all her fears to rest. She was sixteen now, nearly a grown woman. So what if all those at court did not welcome her into their circles? She was still the Princess. After another glance in the mirror, she rose with faux confidence that she did not quite feel yet. If she did not act the part, she would disappoint her mother, and she could not do that. She had to face her fears one way or another.

"I am ready now," Princess Ellyria said.

Queen Anna extended her hand to her daughter. This was her daughter's big moment, she thought with pride in her smile.

"Then let us not keep them waiting. Shall we?"

Linking arms, they left the room to attend to their waiting guests.

At the top of the stairway leading down into the royal ballroom, Princess Ellyria paused and looked at all the elaborate decorations. Lanterns were hung from the cathedral ceiling, garlands of flowers had been draped in every archway, and an ice sculpture of a mermaid spouting wine from her mouth into a fountain had been placed in the main foyer. It was an amazing sight to behold, she mused.

At the bottom of the stairs stood her older brothers all dressed in the royal colors, and they were as handsome as ever. They looked up at their mother (still very beautiful, even at her age) and sister. With her mother as her escort, she slowly descended the great stairway. As they arrived at the foot of the stairs, two of her brothers held out their arms to accompany the ladies to the royal ballroom, while the other two walked protectively behind them. There King Jason, both a father and a husband, sat on his throne awaiting their arrival.

Once she had seated herself upon her throne, the wide-eyed princess skimmed through the vast throng of people in attendance just for her. Awestruck, she watched all the people as they laughed, danced, and dined in her honor. It was then that her gaze fell upon him as he entered from across the hall. He was announced as Lord Brom, and she could not look away, it was as if she had fallen into a trance. He was very handsome, fair-haired, and quite tall, with broad shoulders and a proud walk. She began to drift off, and started daydreaming of what it would be like if he kissed her.

"Your Majesties," Lord Brom said, snapping her out of her fantasies as he bowed before the royal family.

While she had been distracted with her thoughts, he had walked over and now stood in front of her father.

"I am Lord Brom, and I wish to ask permission to have a dance with the Princess."

"That would be up to her, Lord Brom," the King replied with a smile aimed toward his daughter. He was pleased that such a young man of his stature was interested in her.

Princess Ellyria was so nervous that even her stomach turned over in protest. She was intently staring at the marble floor, as if she were trying to analyze its properties, when his shadow crept over her feet.

"May I have this dance?" Lord Brom asked, holding his hand out to her.

Princess Ellyria slowly looked up. She sat there, silent and hesitant, not knowing what to say, until she finally managed some words.

"Yes you may, kind sir," she answered, placing her hand in his.

Lord Brom escorted the Princess out to the middle of the ballroom floor. Everyone else cleared a path, as many onlookers began watching the young couple at the center of the dance floor.

The King nodded for the minstrels to begin playing a galliard. As the music began, Lord Brom took the lead and began to dance the volte. Princess Ellyria was oblivious to the many watchful eyes upon them, as he spun her about the grand ballroom. She could not believe how graceful he was on the dance floor. He looked at her in such a way that made her feel more like a woman than the girl she was. Lord Brom was both enchanting and handsome, with his striking sky-blue eyes, hair the color of golden wheat, and he towered over her petite frame.

Her brothers watched from the corner as the couple danced passed them.

"There is something I do not quite like about him," said Prince Dakota.

"Yes I agree, brother. Something about him just is not right," said Prince Anthony.

The King and Queen also watched their daughter from across the room, both thinking it was the happiest they had seen her in a very long time.

After their dance, Lord Brom asked the princess if she would join him in the garden where they could gaze upon the stars together...

The stars were brightly shining in the sky, and all of the constellations were visible. The warm, early summer temperature was just right for an evening stroll. A cool gentle breeze blew through the trees, the sound setting the mood for a blossoming romance. The couple walked over to the capacious summerhouse to sit in the wooden double swing. They could still hear the music from inside, as the party went on without its guest of honor.

Lord Brom was the first to break the awkward silence.

"It is quite lovely out tonight, is it not?"

"Yes, it is," she replied, avoiding his gaze.

"Is something wrong?"

She took a deep breath and looked at him. His bright blue eyes reflecting the moonlight were mesmerizing.

"No, nothing at all. I am just enjoying the view," she stated simply in a slightly higher pitched tone.

Lord Brom placed his arm around her, and to her surprise she snuggled up to him. Growing bolder, he leaned in to kiss her, only to be interrupted by a distant voice.

"Princess Ellyria Rose!" It was her older brother, Prince Dakota, searching for her.

"We had better get back inside," Princess Ellyria suggested, blushing at the thought of being discovered alone and unescorted in the company of Lord Brom.

"Before they send out a search party," she added.

The two stood and began to walk back towards the castle and the ballroom when her brother arrived.

Prince Dakota approached the couple, causing Princess Ellyria's cheeks to flush, and Lord Brom still looked distrustful.

"There you are! Mother is looking for you," Prince Dakota told her.

"They are about to send out the cake." Prince Dakota added, taking hold of his sister's arm, and pulling her to a stop, allowing Lord Brom to walk on ahead of them.

"What do you think you are doing, dear sister?" Prince Dakota hissed.

She tried to wriggle her arm free from his grasp and walk away, but he held her in a firm grip.

"What do you mean, dear brother?" she inquired innocently.

"I mean with Lord Brom. You know nothing about him, yet here you are, all alone with him and without proper escort. It is not appropriate behavior for a girl your age," he chided.

"Why do you even care what I do? You hardly ever paid attention to me growing up. I am a grown woman now and it would be nice if you treated me as such!" she declared. She left his side to return to her party where everyone was waiting for the guest of honor to reappear.

Once she was in the opulent ballroom, everyone gathered together to observe the presentation of the beautiful cake, specially made by the royal bakers. The cake was seven-tiered, with white icing and pink trimmed roses all over, and sixteen candles were lit to commemorate the Princess's age. While everyone began to sing to the princess, Lord Brom slipped her a note. After reading the note, she could only think of one wish, and then she blew out the candles, as everyone applauded. The princess was given the first slice, and she went to the grand dining table to join her mother and father.

"Are you pleased with your party, my dear?" her father asked.

"Yes, father. I have enjoyed it so," she replied in between bites of cake.

"A toast!" her mother proposed.

"To my beautiful daughter, live life to the beat of your heart, and never lose who you are. To Princess Ellyria Rose!"

"To Princess Ellyria Rose! Here, here!" the guests chimed in unison.

"May I be excused, mother?" Princess Ellyria asked afterward.

"Yes you may, my dear."

Before her mother could ask where she was going, Princess Ellyria quickly left the table.

When she arrived at the smaller fountain in the courtyard off the entryway to the ballroom, Lord Brom was not there as his note had said he would be. She waited for a few moments, before she decided he had meant the larger fountain in the garden instead. She could not believe that she was about to have her second interlude with a young handsome man she had only just met.

The Princess hurried along, barely able to contain her excitement. She grabbed up her skirts, and practically ran to the other side of the courtyard...

CHAPTER 2

The light of the full moon reflected off the water in the fountain and illuminated the majestic garden. Seated on the edge of the fountain was Lord Brom, patiently waiting for the Princess to arrive. It was at that moment she caught his eye, and he arose to her presence just as she had wished. He pulled her to him, and kissed her passionately. As if she were in a fairytale, birds and frogs began to sing, and then fireworks exploded in the night sky above them. Lord Brom gently pushed her away; she looked at him in confusion. Her lips slightly bruised by the roughness of his kiss, not exactly how she had expected it to be for the first time. Though she wanted it to continue, and eagerly waited for him to kiss her once more.

"Let us go away together," he suggested, a note of haste in his voice.

Still blissful from his kiss, she smiled. Without quite knowing what to do next, she simply looked up at him, trying to provoke him into kissing her again. She almost began to pout when he did not. Then she remembered what he had just asked her.

"Why? Where do you wish to go? I am not sure I can just leave my family." It seemed a bit sudden for him to ask such a thing, but she played along. Maybe it was a game?

"Do you trust me?" he asked, still holding her in his arms.

"Yes, but—" She was interrupted as he kissed her again. She grew weak as she succumbed to his fervent kisses.

"Please, just come with me tonight. Let me give you a tour of the city like you have never seen before," he urged.

She pondered his invitation. She had never been allowed to leave the confines of the castle, and now was her chance to do so. Princess Ellyria did not feel uncomfortable around him but wished she could have a premonition of sorts to warn her if he meant her any harm. In the books she had read, there were always premonitions to warn of danger and help guide you. Without ever having had one before, she was not quite sure how to purposely receive one, so she decided to give it a chance and make one come to her. She tried hard to focus her energies to see if she could force a premonition to come, but after a few moments of trying nothing happened. She took it as a sign that he meant her no harm, not noticing the chain around his neck, nor the amulet carefully hidden beneath his shirt.

He looked down at her, and flashed that handsome grin of his.

"We will not be gone too long. The party is scheduled to go on all night. No one should notice your absence," he coaxed.

Princess Ellyria was helpless in his presence, and almost fainted from the unfamiliar feelings he aroused in her.

"Alright, I suppose it will not harm anyone if we are not going to be gone long."

"I can assure you we will not," he told her, sealing his promise with another kiss.

The couple snuck out of the garden and away from the castle, careful not to be seen by the tower guards. Caught in the rush of excitement and confusion, the Princess followed Lord Brom to a nearby field where his horse was tethered and waiting.

"Did you have this planned?" she asked him suspiciously.

"Only after we spent time together under the stars," he said sweetly. He kissed her again before assisting her up onto his big grey steed.

The two rode off into the night, unaware they were being followed...

The cool night air was brisk on Princess Ellyria's face as Lord Brom urged his horse onward. The horse galloped down a winding road that seemed too precarious to walk on foot alone. She could not see through the darkness or the dense fog that had set in. The supposed ride to the nearby town was seemingly taking forever, and she could not shake the strange feeling that they were being followed.

Suddenly, the horse came to a halt. Lord Brom dismounted, and pulled the Princess down from the heavily breathing horse.

"What is the problem? Where are we?" She watched as Lord Brom checked the horse's foreleg and hoof. Princess Ellyria began to worry about what she had gotten herself into.

"Yes, just as I suspected, the horse has cracked his hoof and his shoe is loose."

"What does that mean?" She started to tremble, fearful for being in the middle of nowhere in the dark and possibly stranded. She searched his face, trying to see reassurance that everything was going to be all right, but she saw nothing in his eyes that made her feel any better.

"It means we are going to have to walk, your Highness." Lord Brom took the saddle and bridle off the horse, and then gave him a big slap on the hindquarters, sending him off into the darkness. "He will find his way home."

She was at a loss. Should she leave now, Princess Ellyria wondered, and simply walk back home, in the dark, by herself?

"So what is the plan now? We have no horse, no light, and are many miles from the castle," she inquired. "My family will be getting worried if I do not return soon."

"Do not worry, I know of a nice old lady just around the bend of the road. She will take us in for a while, and lend us a horse," he assured her. "Besides I am sure everyone is still busy having a good time at your party."

As they walked the remaining few miles to the little house in the woods, she became uneasy in her surroundings. The howling of coyotes and wolves in the distance, made her walk just a little faster, in order to get to the cottage sooner.

Little did Princess Ellyria know, that is exactly where she did not want to be...

CHAPTER 3

Nestled deep in the woods was a quaint little cottage. Humble in its appearance, and quite worn from time, the structure still held firm, unlike its small clinging shutters. It had a small paddock just off to the side of the house and an old dappled mare was neighing softly into the cool night air.

As they approached the door, cold chills crept up on Princess Ellyria's arms. She felt a strange knot form in the pit of her stomach, perhaps it was a warning of sorts that they should not be there.

Lord Brom knocked on the old oak door, and an old, hunched-over lady appeared.

"Come in, come in," she said with a raspy voice.

The old woman appeared harmless enough. Her white hair was pulled into a tight bun, she had wrinkly skin, and her big grey eyes seemed to look right through you.

"Whom have you brought to visit an old lady at this hour, Lord Brom?" she asked as she motioned them into her home.

"This is Princess Ellyria Rose."

"Oh, a Princess! Well this is an honor, your Highness," the old crone said as she knelt before Ellyria.

"No please, not on my account," the Princess said, motioning for her to rise. "We just need to borrow your horse, I promise to have her fed and returned in the morning." She really just wanted to leave.

"No worries, child. Stay here, the hour is late, and the darkness will make it impossible to see," advised the old woman.

"I really must get back. My family will be very concerned, and will send out a search party looking for me," she said in a more formal tone. Although it made her ponder, had anyone even noticed she was missing yet?

"Maybe you should stay here, Princess. It is only for your protection, as it can be perilous out in the darkness with no lantern," Lord Brom said.

"If it makes you feel better child, I can send word to your family by one of my carrier pigeons," the old woman said. She gently patted Princess Ellyria's hand before hobbling over to get something to write with. She began making marks onto some parchment she pulled from an old cabinet.

"Lord Brom, get one of the pigeons and send this message to her family with haste."

He did as instructed, taking the rolled up paper and leaving the two in the cottage alone.

"Care for a drink, Princess?" the woman asked, offering a cup.

"Thank you." Princess Ellyria took it and looked questioningly into the cup.

Seeing the confusion on her face, the old woman explained, "'Tis' but chamomile tea dearie, to calm your nerves."

"I never caught your name," Princess Ellyria said as she took some sips of her warm tea, taken aback by its flavor. It tasted pleasant enough, but strange and slightly bitter, not like any chamomile her mother had ever prepared for her.

"I apologize. I had almost forgotten my manners, and you must forgive me. It is Liza, dearie. I am an old friend of the family." The old woman had a wild glimmer in her eyes as she added, "I knew your father a long time ago, when I was much younger."

Princess Ellyria blinked her eyes, rubbed her head, and before she could make out any words, dropped her cup. It crashed and broke on the floor, and she went tumbling after it into sleep.

As the drug Liza placed in the tea began to wear off, Princess Ellyria awoke to find herself in a cage made with crystal bars. Her vision was still a little blurry, her head ached, and she felt quite scrambled. She observed through the bars what looked to be an old drafty barn, it was dark and only a few lanterns were lit. Although the partial light was still enough to see her surroundings, her gaze fell upon her betrayer.

"You! Why have you done this to me?"

Lord Brom came out of the shadows from the corner of the barn. He was unable to look her in the eye, and avoided her glare.

"I am sorry for my betrayal, Princess."

"That is not an answer!" the Princess replied. "As your Sovereign I demand you answer me at once!"

"I was hired by Liza. It is nothing personal, nor does it change how I feel about you." Lord Brom hung his head in shame. "I never meant to hurt you."

"Well if you cared for me at all, then you would have never led me astray and would release me!" She shook the cage door as if it would miraculously open. Choking back tears, she plopped down to the floor of the cage.

A sinister voice drifted through the darkness.

"No use being angry with him, and wasting all of your energy, Princess."

"Who goes there? Show yourself!" the Princess demanded.

An older woman emerged, not the old white-haired woman, but a younger looking woman. Her hair was a tawny brown in color. Her face held a slightly smoother complexion. The eyes, though, staring right through Ellyria, were the same grey eyes as the old woman she had met only hours before.

Princess Ellyria stood up and spat at the older woman. How could such a harmless old woman have fooled her? By being naïve that's how, she thought miserably.

"Not very princess-like of you, my dear."

"I am not, 'your dear,'" Princess Ellyria scowled at the evil woman. "What do you want from me?"

"I want you to use your powers for me," replied the woman.

"What powers?"

"Do not play dumb with me, Princess, I am well aware of

your special gift you inherited from your mother."

"I will not do it, and I am not your prisoner either! Just wait until my father hears about this, it will be the last thing you do!" she threatened. At least she hoped that her father would come for her soon, and punish this woman for what she had done to her.

"We will see about that," Liza turned to Lord Brom. "Keep an eye on her, make sure she stays in her cage," she turned back to Princess Ellyria. "Oh, and Princess, do not try to use magic. The cage will deflect anything back on to you," she laughed wickedly and left the barn.

The next morning came, and Princess Ellyria awoke to the familiar sounds of roosters crowing and birds chirping. She rubbed her eyes, hoping it had been a dream, yet knowing it was not. Not a dream at all, but a nightmare that had come to life. Alone and helpless, she kept going over how she had found herself in this mess, wishing she was home with her family and Isis. She wiped a tear from her cheek. If anyone had noticed she was missing, they would come looking for her soon.

"I am sure Anthony will call out a search party to look for me," she whispered to herself. She was not enjoying being the damsel in distress at all. Princess Ellyria went to the opposite end of her prison cell and wept quietly to herself. She did not want Lord Brom to hear her since he was sitting obediently next to the cage. Not that she cared really, but she did not want him to think of her as being weak. She just wished that someone, anyone, would come to her rescue.

If the Princess had but known, as much as he wanted to, Brom could not let her go. Too many lives were now at stake...

CHAPTER 4

King Jason sat alone in his study worrying about his daughter. Where was she? He had believed that after everything he knew of her destiny, he would have been more careful. The castle had been completely surrounded with his best knights. He should have done more. But he was not prepared for his daughter to have possibly willingly run off with a man she had only met hours before.

What would his father have done in this situation? He gazed towards his father's portrait hung high on the wall. Jason wished his father had survived to watch him grow up and become the man he was today.

"You would have been able to advise me on what I should do," he said to the portrait. King Frank had been the last in a long succession of a pure royal bloodline. His grandfather, King Charles, had broken this legacy by allowing his son, King Frank to marry for love even though he was betrothed to another.

The young couple were married for only a short time before she was with child. While giving birth to their son, she developed a fever that took her life. Mourning her for years after her death, King Frank had never wanted to love another. Eventually the royal advisors suggested that his bereavement had gone on long enough, and that he should take another wife. They thought it would be best that his only son had a mother figure. So, the King took a new wife, a woman named Liza, who was the daughter of a Lord from a neighboring kingdom.

Then the King fell ill, and this left young Prince Jason alone in Liza's care, for many months. Seeing an opportunity, Liza used this time to keep Jason from his father's side. Liza told King Frank that his son could no longer stand to see him in his present state, because he was disgusted by his appearance. She told young Prince Jason that his father had always resented him. She said King Frank blamed him for Goldie's death, and that if it were not for him being born, she would still be alive. Neither Prince Jason nor his father wanted to believe the stepmother's lies, but they took their toll on them, causing self doubt.

Just after Prince Jason's eighth birthday, the King died. Liza became Queen by proxy, until the Prince came of age, and she ruled the kingdom without mercy. All who crossed her met an untimely demise, setting an example for anyone else who might dare to speak out. Liza was awful to the young Prince as well, she punished him severely for even the slightest offense. She would even tell the young boy horrible lies about his father, making him out to be a monster that had been terribly cruel to her.

When the eve of his coming of age began to draw near, Jason set out to discover what he could about his stepmother. One day while Liza was out, young Prince Jason went to the tower in search of his father's papers. Candlestick in hand, the young Prince searched through many old trunks trying to find his father's. At last he came across a large copper trunk, which looked familiar. As he neared the trunk he saw emblazoned on it the family crest. This had to be it! The lock on the trunk was so worn with age and rust it came off with ease. Inside he found his father's crown, robe, and some letters bound together. He was not surprised that Liza had thrown all his father's things into this trunk as though they had meant nothing. To his surprise the letters were addressed to him. Opening the most recent letter carefully, he was shocked by what he read. Everything made more sense to him now. Liza had manipulated King Frank into marrying her all those years ago. Grabbing his father's letters, he quickly left the tower to find the magistrate.

Liza had been at the market and was thus completely unaware of her stepson's discoveries. The guards were waiting in

Liza's chambers upon her return. She was shocked to find herself being arrested for treason. But Prince Jason had taken pity on his stepmother, and instead of having her condemned to death for her crimes, he had simply banished her.

When Prince Jason was finally crowned King, peace swept over the land once again. No longer under Liza's tyranny, the kingdom had regained all the former riches and splendor it once had long ago.

Years later, the young King Jason married for love, to a beautiful gypsy named Anna Marie. She had the gift of premonition, a gift that would only pass on to a daughter. A few months after they had wed she was with child, the first heir to the royal throne. The news spread all over the kingdom and beyond. King Jason's stepmother also heard the news, and came back to the kingdom begging him to forgive her. Caught up in the joy of becoming a father, he agreed.

Then the magical day arrived for the entire kingdom, the Queen gave birth to the next heir to the throne, a Prince. Then as the years went by, the royal family was blessed with three more sons. The proud father held celebrations for each one, each grander than the last. And then, finally, a daughter was born.

King Jason smiled thinking about his children, he loved them, and knew his father would have too. He wiped tears from his eyes. He missed his father, and it had taken years for him to feel that way after being angry for so long at his father for leaving him. He knew it was not his father's fault, as he still blamed his stepmother for that. Even though he had forgiven her, in many ways he was still the angry boy that his father had left behind.

A knock at his door brought him back from his memories.

"Come in."

"Sire, we have searched the entire castle. No one has seen or heard from the Princess since she was last seen with Lord Brom in the courtyard, and Isis is missing also. What should we do now?"

"Let me handle this right now. Tell no one until you have further instructions from me. Now I must go and tell the Queen this unfortunate news. It will break her heart for certain. I will send Prince Anthony with my orders."

The King's squire bowed and departed, leaving King Jason to prepare what he would to say to Princess Ellyria's mother.

CHAPTER 5

Queen Anna Marie was pacing back and forth in the great hall, trying to figure out where her daughter had gone and why she would have left. She turned quickly at the sound of the large double wooden doors opening, it was her husband, the King.

"Where is she?" the Queen exclaimed in tears.

"There, there." The King embraced his wife, trying to comfort her, as he took her small hands in his. "I have some news. Isis is not to be found anywhere either, so maybe they are together."

"Isis would definitely look out for her," his wife said, trying to remain calm. If only she could see where her daughter was, but her gift was lost to her for it had passed on to her daughter.

The doors opened and Prince Anthony strode into the great hall to join his parents. The young knight's appearance was haggard, as he had been up all night searching for his sister.

"What news have you brought to us, my son?" the King asked.

"Not good I am afraid, father. No one has seen the Princess since she left with Lord Brom for the courtyard," he said.

Queen Anna squeezed her husband's hand, fighting back her anger and frustration.

"Then she might have left with him on a girlish whim." She did not think her daughter would do such a reckless act, and leave the castle grounds with a virtual stranger, but if Isis was indeed with Princess Ellyria then she felt a little better.

King Jason wrapped his arms around her small waist, holding her close to him.

"Send your brother, Prince Rowan, out with his dragon, Gaia. Maybe the two of them can get a better view of the lands from the sky," he suggested to his son.

"Yes, father," Prince Anthony, agreed, leaving the room in search of his brother.

"If anyone can find our daughter, Rowan, and Gaia will," King Jason said, as much for his own sake as his wife's.

Out in the barn, Prince Anthony arrived to discover his brother lying with his dragon, both passed out and snoring on a large amount of hay, as he had expected.

"Get up!" Prince Anthony shouted at his still sleeping brother, Prince Rowan.

"What is it, you fool?" Prince Rowan growled back. Being startled awake was one thing however being startled awake along with a dragon is another thing entirely. Beds--not to mention rooms, houses, and even barns-- got burned up that way.

"Your sister has gone missing and I need you and Gaia to take to the air and find her!"

Once a tiny blue lizard that Prince Rowan had hatched from an egg, the dragon had grown and grown to the giant dark blue monster curled up in the barn built specifically to accommodate her size. Prince Rowan gave a whistle to wake up his sleeping dragon. He tried to not startle her, but it was too late, and she let out a breath of fire. Both brothers ducked out of the way. Prince Anthony rushed over with a thick blanket to put out the fire on a nearby haystack.

"Whoa, Gaia," Prince Rowan said to her. "We must take to the sky and search for the Princess." Nodding her head that she understood, Gaia crouched down on her belly to let Prince Rowan climb up on her back. "I will be back as soon as I find her," he shouted to his brother.

"Good luck!" Prince Anthony called back to him. As he watched them rise into the air, he held great expectations that his brother would not fail.

CHAPTER 6

Princess Ellyria was asleep inside the crystal cage. Lord Brom had also fallen asleep while on duty, supposedly watching the Princess.

"Wake up, you fool!" shouted Liza, slapping Lord Brom in the back of his head, "You are supposed to be watching her! You could have let her escape!"

"It will not happen again madam," he said rubbing the back of his aching head. He decided to probe Liza for information. "Liza, when are you going to let her go?"

"When she decides she's going to aid us by giving us her visions. Until then she shall rot in this cage until she dies, for all I care."

"As you wish." He bowed his head in shame; feeling sorry for his actions, he decided he could no longer stomach Liza's cruelty of her. He removed the protection amulet she gave him and threw it down on his way out of the barn...

Princess Ellyria pretended to be asleep, but heard every word. If that is what Liza wanted, then she would be sure to give it to her. It also gave her an idea.

"Wake up, Princess," the old woman crooned. "Tell me, Princess, how do your visions work?"

Princess Ellyria got up and walked towards the old woman. "I must touch someone for my gift to work. I can sometimes receive premonitions in dreams too."

"Well then, here is my hand. Tell me what you see, my dear." Liza extended her hand between the bars.

Princess Ellyria touched the older woman's hand; it was ice cold and without feeling, just like her. She closed her eyes to persuade her captor that she was attempting to receive a vision. After waiting a few moments she opened her eyes, giving her a perplexed look.

"I am getting nothing," Princess Ellyria said in an abrasive tone.

"Try harder, dearie," Liza pressed. "Maybe you are not concentrating hard enough."

The Princess closed her eyes, and then pretended to become weak. Grasping the bars with her hands, she acted as though she could not hold herself up.

"It must be this crystal," she said breathlessly. "You said it could block magic."

"You may be right, but I still do not trust you though. Try harder, focus," she coaxed.

The Princess closed her eyes, and dropped to the floor of the crystal cage.

"Wait, what is this!" Liza exclaimed. "Lord Brom get the key! Quickly, you imbecile!" Lord Brom brought her the key; he was incredibly worried for the girl. The Princess's breath was very shallow, as she lay motionless on the floor.

"Maybe your magic cage drained her while she was trying to use her gift for you," Lord Brom said with disdain.

"Well pick her up, and take her into the cottage," Liza ordered.

Lord Brom knelt down to pick up the Princess. She was so beautiful and vulnerable at this very moment. How he wished he had not brought her into harm's way. He could have easily seen himself fall in love with her. What might have happened between them, if the circumstances had been different? He proceeded to carry her into the cottage, fearful about what might happen to her next.

"Take her to the bedroom and lay her on the bed. I shall fetch her some water," Liza stated as she left for the well.

Lord Brom stood over the bed looking at the Princess. She was lying there motionless; only the slow rise and fall of her chest alerted him that she was still alive. He wished he could take responsibility for his own actions and ask her to forgive him. He knelt down beside the bed, succumbing to her beauty, and watched over her. Then after a few moments, unable to resist, he leaned in to kiss her. But before he had the chance to follow through, Liza had returned from the well with a pitcher of water in hand.

"What do you think your doing? I leave you alone with her for just a few moments and I return to find you trying to molest the poor girl." Liza pushed him aside. "Go! Leave now, Lord Brom!" she demanded.

Lord Brom left the room like a scolded dog, sulking with his tail between his legs.

Liza poured water from the pitcher into the basin beside the bed, and then began to sponge the Princess's forehead.

"Wake now, young lass, we have work to do. Well, perhaps you should rest instead," Liza, cooed at the still sleeping girl. Liza decided it was better to let the girl rest now in order to get what she wanted later. Then Liza turned around to collect the blanket folded at the foot of the bed.

When she was not looking or paying attention to the girl, Ellyria sat up, grabbed the water pitcher, and then smashed it over the old woman's head. And then quick as a cat she leapt over the motionless body and hastily headed for the bedroom door. She glanced back just for a moment, to make sure Liza had not gotten up yet, then swung the door open.

Lord Brom stood in the narrow doorway blocking her escape route.

"Are you just going to stand there or help me escape?" she asked out of breath.

"Yes, Princess, come this way."

Lord Brom grabbed her hand and led her outside to where he had saddled the old dapple mare. He assisted her onto the horse, and then without hesitation, he led the horse away from the cottage.

He reflected on the plan of escaping with the Princess. In actuality it was her plan, he had just aided her in it.

When he leaned in to kiss her in the cottage bedroom, she whispered to him of her plan to escape, and then asked if he would help her. Brom agreed and made preparations while Liza was with her in the bedroom. It was the least he could do with all the hurt he had already afflicted on her. He had to make it up to her somehow. From now on, he swore to himself, he would prevent anything from harming her again.

"We must make haste and get as far from here as possible, before Liza wakes up and discovers you are gone."

He leapt up behind the Princess and kicked the steed into a hard gallop. And they left the cottage and did not look back, riding as hard and as fast as they could to get away.

The Princess barely looked back, as they began to put a few miles between them and the cottage. Grateful to finally be free from Liza's evil grasp, she wanted nothing more than to put this nightmare behind her, and return home to reunite with her family...

Liza slowly rose to her feet clutching the side of her aching head, and then noticed a considerably large bump, barely remembering what had just happened. She peered around her surroundings and saw broken pieces of the vase in the floor, observing the empty bed where a once sleeping Princess had been.

"So tricky she was in her escape. Well, it is not over for her yet," she said out loud. She would have her revenge if it were the last thing she did. She got up and began to search through the house. There was a missing Lord Brom, and then she took notice of the empty paddock where her old mare used to be. There was no doubt in her mind that he was the one who had helped her escape. She would see to him as well and send word to her men to go ahead and execute his father for his betrayal. No one crossed her without feeling her wrath; she always made sure of that.

There was nothing left Liza could do now, she tended to her wound, while organizing a new plan of action to get the Princess back…

CHAPTER 7

Princess Ellyria Rose spared no more concern for Liza, as she was too excited that she was far, far away from that terrible woman. She could not wait to get back to the familiar surroundings of home, and by the looks of things, should be just around the corner. She was smiling inwardly to herself, happy that all of this mess was almost at an end. Everything was going to be all right now. She must have jinxed herself. And when it all seemed too good to be true, the horse came to a complete stop.

"What is the problem now? Why did we stop?" The Princess asked looking down at Lord Brom with her hands fixed on her hips.

"We are far from immediate danger, and this old girl needs a rest." He dismounted from the tired horse, then turned and assisted her down.

Before she could see what was coming, he quickly grabbed her and kissed her. Shocked by his kiss and out of complete reflex, she slapped him hard across his face.

"What was that for?" he said rubbing the side of his face.

"That you ask? You have the audacity to ask that of me? When you lied to me and kidnapped me; only to place me in the hands of that evil woman!" Her eyes were now a deep emerald green. She began to pace back and forth in front of him, rage boiling from deep within her matching the dust cloud forming around her. How could he be so unscrupulous?

"I never meant to hurt you, I had no choice," he said offering an outstretched hand, but she waved it away.

At this moment she wanted to run, getting away from him entirely may be the only intelligent decision she could come to. She would not leave him though and could not explain the feelings either. When she regained control of her emotions, and pulled herself together, knowing this had gone far enough.

"Yes, you had a choice. We all make choices. It is what you choose to do that makes the difference!" she shrieked at him. She continued to pace back and forth in front of him, wearing a new path into the dirt road.

"She has my father, Princess," he confessed.

Princess Ellyria paused to look at him. He was so handsome and boyish. Why did she feel as though she could melt when he looked at her so? She still didn't understand. She reached out and touched his hand, and then looked deep into his blue eyes. She knew he was telling the truth. Her empathy towards him yanked on her heartstrings.

Suddenly, Princess Ellyria began to see flashes of images invading her mind uncontrollably. She saw an old man locked in the dungeon of an old castle. The vision was jumbled together, and she did not recognize anything around her. The trees began to spin before her eyes, and then she collapsed. It was her first real vision. One she had not expected to come right now. And without much rest, it was too much to handle.

Lord Brom caught her just in time. He set Princess Ellyria gently on the ground, and then cradled her in his arms.

"Are you alright, Princess?"

She opened her eyes, and they were again the brilliant sapphire blue that he had known before.

"Are you alright?" he asked again.

She looked at him, still blurry eyed and nodded her head yes.

"What happened back there?" he questioned.

"I had a vision. It is your father. I know where Liza's keeping him. But I do not know the area." She rubbed her head and added wearily, "I have not had a vision so strong before." In actuality it was her first, but she kept that to herself.

"We must save him. Do you remember where he was being detained?" he urged.

Princess Ellyria tried hard to recall the events that flashed through her mind. She cleared her thoughts to try and focus.

"He was in a castle, in a dungeon. It did not look like anyplace I would ever want to visit. How would we even find it?" She closed her eyes for a moment; her head was still spinning from her vision. Now she knew why they had been brought together, to help him rescue his father.

"I remember Liza telling me of this old castle left to her by her late father. I will bet that is the place where she is keeping him too. Come on let us ride, I know the way." He gently picked up the still weary Princess in his arms, hoisted her onto the horse's back, and then climbed astride behind her.

Lord Brom urged the horse into a fast gallop; on to Liza's castle they rode...

CHAPTER 8

Prince Rowan had been riding a very travel-worn Gaia. They had been searching the lands of all the kingdoms, far and wide from their aerial view. He knew she had become weary when she let out a growl, so they touched down for a moment to rest.

Rowan pulled a few of Gaia's favorite tasty treats from his bag, and she gobbled them up.

"We shall rest here for a bit, and then head on home," he said while patting her large head that was bigger than his entire body. Even though she was a monster in size it matched her gentle monster-sized heart as well. Gaia never harmed any other small animals, and only attacked humans when commanded by her master.

After searching the kingdom for days, he had almost given up on ever finding her, when suddenly Gaia heard a noise in the distance coming from the woods.

Prince Rowan drew his sword, taking extra precaution in case of foe.

"Who goes there? Show yourself!" he exclaimed into the shadows.

Gaia raised her head and sniffed the air, and began to wag her giant tail excitedly. Gaia could cause a slight earthquake when she became too excited. The ground beneath began to shake; Prince Rowan knew he must calm her down before she accidentally caused a small natural disaster.

"What is it girl?" he asked still trying to calm her.

A big black wolf emerged from the woods; it was Isis.

"Isis, here girl," he called to her.

The wolf came to greet him with a large paw placed in his hand, and some sloppy wet kisses to the side of his face.

"How are you, girl? Where is the Princess?"

Isis barked, and then began to turn excitedly in circles.

"Do you know where the Princess is? Can you lead us to her?" Prince Rowan asked patting her head. Isis barked once more, and then grabbed Prince Rowan's shirttails with her teeth, pulling him to follow.

Prince Rowan accompanied her; Isis put her nose to the ground, retrieving the scent from the horse's hoof prints. He knelt down to examine them, running his fingers through the dirt. The tracks were still fresh and it looked as though the riders were heading north.

"Thanks girl, good work."

Prince Rowan walked back to Gaia, the giant dragon lowered herself onto her belly, and he pulled himself up onto her back.

"Let us ride, girl. To the sky! We follow Isis," he commanded leaping onto Gaia's back.

Isis stayed on the ground to keep track of the scent since Prince Rowan could not see the trail from the sky. They could however keep watch on her black figure, and then follow her as she tracked the scent.

Isis had been on the trail of the Princess and Lord Brom since they left the castle on the night of her mistress's birthday celebration for days now but lost them at the cottage. It was where they rested the horse, that Isis picked up the scent again...

Prince Rowan knew not of where they were going, only that they were headed north. He did not know of anyone who lived that far away. Why would his sister be heading in that direction? As Gaia soared through the sky, her massive muscles hard at work flapping her wings against the wind, Prince Rowan kept a constant watch for any signs leading to his sister's whereabouts. The wind whipped warm air across his face, and his eyes closed for only a moment; he usually sat back and enjoyed the ride, but he could not today under the present circumstances.

The search continued for his sister, and Prince Rowan was determined to find her now...

CHAPTER 9

Lord Brom, and Princess Ellyria had been steadily making their way to Liza's castle for the past several days. Now reaching the outskirts of her kingdom, they had to be cautious of those who might be looking for them. Lord Brom slowed the worn out steed to a walk, so that the mare could catch her breath.

"We are nearing town, talk to no one. We must be inconspicuous, and not alarm anyone that could be one of Liza's many informants," he paused, keeping a close eye out for Liza's guards, "she will have a price out on my head too for my arrest, accusing me of kidnapping you. Of course, they will try to get you back as well."

"Well my tattered dress will blend in with all the other peasants," she jested. She looked at him, and his face was blank, obviously not amused by her whit.

"This is no time for joking around. We must have a plan set in motion before we reach the castle, on how we will get in, and get my father out." he chided. "We must seek refuge before dark, and I know a place where we can go."

They began to ride through the market to blend in amongst the peasants, since their current appearance made it easier for them.

Before they knew it, they had been spotted by one of Liza's men, disguised as a farmer. The guard began to chase after them, urging his horse on to catch up with Lord Brom and Princess Ellyria. Darting in and out between the many pedestrians in the market, Lord Brom tried to lose his fast-paced antagonist; just when he thought he only had one guard to lose, another flanked him from his left. Now riding out of the market, he was able to urge his horse into a faster gallop.

Shrieking with fear, Princess Ellyria wrapped her arms around Lord Brom's waist, and then pressed her face onto his broad back. The chase continued to the edge of the woods; Lord Brom glanced behind him to see if the other riders had given up. The next thing he knew, they had quickly caught up with him. The rider on the right joined the rider on his left, and another trailing behind them. Now there were three after them. Princess Ellyria was desperately trying to hold on, but the rider on the right tried to grab her from the running horse, making it impossible to remain seated. Her attacker was finally able to grab the sleeve of her dress, she screamed while being pulled to the other horse. Lord Brom grabbed her legs, trying to keep his balance and hold onto the Princess.

Lord Brom gave his mare a swift kick and rammed into the other horse, the attacker had to let go of Princess Ellyria, or fall off his horse himself. Lord Brom turned his horse about and urged her into a faster gallop, but they were still unable to outrun the other horses. The men's horses were only carrying one rider so they were able to move at a faster speed, easily catching up to them once again. The guard to the left decided to try his luck with grabbing the Princess. He soon found himself punched in the face by the fast fist of Lord Brom, knocking the rider completely off his horse. With one down and two to go, he had to come up with a plan to lose them.

Lord Brom rode the horse further into the thicker part of the woods. The mare graciously leapt over a fallen tree, clearing it with ease, but the guard on the right did not make it, his horse buckled up right before he should have made the jump, sending the man flying over his horse's head, and then landing flat on his back. Chuckling to himself, Lord Brom rode on, now only needing to rid himself of the third rider who had been able to keep up the entire way.

The further they rode into the dense woods; the branches

from the trees cut into Princess Ellyria's arms and scraped her face. She tried to keep her head down but had to keep watch to make sure she was not grabbed from the horse again.

The chase continued, they rode as fast as they could go, but the other guard had caught up and was on their heels. Lord Brom made a fast turn around the bend, sending the Princess flying off the back of the horse. Unable to catch her in time, Lord Brom quickly pulled up on the horse trying to get her to slow down, fearing the other rider would stop and grab the girl. He was finally able to slow down his steed when the other rider rode right into the side of Lord Brom's horse.

The mare was knocked over on her side, trapping Lord Brom's leg beneath her. He scrambled quickly out from under the horse and went to check on Princess Ellyria, who was motionless on the ground. Lord Brom feared the worst for her, because a fall like that from a fast moving horse usually meant a serious injury. Before he was able to arrive at her side, the guard grabbed him from behind. Lord Brom turned around to face his attacker, and then punched him hard to the stomach, then to his ribs. The other man fought hard in return. However he was no match for Lord Brom's strength. Without backing down, the man went after his knife in his boot, slashed Lord Brom in his arm, and then lunged for his stomach, stabbing him. Blood poured out from an exhausted Lord Brom, and he fell to his knees. The other man quickly pounced on Lord Brom like a cougar, straddling him as he tried to give him one last fatal blow to his throat.

Then to both men's surprise, Princess Ellyria had grabbed a fallen branch, and then swung at the assailant, knocking him over with one hit. The guard charged after her, but before he could grab her, Lord Brom had pushed the other man to the ground.

After a few moments of rolling over and throwing punches, both men were tiring, but not yet giving up the fight. A frantic princess had become worried as the men neared the edge of a cliff.

"Watch out!" she yelled out to Lord Brom.

When he looked up, he saw his opportunity and grabbed the guard by his shirt, pushed off with his legs, and then hurled him over the side of the cliff. Lord Brom tried to stand and fell.

Princess Ellyria rushed to his side, sliding to her knees in her efforts to reach him in time. His wound was already festering and blood was still spilling from it. She ripped a part of the hem of her dress off, utilizing it to wrap around his waist. Lord Brom had lost a lot of blood and was exhausted from the fighting; he had no energy to get up. She had to try and get him to his feet herself, before someone else might come along, and needed to get him some water.

Princess Ellyria remembered passing a small stream that she had seen when they ran into the woods. She needed the mare, to get the water pouch from the saddle bag, not to mention help to get them out of the woods before dark. She whistled to the horse, worried that after she had gotten up from her collision with the other horse that she had ran too far to hear her call. Much to her surprise, the mare did return, her neck lathered with sweat, and trotted right up to the Princess.

Princess Ellyria retrieved the water pouch made from a sheep's stomach; she ran as fast as she could to the stream. Filling the pouch full of the fresh cool water, she made haste back to where she left Lord Brom. She found him sitting up on his own, a good sign that he was going to be just fine.

"I am so glad you are alright." She was worried he could have been killed. She handed the pouch to him and he began to drink heavily.

He wiped off his bristly chin and looked at his champion and smiled.

"You saved my life, Princess. Thank you," he said trying to stand up.

Princess Ellyria assisted, letting him use her for support.

"You are quite welcome," she replied breathlessly, helping him over to the horse. He held his side and stopped for a moment.

"Are you able to ride again?" she questioned him.

"Yes, I will be fine, it is actually not as deep as you would think, it is just a scratch," he told her.

"It does not appear like just a scratch to me."

She looked up at him, keeping his gaze with her for just a moment.

He pulled her close to him and kissed her with ardency. After a few moments of bliss, he stopped and looked at her.

"We must get going, it will be getting dark soon," he advised. "I know where we can go."

She helped him onto the horse, and then he hoisted her up behind him. Together they rode out of the woods, the mare still tired from before so they just kept at an easy pace. Lord Brom was confident no one would be looking for them now.

"Where are we going to go?" she inquired, her knees stung from the air caressing her wounds, and covered them with the remaining hemline of her dress.

"We are heading for the abandoned corn mill. It is close to Liza's castle. With us being right under her nose, no one will think to look for us there." It was the only place he could think of.

The young couple rode on, carefully keeping an eye out for anyone that would have picked up their trails, and headed for the mill...

The abandoned windmill had not been used in quite some time. It was the perfect place to hide out because it was in the castle's direct path, separated only by the neighboring empty field.

Lord Brom and Princess Ellyria arrived at the outskirts of the forest leading to the old mill, careful to not attract attention, but unfortunately this was the only way to get there. The villagers used the old mill, to grind the corn that used to grow in the field nearby. Now it is abandoned, and no one has used the mill in years. Which gave Lord Brom the advantage by hiding out in plain sight, aiding in their quest to rescue his father.

They reached the open field; Princess Ellyria sighed in relief when they were not followed. Just as the sun had begun to set, it still gave them just enough visibility left in the fast approaching night. From there, they could see Liza's castle ahead of them as they finally reached the mill. They tied the mare to a post out back, where some tall wheat grasses had grown up, and then fetched her some water from a little stream that ran just below the small hill.

Lord Brom had not spoken to the Princess the rest of the way to the mill. She saw he was in a lot of pain, and decided to tend to his wound herself.

"Let me see that," Princess Ellyria began to pull away the makeshift bandage but paused. "The material has stuck to your wound, it has pulled it open again."

"Ouch, easy does it! Did you take skin with it?" he took the makeshift-bandage from her hand. While clenching his teeth together, he quickly ripped the rest of the dressing off; tears stung his eyes. "Go fetch my saddle bag over in the corner there."

Princess Ellyria retrieved the item and set it on the table next to him.

He reached in and pulled a wrapped deerskin package from the saddlebag, and then opened it up to reveal clean bandages, a needle, and some thread.

"Here, Princess, you are going to have to do this for me," he said handing her the freshly threaded needle.

Princess Ellyria shook her head.

"You have to, I can not stitch myself at this angle."

She took the needle from him, but before she began to suture him, she carefully cleaned his wound with some of the fresh water from his pouch. When he flinched, she was not certain if it was from the pain, or the cold.

"Are you positive, you want me to do this?"

He nodded his head.

She had never stitched up a real person before. Only her doll from all those times her brother Prince Rowan had taken it apart when they were kids. So putting her expert stitching to an open wound was completely new to her, making her very nervous. She did not let on to her inexperience for sewing up people. She carefully pressed the flesh together, and slowly pierced his skin with the needle for the first stitch.

"Ouch! Can you stitch a little faster? It actually hurts more going in and out slowly with the needle like that," he complained.

Taking his advice, Princess Ellyria hurried with her stitching and finished tying it off at the end. Then taking the fresh bandages, she carefully wrapped the cloth around his waist several times to hold in place the fresh sutures.

"Thank you. I really could not have done it without you, I feel much better now."

He drew her body closer to his, and kissed her gently on her cheek.

Surprised that he did not kiss her as he had always done before, she was curious if he no longer enjoyed her in that way. It most certainly did not deter her from grabbing his face in her hands and kissing him with fervor.

He definitely did not expect it. A nice surprise indeed, he equally matched her kisses with his, as they were oblivious to the task at hand, and the reason they were there to begin with. When they ignited the fire between them that was beginning to consume them both, he knew he had to be the gentleman and put out the fire.

Left with the feeling of wanting more, Princess Ellyria was unsure about these new feelings that she felt burning inside her.

To distract her from wanting to go any further, he tried to get back to the quest at hand. He was not ignoring her, but he began to finish preparing for the rescue of his father.

Seeing that he was now preoccupied with packing for the journey, she was curious as to what they were going to do.

"So what is our plan of action?" the Princess inquired.

"The castle should not be too heavily guarded on the outside," he gasped, wincing with pain. His wound still felt sore from his sutures and was pulsating from the ride. "To not look suspicious, we shall need to go in through the cellar. Then to the dungeon; where there may be a guard or two. Not anything I can not handle." Confident about his plan, he continued to gather what means he could for the quest ahead, while pushing through his pain.

"Okay, what do I do?"

You will stay here out of harm's way," he ordered. Lord Brom looked at her in amusement as her lip slightly pushed out, and her eyebrows scrunched together. He could not believe she was actually pouting. He had to remember she was practically a child still, and he was nearly ten years her senior.

"No, I am coming with you. It was my vision, so I know where to look for your father. You need me," she stated brazenly. Princess Ellyria was not letting him get away with leaving her behind, especially after almost losing him.

Suddenly, they heard a loud noise, followed by a slight tremble of the floor.

"What was that?" they said simultaneously.

They both looked at one another and smiled. Finding humor at such a stressful time was needed. Finding out he did have a sense of humor hidden in him somewhere, put her at ease. Even under the present situation.

"I shall check outside, you stay put," Brom said sternly to a still pouting princess, "I will be right back."

"Be careful."

She did not care for being left behind and yanked a chair out from under the table; she plopped down and crossed her arms.

Lord Brom went out the back entrance and slowly crept along the sides of the mill, always checking behind him and in front of him. So far, he had seen nothing, until he heard something coming from the edge of the woods.

He looked towards the sound and saw giant green eyes staring back at him through the trees.

"Who goes there? Show yourself!"

From out of the canopy, emerged a giant dragon.

Lord Brom quickly ran back inside the mill, slammed, and barricaded the door with bags of corn. Not even taking consideration for his injury to be careful.

"What is it? What did you see?" the Princess asked, worry in her voice.

All the color was completely gone from his face, his heart was beating right out of his chest, it seemed. He did not want to alarm the girl, nor let on he was afraid either. He looked down to check the binding, making certain he had not torn his stitches. With no blood showing, he felt a little more at ease.

"It was a giant dragon," Lord Brom replied out of breath.

After hearing that news, the Princess ran as quick as a cat outside, away from the sanctuary of the mill. She knew it had to be Gaia, and maybe Prince Rowan as well.

"No, Princess wait! I said there is a dragon outside!" he exclaimed frantically.

Not waiting a moment longer, he chased after her, trying to not disturb his wound, only to find her heading straight for it. Why did she have to be so stubborn? He was so infuriated with her right now. What would he do after he caught her? He was just within reach to grab her and pull her from harm, when a young man appeared from the woods; Lord Brom lost all fear for the dragon.

"Halt right there!" he shouted.

The stranger was not stopping and was running straight for the Princess. Then it was too late; the young man had reached her, but to his surprise, the two were now embracing.

When Lord Brom approached, Princess Ellyria was laughing with the stranger, and then finally turned her attention towards him.

"Lord Brom, I would like to introduce you to my brother, Prince Rowan," she said to the two very confused men. "I knew who it was the moment you mentioned 'giant dragon,'" she added with a giggle.

"Look who I brought with me." Prince Rowan waved for the black silhouette to emerge from the shadows of the woods.

"Isis! I'm so happy to see you," she added as she began to hug her big black wolf friend.

"Looks as though she missed you as well," he said smiling as he watched Isis give his sister lots of sloppy, wet kisses.

Lord Brom was relieved to see it was one of the Princess's brothers, and not one of Liza's henchmen.

"We need to devise our plan, milady, if we are to implement it before sunrise," Lord Brom advised, and then touched her arm affectionately.

Princess Ellyria quickly pulled away, worried what her brother might think.

Prince Rowan did take notice, but tried not to let on that it bothered him, even though it did. Who does he think he is anyway, being that intimate with his sister?

"So, sister, where have you been all this time? Everyone is worried sick over your disappearance." he mentioned.

"There is no time to explain now, we need to send Gaia home to get word to Anthony, and our father," she said, taking control of the situation.

Prince Rowan took parchment from the saddlebag and wrote the message for help. He rolled it up and placed it inside the side of saddlebag that was on the giant dragon's back. His father, and his brother would be sure to find it, once they notice he was not accompanying Gaia.

"Gaia, take to the skies and get this message home straight away. Now fly!" he told her, waving her on. Prince Rowan turned back to Lord Brom, and his sister. "So what is the plan?"

"We are rescuing my father from Liza's castle. She is the one that has been behind all this. I can explain more on the way," Lord Brom informed him.

"Well, what are we waiting for? Let us go, we shall take Isis for protection," the Princess chimed in. The three left to embark on the rescue mission of Lord Brom's father, before the break of dawn.

Little did they know it would prove to be more dangerous than even the Princess could foresee...

CHAPTER 10

The full moon was high in the night sky, casting enough light to see about them in the open field. Lord Brom, Princess Ellyria Rose, and Prince Rowan were on a mission to rescue Lord Brom's father; who was being held prisoner in Liza's castle.

The plan was to get into the castle by the way of the old cellar. With the possibility of a guard patrolling the back of the castle, they were taking extra precautions. The Princess Ellyria would act as a distraction if needed. Isis was trailing behind for protection in case they were discovered.

As they approached the castle, there was no guard in sight. In the darkness they had to take heed, in case one came around the corner making his rounds. Lord Brom motioned for the Princess Ellyria to walk up ahead to see if the coast was clear, and then motioned for Prince Rowan.

"Let us go ahead and check to see if those cellar doors are locked or not," he ordered.

They slowly walked to the cellar doors and Prince Rowan tried to open them first. The doors would not budge, so Prince Rowan tried harder. With Lord Brom injured, he needed to try to get them open on his own, but he was unable to.

"I do not think they are locked, just maybe stuck," Prince Rowan whispered to Lord Brom.

Taking care not to pull open his wound again, Lord Brom had to assist Prince Rowan. Both men yanked hard on the heavy double doors and they nearly fell backward when the doors finally gave way. Checking himself, he was surprised to see that his sutures had not come open.

The dust rose up stinging their eyes, after it had cleared, the two men peered inside to see if anyone, and or anything might be standing guard at the entrance.

"I do not believe those doors have been opened in years," Lord Brom stated out of breath.

The two men were ready to descend into the cellar, and then they saw the Princess Ellyria wave her arms frantically at them. Expecting she would be all right since she had Isis to protect her, they decided to go ahead down into the cellar in search of the dungeon. Even though they were still concerned for the Princess's Ellyria's safety, they needed to go now in order to not be seen.

"Hurry, someone is coming," Lord Brom said, as they hurried down into the cellar, leaving the young girl as the lookout.

A guardsman was coming from around the corner, his footsteps were heavy, and Princess Ellyria heard him coming her way. She stepped back pressing her body up against the castles stonewall, but it was too late.

"Miss, what are you doing back here?" the guard interrogated her.

Staring at him blankly, Princess Ellyria tried to act as though she did not understand his question. When she tried to turn away from him, the burly man reached out to grab her arm. Isis jumped up between them and attacked him. When the Isis finally let go of the guard, he tried to run away. Isis then jumped on him from behind, and the guard fell hitting his head on a large stone that was embedded in the ground.

Princess Ellyria crouched down slowly to see if the man was still alive, and pushed him over to see if he was still breathing. He was just unconscious, so she decided to hurry and go on down into the cellar before he came to.

"Good work, Isis. Now stand guard and let out a howl if someone comes. Okay, girl?" she said patting her friend's head.

Isis wagged her tail and gave a nod as if understanding what was asked of her, and then sat at the entrance as instructed. The

The Amulet of Elements

Princess Ellyria headed on down to the cellar in search of Lord Brom and Prince Rowan.

The cellar was cold, dark, damp, and musty. Princess Ellyria could barely see with such thin light coming in through the corridors, so she let her instincts guide her. Now that she was alone, she tried to recall the images from her vision in order to find the entrance to the dungeon below.

While the Princess was trying to find the dungeon, Lord Brom and Prince Rowan had a head start and had already discovered it. The dungeon was not hard to find with the constant moans and screams of pain coming from the distant stairwell. The cries became louder as they neared the dungeon. Cautiously, they began their descent into the prison below, unaware of how many guards there might be. A horrible stench made invaded their nostrils as they reached the midway point of the stairwell. Covering their faces with their hands, trying to mask some of the odors, they were positive that they had finally made it to the dungeon. Periodically, Lord Brom checked his wound, making sure the bandages were still in place. After he felt they were secure, they moved onward to find out where the prisoners were being held.

Not far behind the men, Princess Ellyria had finally found the same set of stairs and began her journey to the dungeon as well. Unsure of what may lie ahead, she took extra care not to alert any more guardsmen of her presence. Which was not an easy task at all with all of the spiders, bugs, and rats scurrying about the stairs and sometimes across her feet. She held her breath to prevent herself from shouting her fears of the vermin out loud. Composing herself, she continued down the endless staircase that seemed to drag on forever.

Lord Brom, and Prince Rowan found themselves within a maze of dark corridors that seemed to lead to nowhere. They found many rooms, some were used to inflict torture, but it was not where the prisoners were being held.

"Maybe we should split up?" Rowan suggested.

"I agree. We will cover more ground that way. Be careful and keep an eye out for guards," Lord Brom suggested.

The two men split off going in opposite directions, Brom to the right corridor and Rowan to the left.

While the men went their separate ways, the Princess Ellyria had finally made it to the dungeon. The combination of smells between human blood, urine, feces, and even death itself was enough to make her want to vomit. She pressed on to find Lord Brom's father who could be anywhere down here. Luckily the dungeon was pretty well lit with torches, although it was enough to see, and avoid stepping on rats anyway.

As the Princess Ellyria turned to come around the corner, she saw the shadowy figure of a man. Quickly she stopped and leaned into an alcove hidden in the wall so he would not see her. It would have worked, had she not stepped back into a huge spider web. She sucked in her breath just in time to not yell out. Her heart began to race as insurmountable fear gripped her, she was deathly afraid of spiders, and prayed this web she had stepped into was empty. She was finally able to calm herself and had regained her composure until a giant, hairy, black spider dropped down onto her shoulder. She let out a shriek of terror; but quickly covered her mouth with her right hand, and flung the spider off with her left hand. It was sent flying into the wall, and then fell to the floor with a horrible thud.

The spider scurried off, making scratchy noises as it walked across the stone floor. Princess Ellyria had to take a minute to take deep breaths to allow her heart to slow down the heavy beating in her chest. She hated spiders, and began to think she hated the web even more as it was not coming off as easily as she thought it would. She moved out into the light so she could see, to make sure she had finally gotten it all off.

It was then she heard the sound of footsteps, and feared she must have been discovered. Princess Ellyria tried to hurry around the corner, when she was suddenly grabbed from behind. A heavy hand went over her mouth and in her ear a deep voice whispered.

"Do not scream, Princess Ellyria, it is me Lord Brom," he said.

She quickly turned around and hugged his neck tight. She was glad it was not a guard. "I can not believe you just did that," she whispered back, "you scared me to death."

"Come on, we do not have a lot of time. Prince Rowan and I split up. This place is one big circle with lots of separate chambers and corridors," he whispered.

"I think I know where your father is. The path I have been following looks familiar from my vision. Maybe we will find Prince Rowan on the way," she said softly.

Hand in hand, they continued through the corridor in search of the missing father, and now a missing brother as well.

Prince Rowan was fumbling around each of the chambers in near darkness. He had strayed from the main hall looking to find the prison cells with no luck so far. He continued on in the direction he was already facing.

When he heard footsteps coming from the other corridor, he slipped back into a dark corner and waited to see who was heading his way. The sound of chains rattling along the stone floor was followed by heavy footsteps, so he knew someone was coming closer. Prince Rowan peaked around the corner and seen a guard was dragging a prisoner along. Finally, this was his chance to find the prison cells. He needed to stay behind a few feet and just keep them in his sights to not make his presence known. Down a long hall to another chamber was the entryway to the prison cells. Prince Rowan heard the guardsman open and shut the door, which throwing in his prisoner. The guard continued down the long line of cells clanking on the bars to see who stirred from unconsciousness and who did not. The cells that had no response were opened, and then checked to see if anyone were alive or not. The guard would then leave the cell ajar and would proceed with his rounds.

After a long search, the guard made his way to the last cell, then turned back. Rowan heard the guard instruct the other guard on duty, 'to remove the lifeless bodies from the prison cells, before they decompose and get rid of them.' Finally, the two guards were out of sight with a load of bodies in the dump cart. Prince Rowan began to walk through the rows of cells. He looked in each one, in anticipation of finding Lord Brom's father.

Prince Rowan heard footsteps and ducked into one of the newly emptied cells, and then covered himself deep in the corner with the straw while leaning upright against something. He looked behind him and was not surprised to see the remains of a skeleton.

"Pardon me, sir if I am crowding you here, but I do not want to end up like you, no offense," he whispered to the corpse. Prince Rowan stayed very still, waiting patiently before leaving the safety of the cell and his newfound companion. He remained hidden in the far corner, as he heard voices coming. He listened closely in case it were the guardsman, and then recognized a familiar voice.

"Father, it is me, Lord Brom. Where are you?" Lord Brom called out, as he stopped and check each cell.

"I do not think he is here," Princess Ellyria observed. "It looks nothing like what I saw in my vision."

Prince Rowan came out of the jail cell and startled his two companions.

"It is just me, do not be alarmed," he motioned to the empty cell, "I was hiding in there. I thought you were guardsmen returning, or my new friend I made in there started talking to me," he jested.

"No. It is just us. What are you talking about? Are there any more prison cells down that way?" asked his sister giving him a bewildered look.

"Never mind, do not ask. I am not sure, I have not made it passed here."

"Then let us go check it out," Lord Brom replied as he looked at the two siblings while they continued their jesting. He was confused, but it was amusing nonetheless.

They went further down the next corridor, where the prison cells appeared much older. The steel bars were rusted, and much smaller in comparison then the ones they had just passed, these cells must have been the originals built with the castle.

"This place looks familiar," she observed. If her memory served her correctly, it looked like the block of cells from her vision. "I think he is in the far-right corner."

As they came closer to the end of the row of prison cells, a guardsman came up from behind them.

"Just what do you think you are doing down here?" asked the guard. He was a huge and grotesque man who reeked of rotten corpses.

"I was lost and these two gentlemen here were just escorting me out," the Princess Ellyria said coyly, covering her nose, and trying to hold her breath from the foul stench of the man.

"I do not mean just you, I meant all of you," grumbled the guard. Sweat ran over his robust, shirtless body, and he towered over both men in size.

"Oh, well let me explain it to you then," Lord Brom interrupted and punched the guard square in the nose, knocking him out cold.

The guard made such a loud thud, they had to hurry and move him out of the way before someone else came along.

"Come on, let us get him into one of these empty cells before he comes to," Prince Rowan advised.

Prince Rowan and Lord Brom began to drag the unconscious and extremely heavy guard into the empty prison cell and locked the door to prevent his escape.

"That will hold him for a while. Now let us go find my father," Lord Brom suggested.

They continued their search, finally making it to the end of the row of prison cells. In the corner at the far end of the dungeon was the last cell. This was the one from the Princess Ellyria's vision. Lord Brom's father was detained in that cell, she was sure of it.

"Father," Lord Brom called out softly to the darkness. "It is I, your son Brom." He heard a rustling sound scrambling about in the dark prison cell.

The shadowy figure of a man stood up.

"Son. Is that you?" a husky voice called out from the darkness.

"Yes, father, it is I," he responded still focused in the dark cell of the silhouette of his father.

The tall man in the cell came forward and grasped the bars with bony hands. His face had an overgrowth of grey hair and the pale skin of his cheeks was sunk in. His overall appearance was haggard and sullen, like he had barely slept or eaten in weeks.

"You must hurry and get me out, before the guards come back, Brom. Liza has plans to have me executed in the morning for your betrayal."

"Yes, father. I will find a way to get you out," his son replied. "Rowan, would you take Ellyria, and go take the keys off the guard we left back in that cell."

"I already did that," the Princess Ellyria boasted, swinging the keys around her fingers. "It was my vision after all. I grabbed them off the guard, right after you knocked him out."

With keys in hand, she went to the cell door and tried each individual key. She finally found the correct one and unlocked the cell door.

"Thank you, child," he took her hand and patted it. Are you the one Liza is after?"

Princess Ellyria looked up at Brom's father, understanding exactly where he had gotten his height. "Yes, but she will not capture me again," she replied confidently.

"This is my father, Lord Thomas. Father, this is Princess Ellyria Rose, and her brother, Prince Rowan," he said leading the introductions.

"Alright, now that we all know each other, I suggest we get out of here rather quickly, before anymore guards show up," Prince Rowan suggested.

Lord Brom led the group out from the dungeon, passing the jail cell where they had left the guard, noticing he was still passed out.

"Wow, you definitely pack a punch, he will be laid out for quite some time," Princess Ellyria said to Lord Brom.

Lord Brom laughed out loud as they walked past the cell.

"I suppose I did. Now let us get out of here, before we bump into any more guards. I would hate to have to knock anyone else out," he said chuckling.

CHAPTER 11

The rescue of Lord Brom's father seemed to go off without a hitch, until they reached the entrance to the cellar doors. There waiting was Liza, and a group of her soldiers. The man that had been knocked out beside the cellar doors had finally come to and went for backup, while alerting Liza of the situation. The Princess Ellyria, Lord Brom, Lord Thomas, and Prince Rowan were completely surrounded by the guards with no way out.

"You are very courageous, Princess Ellyria to have come here, right to the place I wanted you to begin with," said Liza.

"Oh, no you are not getting her this time Liza. It is over. Give up now and we will let you go in peace," Lord Brom said, shielding her body with his own.

"You can give up the Princess Ellyria. Lord Brom you are surrounded, outnumbered, and there is no way out this time. It appears as though you are not in much of a fighting condition anyway," Liza stated, observing his bloodstained shirt.

Princess Ellyria leaned over to check on his bandages, but he pushed her out of the way.

"There is no time for that now," he whispered to her.

Prince Rowan moved in front of Lord Brom and Princess Ellyria.

"You will have to get through me first to get to her," Prince Rowan said, while unsheathing his sword.

Courageously and presently unarmed, Lord Thomas's valor stood unmoving even with his body challenging itself against him, as he stood beside Rowan.

"As I will also defend her," added Lord Thomas.

The three men surrounded the Princess Ellyria and was ready to fight in her defense, when a mighty roar was heard from outside the castle walls. Everyone turned towards the sound that seemed to shake the very walls with the amount of force it created. Completely unaware of what it was, Liza and the guards made no sudden moves until they had decided what, or who it was outside the cellar doors.

Prince Ian arrived astride his giant lioness, Migata. Sword raised high in his hand, as the sun was shining bright upon it's perfectly made steel. Following behind him was Prince Anthony on his great steed named Odin and Prince Dakota on his giant white owl called Luna. Flying from high in the sky came Gaia. She shot out bursts of flames from her massive jaws, followed by a loud roar, as she brought the cavalry. The Princess's brothers were not the only ones that had arrived. King Jason himself, as well as over a hundred of his best men in armor, was right behind them.

"Go see what is going on out there," Liza ordered her guards. "That goes for you too," she added motioning to her captives.

The group was escorted out of the cellar by the remainder of the guards. When they arrived outside, the King, his sons, and hundreds of soldiers were outside waiting for them.

"As King, I order you to release the prisoners, Liza," he commanded. "If you do not surrender I will have no choice, but to use force against you," he added.

"As you wish, Sire," Liza said as she took a bow. "I suppose if it is force you want, it is force you will get." Liza gave the signal to her men to prepare for the attack. Then she signaled the rest of her soldiers to flank around them, and to attack from behind. Several hundred more men, and fifty of her personal guards came from around the other side of the castle, ready for battle.

*The King and his men were now outnumbered.
Although they had the upper hand, having a
giant dragon, an oversized lioness, and a giant
owl for allies...*

The battle began and Liza's men wasted no time charging upon the enemy. Swords clashed and horses collided with one another, soldier-to-soldier and blade-to-blade, men fought for their lives and for their cause. Unmercifully, blood did spill forth from deeply wounded men, as each one that met the other end of the blade fell to their knees. During this vicious battle, horses fell on top of their riders as the enemy slit their throats to get to their masters and leaving them to die where they had fallen.

Migata and Gaia teamed up to attack Liza's men, flinging the men's bodies left and right. Luna flew down and grabbed the enemy with her sharp talons ripping their heads clean off. Gaia flew as low to the ground as possible, igniting all in her wake. Screaming ensued as flames engulfed the enemy, they ran around in circles as to try and put their flaming bodies out.

Some of Liza's men could not stomach what was happening to their fellow soldiers, so they ran like cowards leaving the rest of the battle to the others. King Jason's men fought fearlessly, and then utilized the assistance they had with their giant allies. Helping them to become the victors in this reckless battle.

In the midst of all the chaos, Princess Ellyria was left stranded. Lord Brom, Lord Thomas, and Prince Rowan had left her side to join in the battle, leaving her defenseless. Princess Ellyria decided to call out for Isis, but she was nowhere to be seen. She was helpless at this point, fearful for all the men in her life that were in battle, and at the moment in fear of her own life. Standing next to the cellar entryway, she thought it may be best to go back inside, but she was not leaving without Isis. She tried to call Isis once more, but her call was stifled and replaced by a gasp when she was grabbed from behind by one of Liza's soldiers. Princess Ellyria tried to scream, but was quickly silenced by the large hand. She tried to fight him, but was no match for his brutish strength. Hearing his low laughter in her ear, he licked the side of her face.

"Settle down now pretty, I want you," he whispered.

All of a sudden, he was groping her, grabbing her breast with his free hand, and then sliding it down her stomach to grab between her legs. She bit him as hard as she could until she tasted the bitterness of his blood. When he pulled it back in pain, she tried to scream for help and get away. Before she knew it, he struck her hard across the face and she fell.

Princess Ellyria stayed down, lying still and trying to collect her senses. No man before had ever struck her. Her face throbbed, and her mouth was bloody. She was using her skirt-tails to wipe off the blood, when all of the sudden she was yanked up off the ground. The guard she had bitten appeared quite angry, as he stood her upright and ripped open the front of her gown.

Princess Ellyria tried to cover her breasts with her hands, the dirt on her cheeks left streaks from her tears. Before she knew what happened the man had forced himself upon her once again. She was powerless on the ground, and too weak to fight him off.

Luckily, another guard interrupted his malicious actions. The guard had arrived just in time, to help get the Princess Ellyria back to her feet. Or so she thought anyway. He bound her hands together, preventing her from fighting them any further. She was not so lucky when the other man began molesting her too. They both took turns fondling her breasts, and then licking her face and neck. Both men made horrible grunting noises, while the stink of them was clinging to her bruised and violated skin. Tears stung her eyes and she was helpless to escape the two guards that had a tight grip on her arms, while they continued their assault of her.

The Princess Ellyria tried to kick them, but it did not affect their heavy legs. They acted as if this was just another hunt to them and she was the quarry. Giving up and losing her strength, she tried to call for Isis once more, but the guard raised his hand as if to hit her again to silence her. Princess Ellyria felt the two men's excitement for her press against her, and she prayed to the Gods that they did not get to rape her.

"No need for such violence, no one can hear her screams above all the chaos in the distance," a voice called out. It was Liza, manifesting from out of nowhere it seemed, with another guard accompanying her. In the nick of time too, because one of the men had already risen up her skirt and was searching for her undergarments with his hand, while the other was undoing his trousers.

Princess Ellyria had never been more relieved to see her. The men quickly stopped their attack on her and bowed their heads to show obedience. Liza walked up to the Princess Ellyria to try and cover her now naked breasts with the shawl she was wearing. It seemed as if she was actually taking pity on her.

"Do not worry my good men, after I get what I need from her, then you can have your way with her. Until that time comes, you will behave yourselves. And do up your trousers," she ordered. She turned to the battered and abused girl, whom she finally had in her clutches again. This time she would not let her get away.

"You are not going to get away this time, dearie. Everyone else is too busy sword fighting to notice you are even in danger. It is so sad, really," she laughed maniacally.

Liza's laughter was cut short by the scream of the large man holding Princess Ellyria. Isis had snuck up from behind him tearing into his flesh with her massive jaws, causing him to let go of Princess Ellyria. Before she could get away, the other guard standing beside Liza shot Isis with his bow and arrow. Isis fell to the ground and did not move.

"No!" shouted Princess Ellyria. She knelt down beside the barely breathing Isis. She took Isis's head into her lap, running her blood-covered hands all over her friend to try and console her. "What have you done?" she screamed.

The arrow had pierced her chest, the wound was deep, too deep to try and pull it out without cutting it out. She glared up at the guard, and then at Liza, if looks could kill they would be dead in an instant. Her body shook uncontrollably with anger and fear.

"You will pay for this," her eyes flashed like emeralds in the sunlight, reflecting the tears cascading down her cheeks.

"No, my dear. You will in spades. Seize her and do not let her get away this time. I have plans for that one," Liza commanded.

The guards grabbed the grief stricken Princess Ellyria from Isis's side, leaving her helpless to die. There was nothing she could do as she was taken away. Feeling victorious, Liza grabbed Princess Ellyria's other arm and led her back into the castle.

Luna had seen what had happened and alerted Prince Dakota to the scene. He did not arrive in time to help his sister, but did stop to help a badly injured Isis, who was barely breathing and motionless. Prince Dakota called for his owl, he had only one shot of saving Isis and that was by getting her home as quickly as possible, but he feared the worst for her.

"Luna, take her home, be gentle and be safe," he instructed. He assisted Isis into the carrier harness and sent Luna on her way. Would his sister's best friend even make the journey home alive?

Since Prince Dakota was a master alchemist, he had no use for a sword. He wished he had one now, as he followed his sister and her captors into the castle. Fortunately he always had a well-stocked pouch, which he carried on his waist belt. Luckily today, he had his favorite black powder to distract the guards with.

The battle between King Jason's men and Liza's men had finally come to an end. Most of Liza's men had fallen, or had run away, leaving the King, and his men victorious...

Tired and bloody from his enemies, King Jason looked around making accounts for all whom survived, only to find one of his sons missing.

"Check around the entire perimeter of the castle, leave no stone unturned," he ordered. "Report back to me, or to Prince Anthony, as to what you find immediately."

A few of his men went on the search, and he turned to look for Luna, but she was missing as well.

"He must be somewhere, father," Prince Anthony said approaching him. Prince Rowan, Prince Ian, Lord Brom, and Lord Thomas all gathered around the King.

Lord Brom looked for the Princess, but she was not where he had left her. Panic began to set in, as he noticed Isis was missing also. He looked around for her, and the wolf in all directions. With neither of them within his sight, he announced his discernment to the others.

"Princess Ellyria is missing, she is not where I left her, nor is Isis," Lord Brom informed the group. He was worried that Liza had captured her once more, in fact he was most certain of it. He was going to get her back whatever the cost. He could not stand the thought of losing her again.

"Let us head back to the castle, maybe they went back down into the cellar for protection away from the battle," suggested Prince Rowan. He was hopeful that his sister had the intelligence enough to get out of the face of danger.

They headed back in the direction of the castle in search of Prince Dakota and Princess Ellyria, when one of Prince Anthony's men came up to them.

"We found some bloody paw prints, and a struggle site, Sire," the young knight said.

They all went and examined the scene left behind. Black fur and blood from a wound as well as footprints left by several individuals, have led them to believe someone or something had been seriously injured.

"That is Isis's fur," Ian announced, squatting down as he picked up the fur and rubbed it between his fingers.

Migata leaned down to sniff the ground where Isis had lain, shaking her massive head, she indicated she got their scent. The giant lioness tracked the scent of Princess Ellyria and Prince

Dakota, which led her to follow it to the cellar entryway.

"Come on, she is on the trail, let her lead the way."

The royal group followed the big cat into the castle, which was a narrow entrance for the giant lioness indeed. She squeezed herself through, leaving behind some of her fur in the doorframe. They trudged on trying to find where Liza may have taken Princess Ellyria, as Migata led the way.

Princess Ellyria found herself back in Liza's clutches again and this time locked up in a prison cell with no way out. Liza had not just one of her personal guards closely watching the cell door, but two of them. She was not taking any risks of the Princess Ellyria escaping again. Heartbroken and despairing, Princess Ellyria mourned over the loss of her best friend. She blamed herself; if she would just stayed home, none of this would have ever happened. How could she have been so foolish to think that she could have aided Lord Brom in rescuing his father? She should have just asked him to take her home instead of this crazy dangerous undertaking, which only caused more heartache. Grabbing up her skirts she just let herself fall to the floor of her prison and sighed, giving up any notions of escaping. Princess Ellyria's clothes were torn and tattered with the stench from those horrible men. Her once beautifully coiled hair was now down in a tangled mess of sweat and dirt. She wept uncontrollably, rocking herself back and forth like an injured child. The remainder of her strength was all used up, and her will to survive slowly diminishing.

The guards laughed at the crying girl in the prison cell. Even though they were told not to molest her, they still waited in anticipation of having her. They raked the keys along the bars, teasing her.

"I will let you out honey, if you are willing to work for it," one of those disgusting men said.

Princess Ellyria did not even look up at them, and ignored their taunts.

Prince Dakota watched closely from a dark corner, planning

a way to break her out. He would place his special black powder in the nearby corridor, down the hall from the prison cells. When the guards go to check on all the commotion, it will buy him enough time to free his sister. He just needed to wait for the right moment.

The small group of men entered the dungeon and decided to split up in pairs to search through the many different corridors. They stopped dead in their tracks, when a round of loud explosions sounded off in the distance.

"It came from down there. This way, follow me," Lord Brom said. Leading the men down the dark, smoke-filled corridor, they could barely see in front of them from the blast. The smoke was so thick they had to stop to cover their faces, as they pressed on to see what had happened.

Along the way, the two guards that had been watching over the Princess Ellyria had rushed out to see what had happened. Lord Brom ran one of the guards through with his sword, unknowingly avenging Princess Ellyria's attacker, while Prince Rowan killed the other with his own blade. They left the bodies and continued to rush through to the prison cells in search of the Princess. They were halfway to the entryway of the prison, when Prince Dakota emerged from the heavily cloaked air with Princess Ellyria by his side.

"Are you alright, my daughter?" King Jason asked. Looking at her present appearance, he thought otherwise. He then pulled Princess Ellyria into a tight embrace. He was afraid to let her go again, but he knew he must, that she would be safer if he sent her on home with her brothers.

Lord Brom was quite taken aback by her ripped dress and disheveled hair. He worried she had been attacked by one of the guards and if so, he wanted them all dead.

"Yes, father. I am alright," the Princess Ellyria choked out. She was still barely able to catch her breath from all the smoke inhalation. She was so grateful to be free from Liza's grasp yet again.

"Prince Dakota and Prince Rowan take your sister home," King Jason ordered his sons. The brothers took care to gather their sister and lead her out of the dungeon, without letting her out of their sights this time. Her tattered clothes shocked them both. They knew how upset their mother would be when she saw her.

"Yes, father. I will call to Gaia and she will get us back home fast," Prince Rowan said assuredly.

"Lord Brom, Lord Thomas, and Prince Anthony, you will come with me, to search for and arrest Liza," the King instructed. "Prince Ian, you stand guard outside with Migata, and alert us if Liza tries to get away. Capture her you may but do not let your kitty have a tasty treat, I want her taken alive."

"We will start the search in her personal chambers," Lord Brom stated. Leading the group to seek out Liza, and arrest her, his thoughts went out to wonder about Princess Ellyria's welfare and hoped she would be all right. He would have offered to escort her himself, but her father may have deemed it inappropriate. So he said nothing and thought it best to go after Liza as instructed by the King.

Liza was indeed in her privy chambers, without any of her soldiers present to protect her. She was trying to gather as many belongings as she possibly could, before the King and his men come to arrest her. She was not going to spend the rest of her life in a cold, dirt-filled prison cell, or worse, be executed.

After hastily cramming as much as she could into her bag, she picked it up and headed for the door. Just as she swung it open, some of the King's men, as well as the King himself, were waiting in the doorway. Liza was not so shocked at the haste they made in finding her, but surprised to see her former stepson.

"Leaving so soon Liza?" the King inquired. "Because you are in luck, we have come to give you a personal escort."

Liza stood there before him, silent. After what she had done to his daughter, the King felt like running her through with his sword, but his people knew he was a merciful King. He would have to wait for his revenge for when she would be put on trial, then he would have his execution and retribution.

"Liza, by order of the King, you are hereby under arrest for the treason and kidnapping of Princess Ellyria Rose. Seize her," Prince Anthony ordered. He stepped aside motioning for Lord Brom, and Lord Thomas to arrest her. Prince Anthony considered killing her right there where she stood, but did not want to displease, or dishonor his father by his actions.

Lord Brom and Lord Thomas grabbed either side of Liza's arms and began to bind her hands tightly. She could only remain calm and still at this point. Liza glared at her captors and would see to it she included them when she sought out her revenge.

"This gives me much pleasure," said Lord Brom.

"To finally see justice done," Lord Thomas finished his son's sentence. The men escorted Liza out of her castle, to her final journey from the life she was familiar with.

Unable to avenge her father, as she had promised, Liza left behind his legacy when she was escorted out...

CHAPTER 12

Gaia let out an incredibly loud roar and shot fire out from her mouth, announcing they had finally arrived in Toledya.

Queen Anna Marie had been patiently awaiting her daughter's safe return, since receiving the message from the carrier pigeon sent by the royal courier that she had been kidnapped by Liza, but had rescued the Princess, and they were on their way back home.

When they landed, Prince Rowan assisted his sister down from the giant dragon's back. Princess Ellyria quickly turned to run towards her mother's waiting arms. Her clothes were barely hanging on, and with tears of joy, they held each other in a long awaited embrace.

"Oh, how I have missed you, my daughter. I was so frightened that I would never see you again," she said weeping, still holding her daughter in her arms, so grateful for her safe return. Carefully addressing her current state of dishevelment, she just gave her daughter a worried look.

"I am fine, mother, I swear. I promise you that I will never run off with strange young men again, who promise me everything and deliver nothing in return," she promised holding her mother tightly. Ellyria missed her so much and she was so happy to be home where she belonged.

"Let us get you inside. I will have a nice hot bath drawn for you and fresh clothes laid out. While you bathe, I shall have a meal prepared for you as well," Queen Anna offered. She was afraid to know just what had happened to her. She saw the bloodstains on her ripped dress that was now falling off of one shoulder, and her once shining black hair was dull and tangled. She feared that her daughter had been attacked and her virtue had been taken.

As they walked arm in arm together back to the castle, Ellyria was most certain that she would never disappoint her mother again. She was happy to finally be home, now only wanting to put this nightmare behind her.

"That sounds wonderful, mother."

King Jason returned to his realm, where he belonged with his family. The battle between him and Liza was finally over. His daughter had been safely delivered back home. The prisoner would face trial, and be punished accordingly. He looked up after dismounting from his horse, when he saw his beautiful wife running towards him, with arms outstretched before her.

The Queen was so worried for his safe return, and embraced him eagerly. She placed many kisses all over his face, and then he found her sweet lips. They kissed passionately for a few moments, both of them ignoring everything else around them. Never wanting them to be separated again, she hoped the entire ordeal with Liza was finally over.

Queen Anna Marie touched her husband's face, smiled, and looked into his eyes. She was so grateful for having such a loving husband and a wonderful father to her children. When they began to turn in the direction of the castle, she paused for a moment and looked up at her husband.

"Thank you so much for seeing to our daughter's safe return and to yours as well."

Still in the comfort of each other's warm embrace, they just stood there staring deeply into one another's eyes. They tenderly kissed each other once more, and then he stopped to caress her face with his large but gentle hand.

"Of course, I would not have let any harm come to our daughter," he said proudly, looking at his wife with loving eyes, and smiled. "I have brought back a prize for you, my dear."

"A prize?" she asked puzzled. What could he possibly have

brought back with him besides their children?

Motioning for Lord Brom, and Lord Thomas, he turned to his wife.

"You will see, " he leaned over and whispered to her. "Bring the prisoner forward."

Lord Brom, and Lord Thomas did as commanded and brought forth Liza and presented her to the Queen.

Queen Anna glared at the woman who kidnapped her daughter. She wanted to see justice done. She wished for her trial to begin now, watching this woman being beheaded would be somewhat comforting. Alas, the only thing she could do was keep her composure, which in this instance was quite difficult.

"Do you have anything to say for yourself right now before your Queen?" the King questioned his prisoner, "not that it will save you." He looked at Liza with disgust. How could she have let his daughter endure such a horrible ordeal? He wanted to have her run through right now.

"I have nothing to say. The crimes set against me are false. I did not commit any such crimes," Liza stated.

How easily the lies spilled forth out of her mouth, it must have left a bitter taste. The Queen knew for certain now this woman was completely insane. For a moment, the Queen was in total shock, and could not believe the waste coming from Liza's mouth. Her brown eyes turned black, her face flushed bright red, tears stung her eyes, and she fought hard not to cry. How could she have the audacity to lie to her face like that? The Queen's emotions came boiling to the surface, she was blinded with rage and could no longer contain them. Without thinking, and acting purely on impulse, she balled up her fist, and punched Liza hard in the nose. Liza squealed in pain as she was knocked completely off her feet and fell to the ground.

Lord Brom, and Lord Thomas just stepped back, taking no care to try and prevent her fall. The two men were laughing to themselves at such a sight. Liza tried to clean up her face from the blood that poured from her newly broken nose with the hem of her dress. However, the King could not contain his composure.

He laughed out loud at the richly–deserving, foul woman that just had been assaulted by his wife. King Jason ordered Liza to be taken away and locked up in the dungeon. Now that the prisoner was behind bars, they could plan for her trial and her inevitable execution as soon as possible. He was completely at rest now, confident in having contained their enemy. The royal family would finally able to continue with their lives and move on.

"This calls for a celebration, we will host a ball in the Princess's honor for her safe return," the King announced. All cheered in agreement as plans were quickly arranged in preparing for the grand ball, in honor of the Princess Ellyria.

While everyone was busy with the decorations and food preparations, Princess Ellyria was supposed to be resting in her chambers, but she could not sleep. She was plagued by horrible nightmares of her painful ordeal. Every time she closed her eyes, she saw those horrible men, and still it sickened her that she could almost still feel their hands upon her. She had soaked for quite some time in the rose scented bath that had been drawn for her earlier, and tried hard to scrub away the scent of the filthy men that touch her and soiled her skin. So in staying awake, she was able to shut them out of her mind.

Princess Ellyria chose to think of more pleasant things, settling on Lord Brom. What was he doing at this very moment? Was he thinking of her? Daydreaming, she recalled the memory of when he first kissed her. It was most extraordinary to her how passionate he was and how gentle he had been with her during their long journey together. If it were his touch upon her body, it would not have offended her so. Fancying herself that she could be in love with him, scared her more than it made her feel good about it. She definitely did not think she was ready for a grownup commitment. Or was she? She would have to ponder it further.

Princess Ellyria grabbed her drying cloth from the table and collected the moisture dripping off of her. She draped it over her changing screen, and swapped it out for her sleeping gown. Lord Brom was still fresh on her mind when she crawled between cloud-like bedding. She closed her eyes keeping the happy memories close to mind.

While her daydreaming continued with most happy memories of Lord Brom, she finally drifted off to a peaceful slumber...

CHAPTER 13

Deep in the forest, darkness had taken over the land, thereby turning day into night. Wolves howled their loneliness in song, serenading the moon, while owls cried out to warn their prey. The dense fog crept over the ground, while enveloping it's thick veil around old and withered trees.

Running barefoot through the woods, she ignored the sticks breaking under her feet and sharp stones cutting into them, while branches grabbed her clothes and slashed into her tender flesh. She was out of breath but could not stop now. She had to hurry to find shelter of some kind if only to hide and rest for just a little while. The full moon in the night sky gave just enough light so she could see directly in front of her, but the dense fog made it difficult to see farther away. She wished she could remember where Lord Brom had said to go, 'the little cottage in the woods.' Where was it? Exhausted, and terribly sore from running for so long, she began to recognize her surroundings. Looking behind her and realizing she was not being followed, she was able to slow down and stop to catch her breath. This was the same cottage that he had brought her to when he brought her to Liza, so long ago. It seemed to be in terrible ruin, as if no one had lived here in a very long time. Peering inside a window, she could see that no one was there, so she went on inside.

The mice were now the only inhabitants, cobwebs covered the corners, and thick dust had lain undisturbed upon the furnishings. The mice scurried away, squeaking their fear of her, as she entered the very room in which she had freed herself from Liza's grasp. Walking to the other end of the house, she turned the knob of the back door, when suddenly she heard a loud crash in the parlor. She decided to go and investigate, thinking it would be wise to arm her person with something, just in case. Taking a piece of broken chair leg she found, she thought it would suffice. She slowly walked back to the parlor, retracing her steps from whence she came in at. Seeing nothing in front of her or up ahead, she proceeded into the room, there was nothing there. Suddenly, a mouse ran across her foot. She screamed, as her heart felt like it was beating out of her chest, and she threw the broken chair leg at the mouse as it ran off.

"Stupid mouse!" she yelled at the nasty vermin. Just when her breathing caught up with her, someone grabbed her from behind. On pure impulse, she reached for the broken chair leg, which she then used to assault her attacker. Eyes clenched shut, she hit her assailant hard with the chair leg, and he yelled out in pain, releasing his grasped on her.

"Wait Ellyria. It is just I, Brom! Take it easy! What did I say about fighting with your eyes closed anyway!" he shouted.

Looking at the man whom she was on a first name basis with now, still called her princess sometimes as his pet name for her. Which made her wonder, if it really was him or not.

"I am so glad you escaped him. I was so worried when you were not behind me that he had trapped you," she said relieved. Searching his eyes for any trickery, she decided to test him.

Taking him into her arms she kissed him passionately, Lord Brom smiled and returned her kisses with fervor. She pushed him away and saw the bewildered look on his face, she knew he was no imposter.

"Why did you stop, Princess?" a very aroused Lord Brom questioned. He looked at her, and laughed as she stood there tapping her bare foot with her arms crossed giving him her classic glare.

"Did you really think it was not me?"

She embraced him again, and looked up into his bright blue eyes. "I am sorry, but I had to be sure. So I tested you."

The Amulet of Elements

"Kissing me was your test? Well if that was your test, I think you had better do it again just to make sure," he teased her.

She pushed him away, and then slapped his arm. She could not believe after all their time apart he was still the charmer.

"I can not believe that after all these years you still have not changed a bit."

"Well, dear Princess, neither have you," he joked.

Surprised to see him in the Dark Forest of Woe, and searching for the same magical object could not have been a coincidence. Then after the giant, terrible, two-headed dog came running after them, there was no time to reminisce about old times together. Especially when that two-headed dog was guarding the wizard's house and they had just been in it looking for the amulet. Of course they would not have found it with it around his neck, as was duly noticed when he had sent his giant dog after them. Her brother Prince Anthony had captured the wizard's apprentice. The boy confessed where his Lord was hiding in the forest and told him of his powerful amulet.

The Amulet of Elements could be used with the heart's desire of its owner; changing anything into one of the four elements, Earth, Air, Fire, or Water. As the wearer, he or she could then imagine anything they wanted and the object would appear. When one already possessed a natural gift of magic like the wizard Raul, the amulet would work more powerfully. Princess Ellyria had the chance maybe to defeat him with the amulet, but not without it. And in her hands, the amulet would be even more powerful. In the prophecy, the amulet was never mentioned, because it was thought of as just a myth. The amulet was very real and must be retrieved from the evil wizard Raul. Princess Ellyria caressed Lord Brom's face wondering what his part was in all of this and why he was there in the first place.

"Why, may I ask, did you so happen to be at the wizard's house at the very same moment I was?" she inquired.

He avoided her gaze, knowing she could look him in the eye and know whether he was lying to her or not.

"What are you not telling me?" Taking his hand she placed it to her heart and closed her eyes. She could feel what he felt in his heart and hear the thoughts in his head. Taking a few steps back she could not believe what she saw.

"My very own father hired you to watch out for me? When did this happen?" she asked angrily. She just stared at Lord Brom, waiting to hear what he had to say.

"When your brother Prince Anthony heard the apprentice's confession, your father sent word to me before you headed out on this quest, asking me to protect you," he informed her.

Princess Ellyria raised her arms and slowly the objects about the room began to float up beside her. Then in a fluid motion, she sent them flying across the room, barely missing Lord Brom in the process. She could see the look of fear in his eyes.

"Does it look as though I need protection?"

He looked at her in awe. Her father had not mentioned she had harnessed all the power within her already.

"I see you have learned to control your powers," he observed.

"Yes, well, it took time over the last few years, but I am finally able to utilize them better. I hope I did not scare you too bad?" she asked tenderly.

"I was not scared," he replied hastily. She gave him that glance again. How she knew, was incomprehensible to him.

"I know," she smiled. Many nights had passed, yet when the full moon was high in the sky and the stars shown brightly, she would always think of him.

Lord Brom looked out the window to see if the coast was clear, and she came up behind him, wrapping her arms around his waist.

"We should head out, but I think it would be best if we remained here for the night, then leave at dawn," he advised.

Lord Brom turned around to face her, cupped her beautiful face into his gentle hands, and leaned down to kiss her passionately. Returning his kiss with equal ardency, she began to feel familiar feelings stir within her. No longer the girl child of his past, she had grown into the woman standing before him.

Their kissing ignited the fires of long ago, the love that had to be buried in the ashes between them like the Phoenix rising from flames. He paused for a moment to look at her to see if she was feeling this between them as well. She pulled him to her and her hands searched his sculpted body.

Picking her up off her feet, he carried her to the bedroom and carefully set her on the bed. He quickly removed the tattered blanket, and then laid her on the flat of her back. They searched each other's mouths with eager tongues entwined. Lord Brom caressed her face with featherlike strokes of his fingertips. She smiled as he placed tiny kisses from her mouth down her cheek to the inside of her neck, his lips caressing her skin so softly. His hands began to explore the hard hidden peaks of her nipples beneath her dress, acknowledging the fact her cumbersome corset was not containing them. Wriggling her body to meet his touch, she had a newfound feeling in her loins she could not ignore. And urged him on to touch her.

She moved his hand to the inside of her thighs pressing her body up into his. Kissing hungrily, he removed his shirt, pausing only for a moment to pull it over his head. It was then she noticed his scar on his abdomen and remembered when he had been stabbed by one of Liza's guards. With his shirt removed, she then caressed his naked chest and explored his body as he had done to hers, placing kisses to his chiseled form like he was like a perfectly sculpted statue. He returned her mouth to his and urgently began to fumble with the ties of her dress, untying the strings to release her beautifully developed breasts. Cupping them in his hands he caressed them as they molded perfectly under his touch. He gently kissed each breast, eagerly taking care each nipple had equal time for him to suckle.

Princess Ellyria arched her back up into his lean body over the sensations he caused to inflame within her. Lord Brom picked her up to sit on his lap, the heat of his desire underneath her equally matched her own. She rocked her body into him, swaying back and forth in rhythmic motion. They continued their exploration of each other's bodies and he could wait no longer. Lord Brom flipped her off his lap onto her back, and then he removed his trousers. He carefully removed the rest of her dress, displaying all of her beauty for him to see. Leaning over her, he returned her sweet kisses, and she arched her body into his, waiting for him to take her. Lord Brom wanted to be gentle with her for her first time. He placed his fingers inside her to help her relax and be able to invite him in without hurting her. She was beside herself with a fever so strong she felt she would burst at his touch. So when he rested himself between her soft thighs, she felt his fever for her as well. When he thought she was ready, and he was about to enter her, she heard her name being called…

"Ellyria. Ellyria, wake up. It is time for your party, Ellyria," her mother said. Princess Ellyria woke up drenched in sweat, and the sacred place between her legs was equally moist. How embarrassing to have such a vivid dream, and then her mother wake her up right before it was fixing to get really good.

"What were you dreaming of? From the sounds you were making, it must have been really disturbing."

Princess Ellyria's cheeks turned a bright shade of red from shame and embarrassment.

"I think it was more of a premonition than a dream."

Queen Anna listened to her daughter tell her about the happenings in her dream, but not all of it of course.

Princess Ellyria told her mother everything she wanted her to hear, and then she sat up in her bed to hug her.

"It was so real like I was there. The wizard, the two headed dog that chased me, and then Lord Brom was there by father's order," she finished.

Queen Anna looked at her daughter and knew this time would come when she would begin to have visions. She only wished her little girl was not growing up so fast.

"We need to figure out what all this means, and more about this Amulet of Elements. You mentioned the wizard was there. When is all this supposed to happen? If we can find out, maybe we can prevent it from ever happening," her mother said.

Princess Ellyria got out of bed and she watched her mother

go to her wardrobe to pull out her favorite gown.

"What should I do, mother?" she questioned searching her mother's face for some kind of answer.

"I am not sure, my dear, but we must get you ready for the ball. I will leave you to get ready and come to check on you a little later."

As her mother left the room, Princess Ellyria Rose went over to her vanity. She looked at her reflection of the girl before her, imagining the woman she was destined to become...

CHAPTER 14

Fireworks soared up into the night sky, exploding into brilliant colors and shapes. The invitations had been sent out with much haste, and had produced many guests that came to welcome Princess Ellyria Rose home.

The Queen had awakened her daughter from a well-deserved nap earlier and had returned to her chambers to see if she was ready. The ball had already begun with guests eagerly awaiting her noble presence downstairs. She entered her daughter's chamber to see that she was at her vanity but had not put forth much effort into getting ready.

"Are you ready, my dear? I know all this is sudden, but you know your father, and how patience is not a virtue of his. When he wants something, he tends to do things without thinking ahead of time," she added.

"Yes, mother, it is okay. I just hope this party turns out better than the last one."

"Oh, it will, dear. This time, perhaps even better, and with a certain handsome young man waiting downstairs."

"I am not sure that I can forgive him mother, after all that has happened," she replied.

Queen Anna looked at her only daughter. She was too young to have to make such adult decisions. She worried for her and wished she could make the decision for her, but she could not. Her daughter needed to learn some of life's lessons on her own, no matter how hard they may be. Anna would give her as much guidance as she could offer.

"I am not justifying him in any way. He did make sure in the end you were safe. And he was forced to do it against his will," she said lovingly.

Her daughter looked up at her and smiled, and then continued to stare at her reflection in the mirror.

"You know if you need to talk about what happened I am here for you," her mother said.

"Yes, I know," she sighed. She began to recall the nightmare that she had yet to wake up from. Princess Ellyria could not help but weep. Tears cascaded down her porcelain white cheeks, and then she found herself in her mother's loving arms. Telling her mother what had happened to her would be hard. She knew her mother loved her no matter what and she felt she would not judge her.

"Are you ready to talk about it, or do you need more time?" her mother asked.

Wiping the tears from her face with her hands, she looked up at her mother, and nodded her head that she was. Taking a deep breath she began to tell her tale.

"Lord Brom sweet-talked me into running away with him, and then took me to Liza's cottage. I had been drugged and locked up in a crystal cage. I felt like I would never be able to get out and how I might not ever see you again."

The tears kept flowing and she wiped her face again recalling painful memories. She went on to tell how she organized her own escape route and was able to play on Lord Brom's sympathies to help her escape.

"I hit Liza right upside her head with the water pitcher, and I was surprised that it actually worked," she said proudly. Taking a deep breath, she paused to collect herself before she went on to continue her story. "We had gotten pretty far from the cottage when we had to stop so the poor horse could rest. Lord Brom, and I had a fight and emotions were high at that moment. That is when I had the premonition about his father, and I felt that it was shown to me so I could help him," she revealed.

Listening carefully, her mother understood that the visions ability to work is tied to their emotions. As Princess Ellyria continued, she watched her mother's reactions to see if she had become upset at all, and she had not yet.

"On the way to the castle, we were chased by Liza's guards, at first there was only one after us, and then there were three. And we barely got away from two of them, before the third caught up to us. I was so scared. I had been thrown from the horse and had blacked out. The next thing I remember seeing was the guard on top of Lord Brom fixing to slit his throat. That is when I grabbed the tree branch and knocked the man off of him. Lord Brom was able to fight him off, and then threw him over the cliff. He was injured, I was able to help him onto the horse, and then after that was when we rode out to the old corn mill. When we finally arrived, I cleaned and bandaged his wound. Soon after, Prince Rowan and Gaia showed up with Isis. Instead of going home with Prince Rowan, as I should have, we decided to all go and rescue Lord Brom's father. Once we had arrived the men went to the dungeon by way of the cellar, while I stayed back to stand watch and give a signal if anyone came. I waved my arms at them that someone was coming, but they went on without me, leaving me to fend for myself and to get rid of the guard. When he tried to grab for me, Isis bit him, and pushed him onto a big rock in the ground, knocking him out. I made my way down into the dark, musty, old dungeon and had to duck into an alcove where I backed into a huge spider web." She watched as her mother cringed upon hearing about it, she hated spiders too.

"I was pretty well hidden, until I got caught in that very sticky spider web. I had hoped it was empty, but I was wrong. This giant, hairy, black spider fell onto my left shoulder. I was able to fling it off and it smacked against the wall. You think it would have killed it, but it just got up and scurried away," she grimaced at the thought of it. She watched her mother cringe again with a horrified look on her face.

"When I had gotten the rest of the sticky web off of me, Lord Brom scared me to death when he grabbed me from behind.

We continued on now not only looking for his father at this point, but for Prince Rowan as well. He had gotten lost when they had split up. Later when we found him, Prince Rowan told us how he had found out what they did with the dead prisoners. When we came closer to the cells from my vision, we were detained for a moment by one of the guards. Lord Brom punched him just once and knocked him out cold. He was twice the size of Lord Brom and yet he still bested him," she said smiling. Her mother saw the proud look in her eyes knowing exactly where her head was at in that regard.

"I took the keys off of him, and then moved on to where Lord Brom's father was. We were able to break him out, and then quickly left before we were caught. We thought we had gotten away, until Liza turned up with more guards and we were detained once more. That is when father, Prince Ian, Prince Dakota, and Prince Anthony showed up to rescue me. We were all made to go outside when father made his first attempt to arrest Liza. Of course she resisted, and then that is when the fighting broke out. I was left alone, scared, and helpless at the cellar doors. I felt completely useless at this point. I did not know what to do. I tried calling Isis, but she never came. The battle was bloody, and so many lives were lost. I worried for my brothers, and for father."

Queen Anna watched her daughter cry and shake uncontrollably, knowing there was more she had not told her.

Tears streamed endlessly down Princess Ellyria's cheeks, and her eyes had become swollen from crying. She did not know if she had the heart to tell her mother about the ordeal Liza's guards had put her through, but her mother was there, and she was still safe at home.

"While I was standing alone calling for Isis, one of Liza's men came up behind me, and grabbed me. I tried to fight him, but he was too strong." She paused for a minute to catch her breath. "He—he started to whisper things in my ear, telling me he wanted me, and then began to lick my face. After that… after that, he started to touch me, grabbing my breasts, he was hurting me!" Princess Ellyria cried out.

The Amulet of Elements

Queen Anna took her grief stricken daughter into her arms as she tried to console her. Princess Ellyria was trembling, and her breathing was erratic.

"There, there, it is alright. You are here, your safe. I have got you now. I am not going to let anyone hurt you again. You do not have to talk about it any longer if you do not want to," she said reassuringly.

Princess Ellyria sat up, wiped away her tears, and waved at her mother that she was all right to continue.

"He grabbed my breasts and fondled them, and when he reached for my privy parts, that is when I bit him. I bit him so hard that I could taste his salty blood. He let go long enough for me to scream for Isis, but then he hit me across the face and I fell to the ground. When I was trying to clean myself up, the angry man came at me again and ripped my dress open. My breasts were now exposed from my corset coming undone. Then he forced himself upon me, and between my legs. I fought him as hard as I could. Then he stopped his assault when the other guard showed up. I thought perhaps he was there to save me, but I was wrong. The other guard joined his cohort in the abuse. I had given up trying to fight them off, as both of them fondled me, I felt their desire pressing into my thighs, and I was so afraid they were going to rape me."

Taking a deep breath, she tried hard to choke back her tears that kept flowing like a river after a long day's rain.

"Then while one of the men held me, the other was undoing his trousers. I tried thrashing about, fighting them again, and for a moment my mouth was free to try to call for Isis again, but he threatened to hit me. They reached up for my undergarments, probing at my privy parts. When the other guard exposed the weapon, he was going to use against me. They both stopped in their tracks because Liza appeared in the nick of time. I was actually happy to see her. I put aside my hatred for the moment as Liza covered me with her shawl. I was not shocked to hear from her that she would let them have me, when she had gotten what she needed from me. She told me I would not get away, and then instructed the men to bring me back into the castle. That is when Isis showed up and bit the guard in the back of his thigh. The other guard shot Isis with his bow and arrow. I thought she was going to die, my heart felt as if it was being ripped in two, and after what the guards had done to me I was blind with fury. They jerked me up to my feet, dragged me into the castle's dungeon, and locked me up. The same two guards, who almost raped me, were left in charge of guarding my cell. With strict orders not to touch me, it did not stop them from taunting me. And at that point, I was in such despair that I did not even care what happened. All I could think about was how it was my fault. If I would have been a proper Princess, remained at home and acquired to become a lady, none of this would have happened in the first place," she said.

Sobbing in her mother's arms, Princess Ellyria felt great comfort in telling her. A great burden had finally been taken away. She continued her story, told her of the loud explosion she heard, and all the commotion that followed.

"The guards that were watching me ran off to find out what the big explosion was. And then right after they were gone, Dakota was at my prison cell, picking the lock on the door. He reassured me that he was going to get me out of there, and then told me how sorry he was for not being there for me when I was little. He said he could not have imagined his life without me, and he was so grateful that I was okay," she said, smiling slightly. "He helped me out of the darkness that was filled with thick black smoke from the explosion and that is when father and the rest of my brothers made their way to where we were. I could barely breathe, my chest hurt and my eyes burned from the smoke, but I had never been more grateful then I was at that very moment to be alive," she said with a full smile.

Her mother embraced her and her heart ached as though it had been ripped out. She felt so powerless that she could not do anything to help her daughter get over this. All she could do now was just listen and be a shoulder to cry on. Queen Anna kept her head low, she did not want Princess Ellyria to see the tears falling from her eyes. She felt it might be best to leave, and would check back with her after she could regain control of her own emotions. Wiping her own eyes, the Queen helped her daughter to her feet.

"Now I think it is time that you start getting ready, young lady, I will be back to see if you are ready a bit later," her mother said.

Queen Anna left the room and cried silently into her hands and quickly headed to her own chambers to be alone. She curled herself up on her bed and needed some time to absorb all that her daughter had told her. The Queen was grateful that her daughter was alive and had remained chaste during this horrible ordeal. When she was able to calm down and put her own reverence to rest, she was able to think more clearly. Having to find out your daughter willingly ran off with a grown man, who then had intentionally kidnapped her, then helped her escape only to go on a dangerous quest to rescue his father, was disturbing to say the least. And then that gruesome attack upon her daughter's body by those disgusting men, was so deplorable and the most horrifying thing to comprehend.

After adequate time had passed Queen Anna decided to go back to check on her daughter, to see if she was any nearer to being ready for the ball...

Princess Ellyria was at her vanity when her mother returned to her chambers. She had been thinking about Lord Brom again, and had decided to ask her mother how she and her father had met. How did she know he was the one she wanted to spend the rest of her life with?

"Mother, may I ask you something personal?"

Her mother looked at her strangely.

"Yes, of course. You may ask anything, darling," she answered her daughter.

Princess Ellyria looked at her mother and slightly blushed, even though she had nothing to be ashamed of.

"How did you meet my father?" she questioned innocently and turned around in the chair to face her mother before she began her story of the past.

"Well, when I was about your age, give or take a few years, I worked at the market alongside my mother. She was a gypsy and a gifted fortuneteller, who also made beautiful jewelry. One day when I was helping her at the market, I saw your father. He was so handsome, that I had to come up with a way to get his attention. So I grabbed a necklace from the table and walked right up to him. He was neat in appearance, looked like a commoner, but did not appear to be poor."

"So you never knew he was the King?"

"No, I never knew, even when we began seeing each other. He had such a gentle heart, so full of life, and was quite the joker. He always knew how to make me laugh, and he was a great kisser," she said affectionately.

Princess Ellyria scrunched up her nose at that last part. She did not want to hear about her parents kissing.

As her mother continued her tale, her eyes lit up in such a way that was unfamiliar to her while she spoke about her father.

"During this time when your father was courting me, he had been hard pressed about keeping his secret to me. He began to be pressured by his advisors that he should not marry me, because I was a commoner. That is when he asked me to marry him. It was very romantic, under the light of the full moon, and the brilliant stars in the sky. Of course I said yes right away, that was when he told me who he really was. I immediately worried it would not be allowed. I was afraid that we would not be able to be wed, and then he assured me it would be all right. His father before him had married his mother for love, and he assured me that he would do the same. We were married shortly after he had proposed. It was on our wedding night when we conceived your brother, Anthony," her mother said beaming.

"Ew, mother, I did not need to know about my brother's

conception. I do thank you for sparing me the details," she teased.

Queen Anna laughed at her daughter, and smiled.

"Is there anything else you would like to know, my dear?"

"Well, how did you know he was the one you really wanted to be with the rest of your life?"

Queen Anna took her daughter's hand in her own and smiled.

"I suppose I just knew. What your father and I had was special. We knew in our hearts that we loved one another as the forest loves the rain. My mother believed that I was too young to marry, especially to a King, but she let me follow my own path. She always said that I had been born with a purpose that I had to see put to good use, she never told me what it was. She had died in her sleep before we were to be married. I always felt that I had killed her by breaking her heart and going against her will. It was my decision to marry your father anyway. He reassured me that was a silly notion and to not put that kind of burden upon myself," she finished her story.

That made Princess Ellyria begin to think that she could never imagine not having her mother around. Her body gave a slight shudder at such a very forbidden concept. She did not want to put her mother through what she went through with her own mother. She paused for a moment to think about what she should do, in retrospect to her own life.

"Are you going to finish getting ready, dear?" she questioned again and looked at her beautiful daughter. Queen Anna was so happy to have her back home safe and sound. She knew it was nearing her time to ready herself for her own destiny.

I will be finished in a moment, mother. I just need some time to myself."

Her mother nodded her head smiling, and then left the room. Queen Anna knew it would be better to leave her daughter for some privacy and to get ready on her own.

Once she was left alone, Princess Ellyria had more time to think clearly. Everything had been clouded, her thoughts, her feelings, and it was all very confusing to her. So many things had happened to her within a span of just a few weeks. She had lost her best friend, rescued a man, was assaulted and nearly raped, and all the while trying to escape from Liza not once, but twice. The one thing that was most surprising to her was finding love out of it all. Never did she think after been locked up in the castle, away from the world outside, that she would have fallen for the very first man she had met. She would always been scared of everything before, terribly unsure of herself, but now the girl in the reflection was so much more confident than before. Maybe she did not yet know what she wanted to be or do with her life, but she was starting to believe in herself. She knew this was just the beginning of the journey ahead. While she looked at the adolescent girl in the mirror, she saw the emergence of the young woman staring back at her.

All at once, everything became so clear to her now. She finally had a decision regarding Lord Brom, and was ready to face what she had to do. With her epiphany fresh in her mind, she left her chambers to make a proper arrival downstairs for all the guests who had come in honor of her safe return.

Trumpets sounded as Princess Ellyria Rose made her grand entrance at the top of the great stairwell. She smiled at all the people that had gathered about in the great hall. At this very moment, she was the happiest she had ever been in her life.

Gracefully making her way to the bottom of the grand staircase, her hand slid down the intricately carved wood. Princess Ellyria's brothers were standing there at the bottom ready to escort her to the great banquet hall. Queen Anna Marie, and King Jason were waiting patiently for their daughter's arrival.

Lord Brom was standing there beside them as well. Princess Ellyria was more beautiful than he could have ever imagined, he simply watched her come down the stairs in such a way that it had appeared as if she was floating down them. Smiling at her, he offered his arm to her to escort her to the ballroom. He was handsome, even more so now that she had come to know him. Lord Brom was a brave and kindhearted young man, who in the end risked his life for her.

The formal announcement was made when she entered the grand ballroom.

"The Princess Ellyria Rose of Toledya, and her escort Lord Brom of Regnuom."

Everyone turned to look upon the Princess. She was so beautiful in her long emerald gown, which embraced her petite figure. The green gown would match her eyes perfectly if she would become angered, and her long shiny black hair was neatly coiffed upon her head in a large braid almost in the shape of a crown, with crimson rose buds barely bloomed woven into it. She greeted everyone with a smile and a nod, and then proceeded toward her awaiting parents in the ballroom.

"Your Majesties," she said while greeting them.

The proud parents arose and embraced their daughter, and then the King gestured that he was going to speak.

"Here is my beautiful daughter, Princess Ellyria Rose, safe in the loving embrace of myself, and the Queen. I give this present for my daughter, a gift in her honor," the King announced as he motioned for Prince Dakota.

The sea of people made a path, allowing Prince Dakota to bring a bandaged and limping, but now healthy, Isis to his sister.

"Oh, Isis!" Princess Ellyria exclaimed as she fell to the floor wrapping her arms around her faithful best friend. She cared not of her formerly made up face, which had now been ruined with tears. The sight of Isis alive and well made the rest of her pain go away. "I thought you were dead!"

"No, she was severely wounded and your brother, and his wonderful potions healed her," her father said proudly.

"Oh, I am so grateful to you, Prince Dakota!" she exclaimed. She gave him a tight squeeze and a kiss on the cheek while tears streamed down her face.

"You are welcome, Princess Ellyria," her brother replied. As he wiped the tears from her cheeks, and smiled affectionately at his little sister.

Her father then raised his wineglass high, and was joined by all the people around him.

"A toast, to my wonderful wife, who blessed me with five healthy children. To my sons, that helped to save my daughter. To Lord Brom, that kept her safe during her escape. And last but not least, to my beautiful daughter. I am so happy you are home with us now," the King toasted, and then emptied the contents of his glass.

"Here, here!" chorused the crowd, and they too drank from their glasses.

The party continued with dancing and dining, and all were having a most wonderful time. Although, no one had paid any attention to the absent guest of honor...

Princess Ellyria had finally been able to slip away from her party with Lord Brom to the gardens. It was where they first kissed under the light of the moon. As exciting and frightening as it was to go back to the very place where it all began, she knew it was also where it had to end as well. Even considering everything she had just been through, and everything he had done for her, this was the hardest thing she had chosen to do. She turned and looked deep into those striking blue eyes of his, and wished things could be different than they were.

"How is your wound?" she inquired.

He reached to where his bandages were hidden beneath his shirt.

"Healing quite nicely thanks to your crafty stitching," he answered.

The somber note between them seemed to go unnoticed as they continued their leisure stroll through the gardens.

Princess Ellyria stopped along the stone path. She knew what had to be done and broke the silence.

"Lord Brom, I want to thank you for helping me to escape. I

could not have done it without you."

"You are welcome, Princess. And thank you, for saving my life," he said.

She was about to make a statement when he placed a finger over her mouth to silence her. He leaned in to kiss her, gently caressing her beautiful face with his hands, as she succumbed to him. She was beginning to lose her head again to the longing in her heart and the excitement she felt for him. Knowing she had to pull away, she pressed her hands up against his chest to get distance between them.

"I can not let this go on any further."

"What do you mean?"

She wiped the tears that trickled down her cheeks.

Lord Brom gently lifted her chin to meet his lips again, and then paused to pull a ring from his pocket and present it to her.

"I want to marry you, Princess Ellyria Rose. I love you. From the moment we met, just a full moon ago. I knew I loved you even then," he declared.

"I am sorry but—" her words were cut off again by his kiss.

He was hard to resist, but she pushed him away.

"I am sorry, but I can not accept this. I am not ready for marriage. I still need to finish growing up, and find out who I am first. After the adventure I just had, I know I am capable of taking care of myself."

She paused for a moment and once again got lost in his captivating blue eyes. How she wished she could be with him. She yearned for him to stay with her just this one night, but she could not, she was not ready. Ellyria knew he was hurt, she could feel it, but it could not be helped.

"I will never forget you, Lord Brom," she promised. She pulled him toward her, and kissed him one last time.

Lord Brom returned her kisses with such passion that it made her regret her decision, and then he was the one who pushed her away. He reached over to caress her cheek softly, as if to commit it to memory. Then he turned, walked away from her, and leapt onto his horse. He sat there for a moment, drinking in her beauty one last time, and smiled.

    She said not another word, only watched as he rode away in the night.

Princess Ellyria Rose was distraught to see him go but had come to understand it was not the right time for her. Love would have to wait…

CHAPTER 15

Deep within the castle's dungeon, Liza was devising a plan to escape. She was already plotting her revenge on the Princess Ellyria. It was not over for her, she would see to that. King Jason had caused her enough pain in the past and the present. She would kill her to have her revenge if she had to.

Liza needed to think fast in order to escape, before she was summoned to her trial. In the opposite cell from hers, someone had expired in the night. If she could somehow switch places, she would be able to act like the dead body and be carried out of the castle by morning.

She pulled a few hairpins from her head, pulled them slightly apart, and then began to pick the lock on the cell door. After working on the lock for a few moments, the latch finally clicked open; she looked around, but saw no one coming. Her opportunity was now available to switch places with the dead body.

To her amazement, the prison cell was unlocked. She supposed no one was concerned with a dead body getting up and walking out. Still, she listened carefully, but heard no signs of anyone coming. She began to drag the body from its cell to hers.

Liza quickly covered the dead body with a blanket, and ran across to the other prison cell. She then wrapped herself in the blanket and lay down to play dead. She waited patiently for the changing of the guards, and for the moment when they would come and carry her out of the castle thinking she was the expired body.

Finally, Liza would be free, and live to fight another day...

The very next day, King Jason ordered his son, Prince Anthony, to retrieve Liza for her hearing. After many years, this woman would be punished for her crimes against his family, and there would finally be justice for his late father. Never again would she be a threat to his family, or to his realm.

Prince Anthony nodded to the guard on duty as he entered the prison. He walked through the rows of cells until he reached Liza's. He began to rap on the bars with the keys, which created an annoyance of sounds.

"Get up, Liza. It is time for your hearing, to stand charged before your King!" he shouted. He banged even more loudly on the cell bars. "Get up, I say. On your feet this instant!"

With no movements or sounds coming from her prison cell, he proceeded to unlock the cell door and walk over to where her body lay. He gave a nudge with the tip of his boot to wake her, but still no movement.

"Get up I say!" he shouted again. With no signs of response, he leaned down next to her and removed the blanket. The body felt cold and lifeless, but even facedown, he could immediately tell it was not Liza's; and upon turning it over, his suspicions were confirmed.

Prince Anthony stood up and rushed out of the prison cell.

"Sound the alarm! The prisoner has escaped!"

CHAPTER 16

Deep in the Dark Forest of Woe, where the trees are barren and no animals dwell, darkness is felt for those who dare enter; while pain and suffering remain for those who can not leave.

Stirring his most recent potion for his benefactor, Raul needed one final ingredient to complete the vilest of his recipes. He reached into his cupboard only to find himself fresh out.

"Damn it. I thought I had a new one," he muttered.

The loud banging on his front door interrupted him. He opened it to find Liza standing in the doorway, completely disheveled and grotesquely filthy.

"Well, you look like shite," the wizard said.

Liza pushed him out of her way, and entered the cottage.

Raul crinkled his nose when she brushed passed him.

"You smell like shite too."

"Oh, be quiet! I just escaped from the King's dungeon," she squawked back at him. "Is my potion ready?"

"No, madam, it is not. I am missing the final ingredient, the final part to its completion," he told her revising over the list in his head.

"I will also need the amulet I gave you. Where is it?"

Shrugging her shoulders, she put her hands to her head as if she had forgotten something.

"I put it on Lord Brom before he went to lure the Princess to me."

"Well, where is it now? Think carefully, because I need it if we are to succeed," he informed her.

"I never got it back, he must still have it. I told him it would protect him," she confessed.

"Do you have any idea what you have done?"

The floor began to shake, and the windows rattled from his anger; bowls, cups, and plates toppled down from high places and crashed to the floor.

Liza feared him. She always believed that he was better as an ally than an enemy. Now she had to come up with a way to get the amulet back.

"You never told me the significance of the amulet, Raul, only that it would protect whomever wore it."

Raul went to his alter, opened the grimoire, and turned its ancient pages to the chapter concerning the Amulet of Elements. An ancient artifact forged from all four elements, Earth, Air, Fire, and Water; all used to create the stone with the blood from a unicorn to fuse them together.

"In its power, it can grant whoever controls it, the power of creation from ones very own imagination," he read the text. "Also protecting whomever wears it from any other kind of natural magic, such as the magic your little Princess possesses."

"So what happens if a magical person wears it?" Liza questioned.

"If a person born with the gift of magic, like myself, and the Princess, wears the Amulet, it multiplies our powers. Which gives us the power to control the elements as well as anything we create from our imaginations," he explained.

"So in other words, one will have control over anything?"

"Yes, but not you, you are not blessed like I am. But I will bring you to power, if you retrieve the lost item. I need it to finally have the ability to harness the Power of Litha."

"What is the Power of Litha? I thought that was what this amulet was?"

"No, no, no!" he shouted. "You are not getting it into your thick skull. The Power of Litha is only conceived during a full Blood-Moon, during its eclipse. Then at the time of the Summer

Solstice, we will be able to draw down its power while it is most potent. Which only happens every five hundred years."

Raul was beginning to become seriously aggravated with her. He tried to calm himself before he destroyed his house again with his temper.

"So I need you to get your guards together to find that amulet, before the next full moon. Time is of the essence!" he declared.

Liza looked up to the sky as she released the carrier pigeon to send word to her head guard, to gather a band of men to find and capture Lord Brom. With only weeks away from the next full moon, she knew she needed to help her ally with haste, so she could finally have her revenge.

"Oh, and Liza. I think you should know that during this eclipse, your little problem will also be getting her full powers."

Liza turned from the window after releasing the bird, she looked vexed.

"What do you mean, her full power?"

"She currently has only the power of foresight from her mother, the Queen, am I correct?"

"Yes, that is why I wanted her, to control her gift. I assumed that was all she had."

"Well, that is why I have always said that people who "assume things" make asses out of themselves," he said sarcastically. "All joking aside, that Princess is the Chosen One, or have you not intelligent enough minions to supply you with that bit of information?"

"No, I was not aware of that fact. What is it supposed to mean?" she questioned.

"I am growing tired of having to explain every damn thing to you," he said irritably. "I will explain this to you only once, slowly, so you can comprehend what I am telling you. The Chosen One is the only person in this world that can kill me!" he shouted angrily, rattling the entire house again.

Objects fell from high places once more, hitting Liza on the head, in the process, and she cringed at the display of his power.

"Are we clear?" he asked calmly, staring at the woman.

"Yes, sire." She bowed her head in submission, now finally aware that she was no longer in control. She accepted it only because he was her last chance at getting back at that wretched girl. Raul was now the one she must bow down to, just like she had done with her own father.

"Now, besides having the amulet again in my possession, I will also be needing the final ingredient for my potion."

"What would that be exactly?" she inquired with a gulp. Afraid to even ask, she already knew of the prior ingredients she had been forced to collect, and they all had made even her stomach turn. Like the tongue from a poison toad, the head of a snail, the wings from a faery, a foot from a rabbit, and the lips from a virgin who had never experienced true love's kiss. Even the last object she could not bear, since she herself could not have retrieved it. She shivered at the sheer idea of it.

"I need the heart freshly removed from a noble and courageous animal that is pure of heart, as a lion."

"Is this a riddle?" she hesitated to ask. Fearing he might turn her into such an animal, just to have a heart to harvest.

"No, it is a horse, you idiot," he disclosed to her.

She gave a sigh of relief.

"Oh, that makes perfect sense now that you pointed it out. You could have just said so, instead of making up riddles," she complained. Thinking they could use Lord Brom's steed, since she was having him arrested anyway. She would see to it they apprehended his horse too. Laughing inwardly to herself, she sent out another bird to include the newly found information. Now that her plan was set in motion, they just had to wait for him to be brought to her, and her wizard ally.

CHAPTER 17

After many long hours of riding aimlessly through the kingdom, a heartbroken Lord Brom decided his horse needed to rest, and he himself needed to find a warm bed for the night. Before the sun in the sky was beginning to set, he spied a small town on the other side of the hill. Thinking that this would be perfect, he traveled on, promising the tired horse he would be able to retire for the evening soon enough.

As they arrived in town, he observed it to be a quaint place. It had all the comforts a man could possibly need; he saw a blacksmith for his horse, a market for the essentials, a seamstress for his clothes, and a barber for his hair. Though to supply the most important of his needs, he saw the local tavern. Which included a place to sleep, food and beverage, and if he was lucky, a questionable woman to warm his bed.

Lord Brom wanted to make sure his horse was taken care of first, so he went to the blacksmith to ask where he could board him for the night.

"Pardon me, sir. Where could I keep my horse for the night?" Lord Brom inquired.

A surly man covered in soot and sweat turned around, exposing harsh features, and smiled to present some missing teeth.

"I am actually the only one to board the horses for any travelers we may get passing through here. I can also make sure he is fed, watered, groomed, and for an additional coin or two, I will put new shoes on him if you would like," he informed him.

The blacksmith then called for his squire to attend the horse. A small waif of a boy appeared, barely the age of ten, and led the horse to the barn behind the blacksmith's keep.

"That was my son, a strong little lad despite his size," the blacksmith revealed. "He will tend to him properly for you."

Lord Brom nodded his head and felt his horse would be well managed.

"Thank you. I appreciate your taking charge of him." Lord Brom gave a few coins, to fill the blacksmith's purse.

"Where will you be bedding down for the night, sire?" the blacksmith asked.

"I am guessing that I will be staying at that fine tavern across the way there," Lord Brom answered. Is there another tavern to bed down for the night? By the way the blacksmith questioned, he made it sound as though there were.

Lord Brom walked out to the dirt road that divided the blacksmith's shop and the tavern. He looked over the neighboring hill towards the direction he had come by. After many hours of having tried to put the Princess out of his mind, she still haunted him. He had to wipe her from his memory as well as his heart if he were to move forward. He decided to cleanse it with much needed libations; hopefully at the tavern, he would accomplish that and maybe more, to finally forget about her.

Lord Brom entered the tavern with low expectations but was surprised at the decent accommodations it provided. From the looks of its patrons, it seemed as though it was a nice establishment. Providing nice edible meals, plenty of ale, and a nice amount of various women to choose from. Deciding to stay, he seated himself in the back of the dining area. He waited patiently for the nice little barmaid with an ample bosom to wait on him, that he first spied when he came in. He watched her as she made her rounds from table to table, pouring more ale into empty cups, and passed out heavy plates of food. While he waited, he watched the patrons as well, some looked to be locals, others dirty from the road just passing through like himself. Some of the men were lucky enough to have a comely wench upon their lap; others not so lucky, for all to be left were the homely wenches. Still, all the same was the ability of the wench to satisfy a lonely man's desires, and to warm their beds.

Arriving to his table was the little barmaid with the ample breasts. She was gentle to the eye, as she was pleasing to his desire. Petite in frame, her little waist would fit nicely in his hands, as he was imagining her in his lap and those breasts that needed to be freed from its confines to satisfy his eyes.

"Pardon me, sire. What can I get for you?" she inquired sweetly. Unaware she had even spoken since his mind was taking leave elsewhere, her voice was as pleasant as she was polite.

"Yes, I would like a pint of your best ale and whatever the day's special is," he answered quickly. He then imagined what she might look like without her clothes, and her golden hair cascading down about her naked flesh.

"Yes, sire. Right away, sire."

Smiling at him, she bowed and went to place his order, and then came back quickly with his pint of ale.

"Thank you, miss. Now enlighten me with what I just ordered."

Blushing at him, she seemed a bit nervous and fidgeted a lot with her apron. "Well, sire, you are having mutton stew, with a small loaf of crusty bread," she answered nervously.

"My name is Lord Brom, you do not have to call me sire," he chuckled. She had to be a virgin, this one, but he could remedy that for her later if she would like.

"Yes, milord." As she walked off, he watched the way her hips swayed as she left the table.

Taking up his drink, he swallowed it down in only three gulps. He quenched his thirst, and then set it down to wipe the froth from his upper lip. He anticipated her seeing that his mug was now empty, and then it would hasten the young girl's return to his table. He wanted to continue his pursuit of her. With having no interest in the woman that he had been observing upon arrival, he had his sights on the young barmaid alone.

Returning with his hot supper, the buxom blonde set the large bowl in front of him, which was blessed with its heaping amounts of stew and accompanied by the promised crusty bread.

"There you are, milord. Can I be fetching you some more ale?"

He nodded, as his mouth was now busy with the food it was consuming rather quickly. He had not realized his own hunger and could not remember the last he had eaten. He had been too busy to satisfy his own appetite, to acknowledge her return to the table with another pint of frothy ale.

"Can I be getting you anything else, milord?" she questioned with a smile. Lord Brom chased his final mouthful of food with a bit of ale and wiped his face before he spoke.

"Yes, but you may satisfy those needs later; if you can take leave from your duties of course. Unless someone might notice your absence?"

Now blushing crimson cheeks, she was unsure what to even say. She considered him to be exceptionally handsome and would be willing to bed him for sure, if it pleased him so.

"As you wish, sire. I can leave here in a short while. I must sneak to your room since I am not to take away from the other girls purse," she informed him. "Do you have a room acquired already, or do I need to make one ready for you?"

Smiling, Lord Brom was eager with anticipation and he quickly finished his second pint of ale. "Yes, that would be so kind of you to do so."

After some time had passed, he decided to see if his room was ready, following his third pint of ale. Motioning for the barmaid to return, he fantasized about all the things he was going to enjoy doing to her, and then finally get the Princess out of his head for good. She arrived to his table, informing him of which room it was, and how to get there by way of the back stairs. Then she tells him she will wait a few minutes to not look suspicious, and will join him later.

While waiting patiently for the pretty little thing to come and join him for a nice romp, Brom decided to utilize the washbasin that was hospitably left with hot water for him. Removing his shirt, he looked down at his wound that was still trying to heal, that he received while trying to save the Princess. A lot of good that did, he thought bitterly. He had already removed his trousers, when he heard a knock at the door. Not knowing for certain who it was at the door, he quickly covered his loins with the thin sheet from the bed, and then opened the door.

Standing in the doorway was the one he had been waiting for, with extra linens for the bed, a trick she obviously used for her excuse to come to his room.

"Please, come in," he offered.

Moving aside to let her enter the room, she looked at his half naked appearance and blushed. Never having seen a man without his shirt besides her father, she kept her head down as she placed the freshly pressed linens upon the edge of the table.

"Will there be anything else that you need for the room? Or anything you need before I leave?" she asked, her cheeks warm and flushed; she had never lain with a man before. She had always been curious after listening to the many whores that always spoke of such carnal pleasures.

"Well, no, the room is fine, I was just fixing to wash up." He was trying not to force himself upon her, but he wanted to give her an idea to keep her here a bit longer. His slight seduction of her must have worked, when she took the sponge from the washbasin.

"I could assist you with that, milord," she offered almost hesitantly. Removing his makeshift cover, he exposed his magnificent statuesque figure and all its glory. She felt as though she should not open her eyes, as she had closed them before the sheet hit the floor. If she were going to wash him, she had to do it with open eyes.

"It is all right, I take it you have never seen a man naked before," he consoled the girl.

"No, milord. I have not," she said blushing. She began to dip the sponge into the water, gently squeezing out the excess, and then let the warm water drip back into the bowl.

Standing there waiting for her to get the nerve to sponge him off, he began to catch chill. He quickly warmed up as the wet sponge caressed his skin, washing the dirt from the road off his hard body. Dipping the sponge back into the water, and then wringing it out again, she returned the sponge to cleanse his broad back. He wished it were the Princess's hands upon him instead, but he did not want her to invade his head right now.

Now the little barmaid was cleansing his chest, strong sinewy muscles, and rippled abdomen, as the water trickled down to his loins. She turned back to the basin to again absorb and squeeze the excess water from the sponge, and then proceeded to wash his backside, taking care not to giggle as he flinched from her scrubbing his tight buttocks. She continued her ritual of rinsing out the sponge, and blushed at the thought of washing his groin area. Already feeling aroused deep within her own loins while washing him and feeling his exquisite body beneath her hands, she was indeed curious to cleans his manhood. She took his member in her hands to wash all around his groin and he watched as her cheeks turned crimson once again. She was amazed as his excitement grew in her hand as she cleansed him. She had never set eyes upon a penis before, and only heard funny tales about size from the other girls. If she had her guess, he was considerably large by what she heard that regulated such a position in stature. Seeing the desire for her in his eyes she was not sure of what happened next, as she was quickly smothered with ardent kisses.

The sponge fell to the floor. She was inexperienced at the art of kissing, but quick and studious as she was, she picked up the lesson with eagerness. Lord Brom could not stand a moment longer without driving himself deep into her moist and tight virgin womanhood. He picked her up off her feet, planted her atop the table, and then lifted her skirt to explore the hidden treasure buried within. Lord Brom proceeded to kiss her fully partaking of the sweet nectar between her thighs, never having been harvested before. The young maiden arched her body into his face, as she had never known such a pleasure was to be had. She cried out in ecstasy, alerting him she was ripe for the plucking. He rose up and kissed her once more, so she could savor what he had just partaken. She was as eager to be had, as badly as he. Without further hesitation, for he could wait any longer, he entered her with such vigor she screamed out with pain and pleasure within one breath. Lord Brom forgot for a moment to have been gentler upon his entry of her, but he did not bother to slow his pace either, thrusting further, feeling the full depth of her. A maid no more, she arched her back, and was given the instructor's lesson of the fine art he schooled her in. He began to get lost in thought with every hard thrust he made, and imagined a beautiful raven-haired beauty, with a petite figure and large bountiful breasts that had yet to be released by him. Shaking her image out of his head, he slowed to free the fair, golden-haired girl's breasts instead. Small in comparison to his love, she had enough of a handful, as he eagerly trapped a nipple between his lips. She squirmed at the pleasured sensation that caused her womanhood to swell even more, aching for its release. Thrashing about into him, he had believed she had gone mad with passion. He pushed himself to the farthest depths of her, urged on by the intensity of her counter thrusts, and plundered her treasure like an angry pirate. She screamed so loud, inviting unwanted company.

Unaware of the impending excitement at his door, Lord Brom drifted to fond memories of his love. He imagined her face being the one with her head thrown back in ecstasy, as he pushed out his life deep into her very core, and met the ardent break of her dam that had been previously kept walled up inside. His pleasure was spent and her own was drenching his loins; just before he could dismount, someone broke down the door.

The girl's father had noticed her missing for a while, and he had just begun to search for her when he heard her screams. Unaware that she was not actually being harmed, he was still quite angry with this drifter for stealing her virtue. The only card he had left to play was a small dowry for her, if he found her a suitable husband and this man was not it. Lunging for a still naked Lord Brom, who was quickly trying to dress, he missed and fell onto the floor. Her father was not a young man and by now was really angry.

"I am sorry, sir. What is it you want for her and I will gladly pay your fee?" Lord Brom offered.

"She is not a whore, you idiot! She is my little girl, who was saving herself for marriage to a good man, not one who would deflower her and leave!" he shouted.

"He is your father?" he asked the girl. Nodding in agreement, the girl watched as the best time of her life frantically pulled the rest of his clothes on. Lord Brom finished tying up his pants, still trying to avoid the angry father's advances, who was nearly out of breath.

"Please, let me give you coin, to see her in a proper marriage," he paused for air, "and then I shall be on my way," he added hastily. Embarrassed for his actions, he left an ample purse on the table before the girl's father chased him down the stairs yelling at him to never come back.

Lord Brom finally made it outside unscathed. He managed to tuck in his shirt, and then proceeded to find the other inn that he was made to think existed by the blacksmith. Even though he was humiliated for what happened, he had to laugh. He did get what he sought out to do, and in the end, it was well worth it. Now since that little adventure was over, it did nil towards eliminating the memory of Princess Ellyria. It was still unbelievable, that while in the middle of his tryst, she still permeated his mind. As he continued to walk through town, he came across the other tavern. Lord Brom peeked in the window, it did not look half as nice as the other but decided that was exactly what he needed, a place to get a little more ale, and then off to bed for him. He thought that if bedding another woman did not release him of the torture she caused in his mind, then he would drink her away. Lord Brom went straight to the bar, asking for his fourth pint of ale, and requesting the male barkeep to prevent his mug from going empty. He placed plenty of coins on the bar, investing in the future of his inebriated state.

By the time the eighth pint of ale was poured, he was interrupted with visions of his siren, which he now believed was trying to kill him. She was so beautifully skilled in her seduction of him, as she dangled the helpless, innocent-girl-act, luring him into her fatal trap. Her long black hair enticed his eyes to fall upon her tiny waist, which was cinched in by her cumbersome corset. The way it held tight to her petite figure, holding up her heavy breasts, that spilled out longing for their release. Her eyes that bewitched him with their ever changing color, distracting him while she placed the unwanted spell upon him.

"Damn her," Lord Brom whispered under his breath, as he finished washing down his tenth pint, of what he thought to be the cure of her. Not having enough sense to pace himself, he began to finally earn back his recent investments. Feeling the sudden urge to relieve himself, he wondered slowly to the facilities he believed to be, and as completely besotted as he was, relived himself on a plant in a clay pot instead. He staggered as he drew up his pants, using a support pillar to keep his balance, and then proceeded back to his seat at the bar, where another of that sweet libation was waiting for him.

Coming in at the number twelve spot in the race of inebriation, to in fact leave Lord Brom in its wake, he spotted what he believed to be his raven-haired siren. Such venal drink blurred his focus. He went to her, entranced by her, drawing him to her by way of her spell, that she had cast upon him. He approached the raven-haired woman, who in reality was quite homely by appearance and much older than his young siren, who spun this web of deceit upon him.

"Hello, my beauty," he said, staggering slightly. He regained balance, and then proceeded to fondle her large breast in his hand, then placed sloppy kisses around the strange whore's open, toothless mouth. He kissed his siren with fervor, grabbing heavy breasts now with both hands, and using them to support himself.

The older woman, who obviously was not his siren, was eager to play along in his drunken games with the expectancy he had not spent all his coins and still carried a heavy purse. In his mind, he was about to embark on his dream to finally take his heart's desire to the bedchamber. He found himself being led upstairs to a small room on the second floor.

The toothless cocotte began to undress, releasing her heavy hanging breasts and her robust waistline from the tightly strung corset that was now in the floor with her dress. She stood naked, waiting for him to take her.

"Place your coin on the table, and then you can enjoy the ride, honey," she said. The raspy tone of her voice was no sirens song, but his ears heard only the sweet melody of his beloved. The remainder of his coin was placed on table, curious that he was being made to pay, but thinking it to be a game, so he continued. The homely woman neared him and with his senses so far from its normalcy, he did not notice the foul aroma from her body. The combination of odors from being unwashed, to the hundred or so men a night spilling forth into her, made her disgustful.

Bedazzled by his venal libations, Lord Brom approached her to fondle her naked breasts, and kissed her again. Feeling himself becoming aroused, he proceeded to see himself free. She pulled him to her, taking care of his sluggish demeanor, leading him to the empty bed. Gently, his kisses moved to her large endowments and she giggled at the way he was doing so. So then she decided to lay him on his back and mount him, he whispered in her ear his undying love, calling her 'princess'. How sweet a young man he was, she thought as she flipped him onto his back and proceeded to be sweet to his manhood. While utilizing her unencumbered mouth upon him, he fell back in ecstasy as she gave him her best talent of the entire ill-reputed house. Lord Brom never felt his member being kissed like that before. He envisioned being devoured by his deadly siren, which he was for certain she was trying to eat him alive, starting with the very thing that got him into trouble in the first place, his manhood. The older woman finished him off, and wiped him from her mouth. She noticed he was fast asleep, and she was curious if he was dreaming of her.

Lord Brom woke up fast to the commotion about him, as he was hearing that old man's voice in his aching head. He was shouting that he was the one that had raped his daughter. The master-at-arms had been awakened from sleep by the old man insisting that they come arrest him now. He had followed Lord Brom to the bar cautiously to not alert him, and then after having the knowledge of his whereabouts, he brought the guards to where he was. During his rude awakening, it sobered him up fast and he was quick to assess his surroundings. There on the bed beside him was a most horrifying sight, as he really wished he had not taken her to his satisfaction, and then in searching the room around him, he observed the shouting old man, and the two guards that were intent on arresting him. Finding himself still clothed, with only his pants undone, he quickly got up and fixed his trousers.

"Let us discuss this civilly," he said to the other men.

With his words ignored, the guards then tried to apprehend him. When they tried to grab him to bind his hands, he punched one of them, and then pushed the other out of his way. Running out of the room and skipping some of the steps to make his escape faster, he accidentally ran into a very large gentleman at the bottom of the stairs knocking him to the ground and ended up finding himself piled on top of him onto the floor.

Lord Brom stood up and assisted the other man to his feet and without any warning, his apologies were lost to the sound of fist connecting to face. Lord Brom was knocked back, about lost his balance; as he regained footing, he returned the man's appreciation for his apology, this time knocking the large man into an innocent bystander, relieving him of his seat. The gentleman got up and eloquently punched the larger man who had fallen on him by no fault of his own, who then was turned in the direction of Lord Brom who hit him once again; ironically sending him into yet another man, sitting at his table. The now furious man sent his table flying across the room, leaving Lord Brom the main focus of his attention. Lord Brom grabbed the closest man fighting on his right, and then quickly used him as a human shield. The man fell limp in his arms from the blow that had been originally been intended for Lord Brom. He then carelessly tossed him aside and continued to fight his way through the crowd. The entire tavern had joined in the fight, each man was throwing punches and using anything they could use as a weapon. Tables were overturned and chairs were broken, while many pints of ale were smashed and wasted on many heads. Lord Brom was smack-dab in the middle of the brawl trying to avoid getting punched, but somehow made it to the tavern door.

When Lord Brom swung open the door he found himself surrounded by guards, then suddenly everything went dark. The men-at-arms had made their way out to call for backup during the fighting. When they came back, it was Lord Brom's misfortune that they found him on his way out, and one of them knocked him out with the hilt of their sword. He was unaware to the further misfortune that his face was on every wanted poster plastered about town for his arrest, put up by Liza's men. So when the guards that had arrived recognized him, they quickly assessed that he was the man from the wanted poster and called for backup.

A still unconscious Lord Brom was carried out to their wagon and placed carefully inside as instructed. His horse had already been seized and was now tethered to the wagon. The small town was close to where Liza's men were staying for the night, and he was quickly brought to them to collect the promised bounty. Lord Brom was worth a heavy purse, and as promised, it was paid to them. The local guardsman then divided it equally between them, while unknowingly sealing Lord Brom's fate in the hands of Liza's personal guards.

Liza's men had strict instructions to bring Lord Brom straight to the Dark Forest of Woe. The guards obeyed, even with the fear that consumed them. The journey would be long, so they prepared to keep Lord Brom unconscious for as long as possible. When he had begun to stir to consciousness, he would again be delivered with a powerful blow to the head, keeping him in a deep slumber until they arrived to their destination.

Deep in the feared forest, the guards pulled the wagon up to its final destination, the wizard's cottage. Where he and Liza patiently waited for Lord Brom and his stallion to be brought to them alive. Dragging inside the still sleeping Lord Brom. They sat him in a chair, and proceeded to truss up his hunched over body, binding it tightly so he could not escape in the event that he came to.

After waiting an hour for him to awaken, Liza became impatient, and splashed cold water in his face.

Lord Brom began to rouse from a hardened slumber, unable to move and still feeling the hard-throbbing pain in the side of his head, he finally opened his eyes. He was confused with his surroundings and angered not only by what he saw, but who he saw. Standing before him, to his surprise, was a very much alive Liza.

"Welcome back to the living," he said sarcastically.

Liza slapped him hard across his face, and then spat at him.

"Yes, I did manage to escape."

He tried to lick the blood from the corner of his mouth, before she struck him again. He was beginning to think she was enjoying herself, so he spoke up.

"How is it that you got away? I am sure they are hunting you down right now," he added before being stuck once more.

"That is not any of your concern. I need to know where is the amulet I gave you, and do not try to lie to save yourself, we plan to kill you anyway," she added.

Raul came around from behind Liza to face Lord Brom.

"Good one, Liza. Let us give him something to really look forward to, if he tells us what we want to know," he said sarcastically.

"Who is he?" Lord Brom asked.

"None of your concern, but I am a wizard, and I can make things very unpleasant for you, if you do not tell this hag what she wants to know," Raul answered.

Taken aback by all this, Lord Brom looked them straight in the eye.

"I do not have it anymore, I left it back at the cottage," he answered.

"Where in the cottage?" Liza asked.

"I do not remember. I just threw it down. I am not even sure where it landed," he informed them.

Raul began to pace back and forth, creating a dust storm right in the middle of the room. Lord Brom watched in amazement as the wizard's powers unfolded before him.

"Send word to the guards outside to search the cottage," he told Liza. "As for you, handsome. I am going to keep you alive a little while longer. I may have some use for you just yet," Raul declared.

Brom just watched in confusion as Raul returned to his alter to retrieve his cauldron, and then hang it over the fire.

"What do you intend to do with him?" Liza asked.

"I am not so sure just yet but prepare the horse. Once the potion has heated, it will be ready for his heart," he told Liza.

Lord Brom could not believe what he had just heard, while the horse was fetched and brought into the house. The wizard began to recite an incantation from the grimoire, raising his atheme high in the air before the stallion. Lord Brom finally realized what was about to happen, he began to panic and started pulling hard at the ropes behind him. Unable to break free of his bonds, he was helpless to aid his friend. The wizard finished his incantation and was now prepared for the heart of the stallion. Lord Brom was tempted to close his eyes from the view of what was about to happen. He watched the wizard raise the knife in the air, but before Lord Brom could turn away, warm blood splattered upon his face. He watched helplessly as the remainder of life grew dim in his horse's eyes.

"Noooo!" Lord Brom screamed.

CHAPTER 18

Prince Anthony had been following Liza's trail
along with some of his best knights. Having left
word with his father about her escape he was
then sent on his way to find her. Unaware of the
dangerous quest he was about to embark on...

King Jason had called for his wife to join him in his study to
break the news to her about Liza's escape. Afraid to even
ask him of the bad tidings that she was certain he was going to give,
the Queen entered his study.

"What is the matter, dear husband?" she inquired.

"I am sorry to be the bearer of bad news, my love, but Liza
has escaped," he disclosed.

She grabbed onto the chair in front of her for support, and
then carefully moved to sit in it.

"How? How did this even happen?"

"I'm not sure exactly, but Anthony discovered her
disappearance when I sent him to the dungeon to collect her for
the trial."

She sat motionless for a moment, searching her husband's
face for some kind of reassurance.

"He has left on a mission to locate her whereabouts and

arrest her once again."

"So did he tell Ellyria yet?" she hesitantly asked. Knowing that this news will devastate her, after everything she has been through already.

"No, I told him we would break the news to her," he answered. He dreaded telling his daughter the fact of Liza's escape, but could not keep it from her. "Where is Ellyria right now?"

"She was in the library with Nan, she was studying her lessons when I left to see you," she informed her husband.

"Well, we must go to her. She should hear it from us first, before word gets out about Liza's escape."

In the library, Nan had left Princess Ellyria to her studies while she went out to fetch her something to eat. Alone in one of her favorite places, Princess Ellyria looked up from her book, when both her parents came in hand in hand. Knowing that something was amiss, she waited for one of her parents to speak.

"Ellyria, darling, I have something that needs to be addressed," her father said. Sitting down in the chairs on either side of their daughter, they began to break the news of Liza's escape and that there was a search party led by her brother, Prince Anthony to find her. "I am so sorry this has happened, my dear," he added.

She sat there for a moment, hardly knowing how to react, or what to say. The silence was deafening, as her mother hated awkward silences.

"Is there anything you need to say, it is alright to speak freely," her mother consoled her.

Princess Ellyria watched their faces as she absorbed what she was being told. Her mother was treating her like a small child.

"I understand mother, and I am not a child, you do not have to speak to me as such," she stated.

Her father was offended by his daughter's mannerisms towards her mother.

"Young lady, you do not speak to your mother in that tone. She is only trying to console you," he scolded. "We have only your best interests at heart dear, and we want to protect you. Even though we can not protect you from everything that threatens to harm you."

Her mother was now crying into her hands, heartbroken from the cruel words of her daughter. Her husband put his arm around her to try and reassure her that everything would remedy itself in time. As soon as Liza was apprehended, the sooner they could be rest assured that she would not harm anyone ever again.

"I am so sorry, mother. I did not mean it in such a way, nor did I mean to add insult to injury and cause you to cry."

Her mother nodded that it was all right and got up from the table.

"We will catch her, I promise," her father said. He held his wife's hand for a moment before she pulled it away. As he watched his wife leave the room, he turned to his daughter.

"I need you to stay here and out of the path of danger. I do not need you getting into any more trouble. Your brother will handle this. Do I make myself clear, young lady? May I have your word on this?" he questioned her.

"Yes, father, I promise. I have learned my lesson the hard way by meddling where I did not belong," she swore.

Ellyria did not want to be anywhere near that woman again, she would not leave the castle until Liza was finally captured...

Prince Anthony and his men had followed Liza's footprints, until they stopped at the Dark Forest of Woe. The horses became antsy and began to rear up, clawing the air with their hooves. As they tried to settle the horses, they saw smoke coming from the center of the woods.

"Come on, let us ride!" Prince Anthony yelled out to Odin. The gallant steed with the heart of a lion was not afraid of these woods like the other horses. It was not until he moved out that the other horses followed.

They ran toward the smoke that gave away Liza's hideout. The men that followed Prince Anthony began to disappear mysteriously the closer they came to the wizard's home. Without looking back, Prince Anthony had not noticed the absence of the four other riders who accompanied him until now. Slowing Odin down, he discovered he was now alone, as he reached the cottage in the center of the woods. His horse became uneasy and they were cautious approaching the house. Odin scraped the ground with his powerful foreleg, kicking up the earth with his hoof.

"What is it, boy?" he said patting Odin to calm him. Prince Anthony then heard screams coming from inside the house, and saw colorful sparks flying up out from the chimney.

Urging his horse to the house faster now, his faithful steed galloped to match the speed of the wind that blew against him...

"What happened?" asked Liza.

"This is not a pure heart!" the wizard screamed. The heart he cut from the animal was not what he desired, but only that of the rogue beast that his new nemesis was brought in with. He watched as Lord Brom wept for this animal.

"You are heartless, and insane," he sighed after he helplessly watched his horse being butchered alive by this wizard's cruel hands.

"Shut him up, I am growing tired of hearing that one speak."

Raul motioned for one of the guards, and then Lord Brom was delivered a nasty blow to the back of his head.

"Finally, some peace and quiet so I can think," he muttered.

Suddenly Prince Anthony stormed the door with Odin, knocking it open. His horse stood unafraid by the sight of his fellow horse standing with his chest hollowed open.

"Glad you could join us," the wizard smiled. He held up his hands and the door closed and locked behind Prince Anthony. "I have him now, the true heart of a lion!" the declared, laughing maniacally.

Before Prince Anthony had a chance, Odin reared up to attack the wizard, but to no avail, the wizard backed away, avoiding its clawing hooves. When Odin came back down, Liza hit the unsuspecting Prince Anthony in the back of the head, while one of the guards took him off his horse and the other guard grabbed Odin's reigns. Lord Brom was once again helpless to escape.

"Take him to the other chair and tie him up too," Liza instructed the guard.

"No, we have no use for him, only his horse," Raul said. "Kill him," he ordered.

"No!" screamed Princess Ellyria, as she sat up in bed drenched in her own sweat.

She could not believe it. She was shaking, her heart raced inside her while tears poured from her emerald eyes uncontrollably...

King Jason called to his wife to join him in the study as she entered the room, he told her of how Liza had escaped. Upset as she was, he tried to console her, and explained how Prince Anthony was on his way to track her with several of his best knights. He would arrest her as soon as he found her. His wife had inquired if their daughter had been told yet and he told her she had not yet been informed; it was up to them to break the bad news to her.

"Where is Ellyria now?" the King asked his wife.

"I left her in the library studying, when I came to see you," she answered.

Just then, Nan passed by the study where Princess Ellyria's parents were, when they called out to her.

"Yes, your Majesties," as she went inside, she waited to be addressed by them.

"Yes, Nan, I thought you were in the library with Princess Ellyria?"

"I was, ma'am, but the girl felt another one of her headaches coming on and she went to her chambers to rest for a while."

"Alright, thank you. That will be all, Nan," the King released her.

Nan left the room, leaving their Majesties alone. After a few moments they too left the study as well, to go and break the news to Ellyria.

As the King and Queen neared Ellyria's chambers to check in on her, they heard her crying quite loudly and hurried in to see what had happened. Bursting open the door, the worried parents saw their daughter sitting up in her bed, her face drenched with her tears and her emerald eyes were swollen from crying.

"What is the matter? Are you alright, my dear?" her worried mother asked.

"What has happened to have you this distraught?"

She took in a deep breath, her mother held her in her arms. Frantically Ellyria began to tell what she had seen in her vision.

"I had a horrible nightmare that Liza had escaped, and there was this wizard who had just cut out this horse's heart that belonged to Lord Brom, and he was tied up in a chair. She took a pause to catch her breath in between sobs, and then she continued. "Then Anthony, and Odin broke down the door, but Liza hit Anthony with something. The guards dragged him off his horse, and the other guard grabbed Odin so the wizard could cut out his heart! It felt so real, as if I were there," she added almost hysterically.

Both her parents looked at one another, they knew it must have been a premonition, and then worried about how much could be actually going on right now, or about to. They decided to keep it to themselves while they tried to calm their daughter.

"There, there, my darling. It was just a dream," her mother consoled her.

" It was real, I know it." She did not understand why they were not listening to her.

"I am not going to lie to you, Liza did escape early this morning, we are guessing before dawn. Anthony has gone to look for her, but he has several men with him, and they would not allow him be captured," he confessed.

Ellyria's mother held her daughter in her arms, trying to wipe the tears from her eyes. Her father decided he would leave the two of them alone, maybe his wife could talk to the girl better than he could. As he left the women to talk, he went to one of his knights to gather another search party to see where Prince Anthony was, to ensure he was alright. After her husband left the room, it gave Anna time to try to talk to their daughter, and explain to her about their shared gift.

"Ellyria, I know how hard this gift is to handle sometimes. I began to get them when I was about your age, but as I grew older my visions came to be less intimidating. I was then able to decipher whether they were real or not."

"I know this was real, I felt their pain," she argued.

"Well, some of it possibly could be, but sometimes you only get pieces of what is actually going on. I know your brother is a great knight and quite capable of taking care of himself. Lord Brom headed home to be with his father, and you are just dreaming of him because you miss him," her mother assured her.

Princess Ellyria took a moment to absorb everything and it now made sense to what her mother was saying. Especially after that most intense vision she had of the two of them being together, that her mother had interrupted by waking her up.

Just then Isis jumped up on the bed and licked her in the face, Princess Ellyria laughed, as her best friend was always able to make her smile.

"See, even Isis thinks you are reading too much into your dream," she said. Maybe her mother was right, and she should put it all out of her mind for the moment. Perhaps she was reading too much into the dream, after all, she has been through so much.

Her mother left the room to allow Princess Ellyria to get more rest, but she was not tired and decided to go enjoy the rest of this beautiful day...

In the Dark Forest of Woe, Lord Brom had awakened to shouting. Still tied to the chair, he could not break free from the binds. His good steed had been butchered open to obtain the still beating heart for the wizard's potion, only to find it was of no use to him. He had been knocked out again by one of the guards to stop him from yelling out. Liza had turned away from his gruesome ritual with no stomach for it, deciding to stay out of the wizard's way. Just as the wizard was going to use Lord Brom's heart instead, as an experiment. Prince Anthony and Odin broke down the door.

"Just in time," the wizard said.

Liza knocked out Prince Anthony, and Odin was the one the wizard was waiting for all along...

CHAPTER 19

The midday sun was fast approaching, and the blue sky was accompanied by shades of pink and orange. The Summer Solstice was still a few weeks away, although it felt like it had already arrived. For well over a month now the weather was quite warm and the desire to want to keep cool was now a necessity.

Playing in the fountain was a special way in keeping cool on this hot summer day. The Princess Ellyria was laughing and splashing Isis, as they both ran around, going in and out of the fountain. Her long black hair had come down from its tightly coiled bun and was already dripping from being splashed by Isis. Even her white cotton summer dress was completely soaked from her hips down, for she had gave up on trying to keep her hem out of the water a long time ago.

Barefoot and carefree, the two best friends romped through the gardens to play and chase each other around, their usual game of choice. Even though she was still aware of the fact that she would be getting yelled at later. She did not care. All that mattered was the much-needed fun she was having at this very moment.

Fatigued and drenched, Princess Ellyria stopped to catch her breath. Isis followed suit, but before she could move away, Isis began to shake the water from her thick black coat, showering again the already washed Princess.

"Isis, quit that. I am already besotted enough, girl," she said giggling to her friend. Princess Ellyria retired for a moment to rest and sat down on the swing in the summerhouse. She began to reflect on the last few weeks. The events that had happened to her and the decisions she had made. The premonitions she had been having of late were disturbing and she tried to get them out of her mind, without success. She missed Lord Brom, but knew it was the best choice to not accept his proposal. What might have happened between them, she did not know. But the memory of that very arousing vision she had of the two of them she could not stop thinking about. Shaking her head, she had to get the 'what if she had said yes' scenario out of her mind. It did not matter now. What is done is done and she can no longer change her decision. She wished only the best for him, even though she still worried about him. After the last horrible vision, she was having a hard time ignoring it, especially when it felt so real to her.

Princess Ellyria Rose remembered her promise that she made to her mother and father, to stay away from trouble. She questioned her ability of whether or not she could keep it. Although trouble had always seemed to find a way to her, she did not feel she would go looking for it. Even though she was worried for her eldest brother, Prince Anthony, since the recent vision of him and Lord Brom. She knew him to be courageous and felt he was capable of recapturing Liza.

She was also grateful of her brothers for rescuing her, and was no longer jealous of them, but found a new respect for what they did. Her brothers had in fact become her heroes, and she had been the damsel in distress after all. That would never happen again, she would not allow herself to fall prey to those who may harm her. Even though she promised her parents to not go looking for trouble, she would make sure trouble did not come looking for her. With Liza still at large, she had to keep her wits about her and get serious with her spell work, so she could better protect herself, if the need should arise. She also had to find out more about the wizard from her premonition, and this Amulet of Elements. She needed to find it before it fell into the hands of Liza, or especially the wizard. Was this her destiny? How did Liza and the wizard fit into all of this? She would have to make sure that Prince Anthony, and Lord Brom were all right. She was not going to stand by waiting to see if her premonition harbored truth. How would she be able to find out without becoming captured again by Liza, or worse the wizard himself? She promised herself that she would not become a victim again. She would stop at nothing to see it met and will come up with a plan to see that it is put into action. Confident of her plan she decided to kick back and relax, she was going to need her rest.

Princess Ellyria looked all around her, at the beautiful royal gardens, the flowers, and the fountain, growing up here was not all that bad. She no longer felt trapped and alone in the home that she grew up in. Princess Ellyria accepted the fact of having been kept here all those years a secret, and being deprived of venturing off of castle grounds, after all it was for her protection. She knew that now and understood. Ellyria was grateful for every aspect of her life, and had even discovered herself in the process.

She reached over and patted Isis, who had her head in her lap, looking out beyond the castle walls.

"It is beautiful, is it not Isis? Those majestic mountains, with their snowy peaks and the rolling green hills down below." she said, as she softly stroked Isis's soft head.

Isis just looked up at her from her lap with her dark eyes that almost seemed to smile back at her in agreement.

What a wonderful world it must truly be, if this much beauty really exists.

What else did it have in store for her?...

CHAPTER 20

Princess Ellyria was tossing and turning in her bed, the nightmares were invading her sleep again. The images were coming in randomly like flashes of the past becoming a slideshow in her mind. She could not wake up, drenched in sweat she felt trapped within her own dreams...

"Brom, no! Wait, Liza! How could you do this to me?" she called out in her sleep. "I do not understand," she cried. "Why are you doing this to me?"

Princess Ellyria ran, not looking back at the woman laid out unconscious in the floor. Lord Brom helped her onto the horse as they ran far from the cottage, and then they were suddenly in the woods. She felt herself falling off the horse and everything went dark. Then she woke up with a dull ache in her head, and finding herself in the corn mill. She walked outside and saw herself, Lord Brom, and her brother, Prince Rowan. Waving her hands to try and get their attention proved to be a moot point, they could not see her. She tried to call out to them, but they could not hear her. When she stepped outside to run to them, she found herself in the dungeon of Liza's castle. It was dark, yet she was able to see a flicker of light coming from around the corner. She slowly walked towards the light, and found herself suddenly trapped in a giant spider web. While she was trying to fight her way out, she felt the vibrations coming from over her head. She looked up and saw the giant, hairy, black spider; its jaws were wide open and heading straight for her. Screaming, fighting frantically to get out of the giant, sticky-web, she suddenly felt herself being pulled out. She opened her eyes to see who her hero was, but no one was there. Standing alone she looked all around her, finding herself to be back outside the castle. It was quiet, and then faintly in the background she could barely hear what sounded like fighting, but the sounds were muffled. They gradually became louder; horses stampeding, swords clashing, men screaming, and the familiar sound of Liza's laughter. All of the sudden she felt herself grabbed from behind, she felt a heavy hand covering her mouth, her nostrils were invaded by the same filthy scent she had tried to scrub off. She could not see her attacker, but felt hands all over her body, like there was more than just one person molesting her. They had her hands bound together, her mouth was no longer covered, and when she tried to scream, nothing came out. No one was there, but she could not move nor fight. She felt her clothes being ripped off, her breasts were being fondled, and someone was between her legs trying to touch her. All of the sudden while she was helpless to fight off her invisible captors, she saw Isis laying beside her on the ground covered in a pool of her own blood, and Liza was standing over her, laughing maniacally. She tried to scream again, but could not. She felt tears cascading down her cheeks, but still could not feel anything else but the hands of her attackers. As she felt herself drifting from consciousness…

When Princess Ellyria woke up, she was back in her bed in her chambers. She could hear music playing and people laughing. Then she got up from her bed and was in her emerald green gown. She went downstairs, but no one was bowing, or even addressing her existence. It was like she was not there. When she walked outside to the courtyard she saw, Lord Brom and herself. She was talking, well, her other self was talking to him. She could feel the pain coming from them. This had to have been when she turned down Brom's proposal. How she wished she could change the past now, and then he would not have been trapped by Liza or the wizard. She walked up to the shadows of her recent past, when she stuck her hand in between the images they suddenly vanished. Quickly she turned around, and then the courtyard began to vanish too, the castle, the fountain, it was as if everything were melting away. She clutched the sides of her head, and when she turned back around, she was standing in the woods. Right in front of her was a cottage. It was not Liza's cottage. She knew that as she approached the side of the house, very slowly, just in case in this scenario she made noise. All of the sudden colorful sparks shot out from the chimney, and she heard screaming coming from inside. She went to the window, it was Liza; she dropped down out of sight, just in case the older woman saw her, and then slowly rose up until she could see what was going on. Liza had moved away from the window, she saw Brom in a chair tied up, and his horse was in there too, his chest was cut wide open. The man standing in front of a big cauldron must be the wizard, but she could not see him very clearly, it was like his image was blurred out. All of the sudden Prince Anthony appeared in front of the house kicking the door in. The wizard was laughing, and then Liza had knocked out her brother with a vase. She got up and tried to run around to the front door, but it slammed shut. She could not get in. Princes Ellyria ran back to the side window, only to see her brother being pulled off of Odin, and the guards holding him tightly by the reins. Then she overheard the wizard say to kill her brother.

"No!" She screamed as loud as she could, but no one heard her.

Lord Brom wearily opened his eyes, as he looked over to Prince Anthony, and then to his horse. He was just as helpless as her unconscious brother was and she was helpless to do anything to save them. She continued to watch as Prince Anthony was tied up, Odin was stretched out and tied down as well. What was going to happen to Odin? The wizard grabbed the knife and raised it high in the air. Odin snorted at the wizard and tried to break free from his bonds, but was too constrained by the ropes that held him. Princess Ellyria watched helplessly as the wizard was ready to bring down the blade into Odin's chest. While at the same time a guard had grabbed her brother by his dark hair to lift his head up to expose his neck, so that the man could place the knife to her brother's throat.

"No!" She screamed again, as she banged on the window, but no one could hear her...

CHAPTER 21

ord Brom woke up to the uncomfortable upright position he found himself in while still tied to the chair. His head ached, his neck was tight, and then as he looked about the room, he saw Prince Anthony; knocked out in the corner of the floor, his hands and feet bound together. His horse Odin was tied up as well, his legs were spread apart, and his neck was stretched up and tied to the back of the saddle. The wizard was busy sharpening his atheme. Liza was standing in a corner looking frightened, and one of her guards had walked over to where Prince Anthony lay in the floor. Lord Brom was not gagged so he decided that he was going to address his concern for Princess Ellyria's brother.

"What do you plan to do with the Prince, Raul?"

The wizard turned towards Lord Brom still sharpening his blade as he walked towards him.

"Well, not that it is any of your bloody concern, but he is of no use to me. I plan to have him killed, and I will sacrifice his magnificent steed. Is that enough information for you?" asked the wizard. Raul took the freshly sharpened knife, and wiped the blade with his cloth, taking care to clean off the remaining grit. He held it up in front of his face to examine his reflection in the blade, and then touched the point with his fingertip, satisfied with the atheme that was now razor-sharp; he decided to test it further.

"So, Lord Brom, is it? What do you suggest that I do with the Prince? Let him go?" The wizard took the knife and traced it along the side of Lord Brom's face not yet piercing the flesh.

Lord Brom began to break a sweat worried what the wizard might do.

"Yes, I do think you should let him go," he said bravely.

Raul stopped, retracted his knife, and looked at his hostage. "What is in it for you, if I were to let him go? Why do you care so much for his life? Do you know him?"

Lord Brom looked up at the wizard, and then looked over at Prince Anthony who was finally stirring to consciousness.

"No, I do not know him personally, but I know who he is related to," he answered.

Raul began to pace back and forth in front of him, and then stopped suddenly as if he had an epiphany.

"I know who he is. I just wanted to see if you knew who he was? And to see what his life meant to you," the wizard added as he walked over to a now alert Prince Anthony. Raul grabbed his dark hair pulling him up onto his knees, and then placed the knife to his throat.

"Now, answer me this, Lord Brom. What is his life to you?" he asked again.

Lord Brom saw the fear in Prince Anthony's eyes, and then thought about the tremendous amount of grief it would cause the Princess if he let her brother die.

"Let him go, Raul. I know it is his sister you want," Lord Brom answered.

Prince Anthony tried to fight the wizard, but with being tied up and the wizard having a handful of his hair made it difficult.

"No! What are you doing, Lord Brom?" Prince Anthony asked. His struggling caused Raul to let go. Prince Anthony fell over in the floor, and then continued to shout at Lord Brom.

"No, Lord Brom, do not tell him anything, I would rather die than to give him any information that he wants, please," he begged.

Raul walked back over to Lord Brom and grabbed him by his hair. He pulled his head to the back of the chair, leaned over him, and then placed the knife to his throat.

"So, tell me. What is it that he thinks you know that could possibly entice me to keep from killing him, or you for that matter?"

Lord Brom felt the cold steal upon his throat once again, he did not want to move in case the wizard slipped and slit it open for him.

"He is the Princess's brother," Liza spoke up and answered for him. She came out of the corner, not wanting Lord Brom to try and talk his way out of his present predicament.

"You, bitch!" Prince Anthony shouted at the vile women. It was her fault they were in this mess to begin with. He was furious, this time he was not going to arrest her, he was going to kill her first chance he had.

"So, this is your little Princess's brother?" Raul asked as he began to wave the knife around in the air in front of Lord Brom's face.

Lord Brom was free of the wizard's grasp, and he was able to hold his head up so he could see what was going on. Liza was standing in front of him, giving him an evil glare, and the wizard had begun pacing again.

"What should I do with that one then?" pointing at Prince Anthony in the corner.

Liza moved to Raul and placed her hand on his arm that had the atheme, trying to get him to lower it away from Lord Brom's face.

"Why not use them both for leverage?"

Raul looked at Liza, and then looked at the two men that were tied up.

"What do you mean by, leverage?"

Liza motioned to Prince Anthony. "He is the King's son, you could ransom him. He is probably worth more to him as an heir to the throne as opposed to his sister. Maybe you could make a trade," she said motioning to Lord Brom. "He is the little Princess's love interest. If you put the word out to her, she will come running to his side. Take your pick, but keeping them alive is your best bargaining tool."

Raul rubbed his chin with the blade contemplating his choices.

"What is in it for you, Liza? Because I really do not give a shite if this is one of your schemes to get the Princess back. I do not need her, and I sure as shite do not need you," he declared. He grabbed Liza's arm, and put his blade to her throat while pushing her up against the wall. "Let me get this straight for you. You work for me now, not the other way around. You will do as you are told, and no longer will you question me. Got it, hag?" Liza shook under his grip, he knew she was deathly afraid of him, and she had no choice in the matter now.

"Now that you understand. I will tell you what I am going to do," the wizard declared. He walked over to Prince Anthony, grabbed him by the hair, and dragged him along the floor to Lord Brom's chair.

Lord Brom looked down at Prince Anthony, and then to Liza who just shook her head at him, and to Raul who had gone over to Odin. The wild glare that was once in Odin's eyes had faded away, he was too tired to fight.

"What do you intend to do with my horse?" Prince Anthony inquired.

Raul laughed maniacally. "What do you think I am going to do, dear boy?" the wizard asked. Raul grabbed Odin's reins, pulling them high to stretch his steed's neck, and then raised the atheme.

"No!" Prince Anthony screamed.

CHAPTER 22

Princess Ellyria woke up in her bed to the sound of her own screams. Sweat covered her body and soaked her bed linens. She sat up, it was still dark out, and she did not hear any commotion downstairs. Was it still the middle of the night, or was it right before the dawn? Getting up from her bed, she walked over to the window, and looked up to the sky. She could still see the stars, so it was in fact the middle of the night, which gave her an idea. If her brother, and Lord Brom was in fact being detained right now by Liza and that horrible wizard, then she was going to go after them. Not having enough sense to think through her plan, like she knew that she had to, as she carefully snuck out of the castle. She hurried to put on her riding clothes since it was the only outfit she had that included a pair of trousers and boots. After putting her clothes on she had to make herself look more like a man, so she tightly braided her hair, coiled it around her head, and then put on her riding hat. She looked at her reflection in the mirror, but still saw her large breasts protruding out from the inside of her shirt. She then decided she needed a jacket to cover them up. Her riding jacket was too form fitting, so she had the idea to borrow the stable boys instead. That would be in the barn, with the stable boy. She would think of something when she got there, as she quietly crept down the stairs to the great hall, and then decided to go out the side door to the garden. She passed by her favorite wading place, the large fountain, on the way to the stables.

The barn was not guarded, strangely enough, so she slowly opened the door and slipped inside. The horses softly neighed at her presence and woke up the sable boy that was always on guard.

"Hey! What are you doing in here?"

She was surprised that he did not recognize her.

"What are you doing in here? Who are you?" he continued to ask of her.

She thought she had better speak up and let him know who she was, but before she got the word out, he was after her with a rake.

"No, wait, it is I, Princess Ellyria!" she shouted, but he was not listening. As soon as he went to lunge at her with the rake she grabbed the upper part of the stall door, and flung it into him, causing the boy to fall into a heap onto the barn floor. She removed his jacket, that was as baggy as she thought it would be, and proceeded to pull his body into one of the empty stalls.

"I am so sorry, but I had too. You will forgive me, will you not? I will try and bring your jacket back," she said to the sleeping stable boy. Now she needed to grab her horse.

"Hey, girl, I need you tonight," she whispered to her friend. Just then Ellyria heard a noise, it sounded like someone had just walked into the barn. She ducked down beside her horse Belle, and then heard a swishing sound, followed by a bark. It was Isis, she had followed her out to the barn, and there she sat wagging her tail.

"Isis, what are you doing here? You are supposed to be asleep," she said to her best friend. Isis just looked at her.

"Oh, all right, you can come with me." Isis wagged her tail and waited patiently for her mistress to saddle her horse.

Princess Ellyria quietly led her horse out into the darkness, making sure to close the barn door behind her. She looked to the tower and did not see the night guard. So she mounted the mare and hurried out of the courtyard. She had the mare jump over the broken wall that led out into the field, and kicked Belle into a hard gallop, as Isis faithfully ran beside her.

Princess Ellyria was not quite sure where exactly she was heading, or what she was going to do once she got there. Driven by her instincts alone she knew the wizard's cottage was in the Dark Forest of Woe, and she was pretty sure how to get there. She remembered overhearing her father talking to one of his knights about it, when he was in his study. She usually did not eavesdrop, but when it concerned her brother, she was sure to listen to what was going on. When her brother went missing, after going after Liza, and the other knights horses had returned without their riders, her father gathered his men to go look for his son. So between the information she gathered from her father, and that of her premonition, she was pretty sure she could find her way to the enchanted forest and the wizard's cottage.

After many miles of traveling Princess Ellyria grew tired, and then decided she needed rest, not only for herself, but also for Isis, and Belle. It was still dark, but the stars had faded from view, to signify the impending dawn. Her parents would soon discover that she was gone and alert her other brothers to come looking for her, but she was careful to not leave a trail. She rode Belle without her shoes, mainly because she could not put them on the horse, but it turned out to be a good thing since her hoof prints could resemble that of a wild horse.

"Come on girls, let us rest for awhile, and then we will get back to our travels," she said to Isis, and Belle. She pulled some food for the horse out and let her nibble the fresh oats out of her hand. When she was finished she gave Isis some dried meat she kept in the saddlebag. She packed some crusty bread for herself, and sat down with her back leaned against a tree to eat it.

When she finished, she climbed back on Belle's back and looked around to make sure no one was around before heading out. Isis tagged along, but kept her distance in the rear, in case they were being followed. They rode out into a steady gallop in the direction of the feared forest. She had heard many tales from the servants, about the forest being haunted or cursed by the wizard himself. They claimed that anyone who dared to enter the forest never made it out again. She was not scared, well maybe a little, however Ellyria was not going to let it get the best of her. She was going to see this quest through to the end.

The fog suddenly was upon them, as she stood amongst the gnarly trees and upon the brown grass. All she heard was silence. This had to be the Dark Forest of Woe. Belle became uneasy, refusing to go any further, she reared up and Ellyria fell off. The horse turned and ran off in the opposite direction, leaving her to walk on foot to her final destination.

"Coward," Princess Ellyria said as she wiped the rest of the dirt off her bottom. "Come on Isis, it is just you and me now." She continued her journey, not quite sure how far she had to walk until she reached the wizard's cottage. The forest seemed to come alive. The trees appeared to be watching her, and their branches reaching for her. The deeper into the woods she walked, the more it seemed as if it was closing in on her. Vines began to wrap around her ankles and dragged Princess Ellyria to the ground. Isis tried to bite at the vines, but they were too strong. Princess Ellyria grabbed them, trying to pull them off of her ankles, but they were not coming off. Isis began to chew the vines and managed to weaken them enough, allowing for Princess Ellyria to pull them the rest of the way off. She hurried to her feet and started to run through the forest, as sharp branches ripped at her clothes, but she kept on running and Isis stayed right behind her. She was determined to get to the cottage more than ever and was not going to stop now.

The forest gave way to a clearing and in its center was the wizard's cottage. Dark and menacing as it appeared, Princess Ellyria would not let it intimidate her. She leaned up against a tree to rest for a moment. To her surprise the tree had not tried to attack her. What she was going to do next, now that she was finally here? Isis had her nose to the ground, as she had picked up on Prince Anthony's scent even though it was faint. Princess Ellyria took notice and followed her. The trail led to the cottage, as she suspected. Isis walked all the way to the door, while she stayed back, way out of sight. Isis walked back to her side and that is when Princess Ellyria heard her brother scream. She went to the window to the side of cottage and peered inside. Lord Brom, and her brother, were tied up, Liza was standing beside them, and the wizard had hold of Odin. It appeared that he had a knife and was about to cut into the horse's chest. Just then Prince Anthony had managed to get out of his bonds and pushed Liza into the wizard who fell on his own blade. She could not stand by for another minute and ran to the door pushing it open.

"Ellyria! What are you doing here?" Lord Brom asked.

Liza got up off the wizard who was still in the floor, and then tried to run after Princess Ellyria. Princess Ellyria ran behind Prince Anthony, who was weaponless and hid behind him.

"Just when you think wishes do not ever come true, here you are, Princess," Liza said smiling.

Liza motioned for the guard to grab him, but Prince Anthony fought him off, disarmed him of his sword that was on his belt, and pushed it into his adversary's stomach. Prince Anthony pulled the sword out and went after Liza.

The wizard rose from the floor and with a quick motion of his hand, that sent Prince Anthony flying across the room up against the wall. Princess Ellyria started to go check on her brother when Liza blocked her path.

"I would not do that if I were you, Princess," the wizard said as he pulled the athame from his side. He was unaffected by the perilous wound that would have killed any other mortal man, but it did not seem to phase him.

Princess Ellyria's eyes were wide. She could not believe what she was seeing. The wizard's wound had sealed itself.

"Do not dare touch her, or I swear I will kill you myself!" Lord Brom shouted at the wizard Raul. Lord Brom was still working on his bonds and had nearly made the ropes loose enough for him to break free, but he needed to wait.

Princess Ellyria tried to make a break for it, ran past Liza to get to her brother, and then dropped to the floor where her brother was passed out but was still breathing.

When Liza turned to run after her, it was enough of a

distraction to keep the wizard busy and not suspecting what would happen next.

Lord Brom freed his hands then quickly untied his ankles from the chair legs. He hit the wizard in the head, knocking him out for the moment. Liza turned to the commotion and picked up the sword from the floor. Lord Brom leaned out of the way of Liza's clumsy lunges, grabbed her arm, took the sword from her hands, and then pushed her to the ground. He was contemplating driving it straight through her heart, when Ellyria shouted at him.

"Quick, just free Odin, grab my brother, and let us get out of here, please!" she shouted.

He did as instructed and freed Odin from his bonds. The tired horse tossed his head around and scratched the floor with his hoof; he was ready to leave too.

Lord Brom helped Princess Ellyria get Prince Anthony on the horse as he was finally starting to come to. Ellyria hopped on behind him, and led Odin to kick open the door. Lord Brom still had Liza cornered.

"Let us go, Lord Brom," Ellyria called out to him.

Lord Brom never let his gaze fall off of Liza, as he backed out of the house. He leapt on the giant steeds back behind the Princess, since Odin was in fact large enough to carry three riders at a time, as Ellyria kicked the mighty steed into a hard gallop.

They left just as the sun was emerging from the distant horizon, but the Princess knew they would not make it back home in time before the entire household discovered she was missing in the first place...

CHAPTER 23

Raul woke up to find Liza staring out the window. The back of his head ached, and now he remembered why.

"Liza, it appears as if everyone has just vanished. Why is that if I might ask?" the wizard inquired as he slowly approached her.

Liza was so scared of what was fixing to become of her, she could not move. When she was standing in front of him she slowly fell to her knees and took his hand, pressing it to her lips.

"Please, sire, have mercy on me. I did not know that Lord Brom, and the Prince, had loosened their bonds. They took me off guard. Lord Brom had gotten the sword from me, and threatened to use it, had I not stayed back to let the others get away."

The wizard grabbed Liza by the hair and dragged her across the floor to where his atheme lay. He let go of her to pick it up off the floor, when she made the attempt to get up, he struck her hard across her face. She fell to the floor: her jaw throbbed, and she could taste red iron in her mouth.

"Do you think me a fool, bitch!"

Liza began to crawl to the open door and try to escape, when Raul waved his hand, and the door slammed shut. Liza was trapped.

"Please Raul, I did not mean for them to get away," she sobbed. Liza had sat up but still remained in the floor.

"Save your tears, hag. I have had it with your incompetence," he stated before he kicked her in the face.

She went down, her nose pouring blood, never having the chance to heal from when the Queen had broken it before. Liza

141

spat out the blood from her mouth and looked up at the wizard, pulling herself up onto her hands and knees.

"Please, I beg of you to let me make it up to you. I swear I will not disappoint you again," she pleaded.

Raul looked down at the sorry shite before him, groveling like a slave, before you take their life. That angered him, and then he kicked her in the ribs repeatedly. She screamed out in pain. He just laughed and continued his abuse.

"I do not work well with those who do not heed my words. You are gravely treading on unstable ground madam, so if you want me to spare your life, you had better come up with a better excuse!" he shouted having stopped kicking her at this point.

Liza lay nearly breathless in the floor. She believed he had broken a few of her ribs, and held her side with her hands as she tried to sit up.

"You, need me," she muttered almost in a whisper, "your hideout has been discovered, we can go to my cottage, and they will never suspect us there. I can help you figure out a way to get the horse back, if that is what you desire," she said added breathlessly.

Raul looked at Liza, his face was emotionless, and she had tried to crawl to his feet in the attempt to grovel some more. He was not swayed.

"Wrong answer, wench! I do not need you, nor do I need you to come up with anymore of your ridiculous schemes," he said, as he kicked her one last time.

She fell to the floor, and remained perfectly still, afraid to make even the slightest movement. The next thing she knew Raul grabbed his grimoire and walked out of the cottage, the door slammed shut behind him. Liza pulled herself to her feet, and hobbled to the window. She looked out, the wizard was waving his hands in a circular motion, and the shutters on the windows slammed shut. She could not see what he was doing now. She limped towards the door, tried pulling it open, but it was as if it had been locked from the outside. She heard the wizard shouting some kind of incantation. Then before she knew it the inside of the cottage erupted into flames.

The Amulet of Elements

The wizard smiled as heard her screams. Smoke rose from the chimney, and through the cracks in the shudders, as the flames rose higher, with Liza trapped inside.

After a few moments, her screams could no longer be heard, and then the entire cottage was engulfed in the red flower.

Raul then turned away from the house and vanished from the forest...

CHAPTER 24

Prince Anthony woke up to find himself laid across Odin's back, in front of his sister, and Lord Brom sitting behind her.

"Welcome back to the living dear, brother," she said cheerfully. She pulled Odin to a stop, so they could all get down for a moment and rest.

They were well away from the Dark Forest of Woe, and were now safely back in Toledya.

"How are you feeling?" Lord Brom asked Prince Anthony.

Prince Anthony tried to stretch his aching body, which was still sore from being hurled into a wall.

"As good as can be expected, I suppose."

Ellyria tried to check his head for him, but he motioned her away.

"I am alright, you do not have to baby me," he chided.

She stepped back and allowed for him to regain his strength.

Lord Brom looked at the rope burns, that Odin had around his neck and ankles.

"Is he going to be all right?" Prince Anthony asked. He was concerned for his horse that he had raised since he was still just a fuzzy colt.

"Yeah, he will be fine," Lord Brom assured him. "He will heal in no time."

"We are not that far from the castle, and I would like to get back before father is even more infuriated with me, more than he already is," she informed her brother.

"You left without him knowing? Oh, you are definitely going to get it for sure." Ellyria shrugged her shoulders and nodded her head.

"We had better be getting you both back home," Lord Brom suggested. He helped Prince Anthony up onto Odin's broad back, followed by his sister, and then hoisted himself on behind them both.

Anthony took the reins and kicked his faithful steed into a fast gallop, to hasten their way home. Maybe his father will be lenient with his sister; after all, she did rescue him, and Lord Brom. They rode off and headed to the castle. Isis spotted them, and followed them back home…

King Jason was furious when Nan informed him that his daughter was found missing. The stable boy had gone to the King and informed him of the intruder that had knocked him out, stolen his jacket, and had taken the Princess's horse Belle. Jason put all the information together and presumed it had to have been Ellyria, since Belle allowed for no one else to ride her. He had not spoken to his wife yet, as she was still slumbering. He did not want to wake her and cause her to panic.

Just then the stable boy ran in out of breath.

"Tis Belle, Sire. She has returned, and without the Princess," he announced.

The King rose up from his seat in his in his study, he was going to have to tell the Queen now.

"Thank you, boy, that will be all. See to it that Belle is taken care of," King Jason ordered. He waved the young man away, and called to the guard by the door to fetch his remaining sons to him.

One by one the King's sons were summoned to their father's study. Ian was the first alerted and the first to join his father.

"What has happened, father?" Prince Ian was his father's announced successor to the throne. His other brothers had no desire to become King, but Prince Ian was proud to follow in his father's footsteps.

"Your sister has run away. I bet she had it in her mind to

rescue your brother, Anthony."

Just then Prince Rowan, and Prince Dakota, had arrived together, and was informed that their sister was missing.

"I could fly out with Gaia and help search for her," Prince Rowan offered.

Prince Dakota stepped up. "As I can with Luna. We can cover more ground that way," he added.

Their father was contemplating what to do, when the tower guard came running in.

"Sire! Prince Anthony, Princess Ellyria, and Lord Brom are approaching the gate!" King Jason, and his sons, followed the guard out and headed for the courtyard, when Queen Anna came running to her husband.

"What is going on? What is all the commotion?" she asked.

King Jason embraced his Queen and motioned for his sons to go on out.

"It is nothing to worry yourself with my love, Ellyria snuck out last night, but now she has returned with Anthony, and Lord Brom," he informed her. Without a moment's hesitation she ran outside, and saw her son and daughter enter the courtyard.

"What were you thinking, young lady? I just found out what you had done. How could you be so foolish, girl?" her mother scolded.

Lord Brom helped Princess Ellyria down from Odin, and walked with her arm linked in his, to face her displeased parents. He would speak to them and see to it that she was not punished too severely.

"Mother, father, I am so sorry. I had to," she confessed.

Her parents looked at their daughter. Without knowing what to say they went to her, and embraced her. They turned to Prince Anthony and embraced him as well.

"I can vouch for her, your Highnesses. Your daughter was very brave, and if it were not for her, we might not have escaped," Lord Brom stated.

Prince Anthony nodded his head in agreement. "It is true, father. If it were not for Princess Ellyria we would not have made it out alive, she saved us."

King Jason was curious if they were just covering for her, but he did not care, he was just happy they were both safe and sound.

"Thank you, Lord Brom, for bringing my children home safe once again. If there is anything that you need, name it and it will be yours."

Lord Brom looked at Princess Ellyria, he did not want to leave her, and she just saved his life again. He saw the look in her eyes; they were the color of the brightest sapphire, and she seemed to want him to stay too. Should he?

"Thank you, your Majesty. A horse to replace the one that was taken from me would suffice, and then I will be on my way," Lord Brom said. He began to worry now that the Princess was giving him her glare.

"Nonsense, you will stay with us for some time. You can freshen up, and I am sure one of my sons can lend you some clothes, while yours is being washed. You will dine with us tonight. I shall have a grand feast prepared in your honor," he announced.

Lord Brom knew that he could not argue with the King. Ellyria smiled as they all walked back inside the castle.

CHAPTER 25

Lord Brom had decided to leave after an extended two-day stay, that was longer than he had intended. Luckily, he had not seen the Princess much, since the great feast, that her father had ordered. He had spent more time at the King's side, and only caught mere glimpses of Princess Ellyria passing through, or during mealtimes. As promised a new horse was provided for him, his clothes were freshly washed, and he felt it would be better that he left now. He did not wish to say goodbye to Ellyria, it would not only be painful to her, but to himself as well. Lord Brom planned to stay with his father, Lord Thomas, for some time to help him tend to his lands.

Lord Brom had gathered his belongings and set out to load his saddlebags, with provisions for his long journey ahead. On his way to the stables he paused to look upon a beautiful and innocent sight in the fountain. Princess Ellyria, and Isis, were playing in the water. It was a sight to behold for a young lady of her stature and age, when it would be more like behavior of a child. He found it quite amusing observing such play, and it continued to prove the point of her still caught between that of a woman, and that of a child. He turned around to head on into the barn not thinking for a moment that the Princess had seen him.

Lord Brom was placing the saddle on the beautiful roan stallion that had been gifted to him, when Princess Ellyria walked in. She was dripping wet, her long black hair was cascading down like a waterfall and hiding the front of her cotton day gown that she was wearing. When she approached him, she lifted her hair away pulling it behind her, revealing that her dress was almost completely see through.

Lord Brom could not think. He rubbed his face with his hands in a downward motion to keep himself from staring at her. One could almost see through the thin material and the striking silhouette of her large breasts that her dress was clinging to. It displayed the perfect peaks of her erect nipples that he could almost see the color of, like that of newly ripened strawberries. Lord Brom was trying to control his urges, when she made it quite difficult for him to ignore.

Princess Ellyria walked around to the front of the stable door and watched him for a few moments before she spoke.

"Where are you going? Were you just going to leave, without saying goodbye?" she inquired almost pouting.

Her eyes were bewitching, he felt that he would fall under her spell once again if he did not leave. He walked out of the stable to fetch the bridle. She met him at the stable door and did not move. He really was beginning to feel uncomfortable being in the King's barn with his daughter, when anyone could walk in and see them; which appeared inappropriate even though it was really quite an innocent situation. He had to get past her, so he placed his hands on either side of her tiny waist and carefully pushed her aside. He was barely able to get her to move, which allowed hardly any space to get by her. He had no choice, but to brush up against her. The thin wet material of her dress, her large breasts and the hardened peaks of her nipples made it quite difficult to ignore.

After trying really hard to resist her, he became instantly aroused by the warmth of her body under the cold material. She tilted her head up to look at him in such a way that compelled him to grab her, and kiss her without hesitation. She returned his kisses pressing her wet body even closer to him, and getting his clothes wet in the process. He reached up behind her neck and grabbed a handful of her wet hair, and pulled her head back ever so slightly, so he could ravage her neck with ardent kisses.

The Amulet of Elements

The couple was in such rapture, they had not paid attention to the stable boy that had come in, and cleared his throat to interrupt them. When that did not work the boy dropped the saddle he had in his hands. That was finally enough racket to make Lord Brom look up.

Princess Ellyria grabbed the horse blanket from inside the stall to cover her near naked breasts, but she could not disguise her bruised lips, swollen from kisses, and her neck that was unmistakably red from Lord Brom's assault on it.

"Could you please give us a moment alone," she asked of the stable boy who turned around without hesitation or response. She then turned and looked at Lord Brom, with those beautiful enchanting eyes of hers that were slowly turning green.

"Were you going to say goodbye, before you left," she questioned again, waiting for his answer this time.

He took her in his arms and kissed her gently, his usual way for getting out of answering the question. When he stopped and looked into her in the eyes.

"No, I am afraid I was not," he finally answered.

She turned away from him, not wanting him to see the tears that threatened to make an appearance. He gently lifted her chin with his hand to make her look at him. Then he wiped away her tears that could no longer be kept at bay.

"Please do not cry, Princess. I know it is hard to say goodbye, but as you said it yourself, you are not ready to be married," trying to comfort her. He finished putting the bridle on the horse, and he made sure the saddle straps were good and tight before he mounted. Without a word Lord Brom rode out of the barn into the courtyard.

Princess Ellyria stood like a statue, unable to find words that carried enough measure to convince him to stay. Nor could she find the words to say goodbye, as she watched him ride down to the end of the cobblestone path. Without really knowing what exactly compelled her, she put effort to her feet and ran to him as fast as they would carry her.

"Wait! Brom! Please wait!"

He turned and looked down at the Princess, who was now out of breath and crying.

"When will I see you again?" she said choking back her tears.

He looked at the beautiful, woman-child standing beside his horse holding onto his leg as if in an effort to try and prevent his departure.

"I do not know, Princess," he reached down, squeezed her hand, and then let it go. He kicked his horse into a gallop and rode out of the courtyard to the road leading away from the castle.

She watched him leave yet again for a second time, leaving her to regret her first choice in denying him what he wanted. She wiped the tears away with her hands, and then walked back towards the castle.

CHAPTER 26

The King and Queen were watching through the window at the heartfelt goodbye, between their daughter and Lord Brom. They had been sitting in the parlor, when Nan had come in and informed them that Lord Brom was leaving. She passed the message that he left stating he did not like goodbyes but had expressed his undying gratitude and thanks to the great courtesy they had bestowed upon him. That if there were anything that they needed, they had only to call upon him, he would be there, and no matter the desired duty that was requested of him. King Jason respected that, yet Queen Anna knew that her daughter would be terribly upset. They had looked to see if Lord Brom, and Princess Ellyria would cross paths since she was playing in the fountain. They both knew he had to travel through the courtyard to get through the gardens, and on to the stables. That is when they happen to see the couple, and what looked like a not so pleasant goodbye.

"Where did he say he was heading?" she asked of her husband.

The King turned to face his beautiful wife, and he smiled affectionately.

"He mentioned going to stay with his father, Lord Thomas in the North, and help him with his lands," he informed.

Queen Anna nodded her head, and then saw her daughter return inside.

"Maybe I should go and check on her. I am sure she is having a difficult time, with losing him yet again," she said as she embraced her husband quickly before leaving the room.

Ellyria was face down in her feather pillow that was now wet from tears. She could not believe he was still able to leave, after she had practically thrown herself at him in the stables. When she came back to her room, she had taken off her wet gown and replaced it with a summer dress, and did not bother to comb out her lovely waist length hair. She was too sad to care about the number of tangles she probably now had, and just curled herself into a ball on her huge canopy-bed.

When her mother walked into her room she did not bother to sit up or greet her. Queen Anna sat beside her daughter on the bed and pushed the hair from her face that it covered.

"Are you alright, my dear?"

Princess Ellyria rolled over to her side to face her mother but did not speak. Her eyes were the color of emeralds, and were red and puffy from crying.

"I can not understand what you are feeling right now, but I can listen if you would like to talk about what just happened between you and Lord Brom." Her mother placed a hand on her shoulder, and then looked down at her daughter, waiting to see if she was going to open up to her.

"Why does it hurt so much?" she asked her mother, who was now wiping tears from her cheeks.

"I cannot answer that, my darling. Only you can answer that question. First you have to ask yourself this, do you love him?" her mother inquired.

Princess Ellyria sat up, her hair falling all around her in such a mess that made her look like a small child. She nodded her head.

"Well, what do you want to do about it?" Her daughter began to cry again, covering her face with her hands, and then falling back onto her pillow.

"Stay here in bed," she replied sobbing.

Her mother shook her head and pulled her daughter's hands away from her face.

"That is not an option, my darling, daughter. You have to get up, wash your face, and brush your hair. If you do not think there is a way to change it, then you have to move on. You had the blessing of experiencing your first love. Now it is time to move on in the direction that you said you had wanted to go in. It was your choice that you turned down Lord Brom's proposal, because you wanted to live your own life first, and go on your own journey. So, get up out of your bed young lady, and start that journey right now."

Princess Ellyria drug herself off the bed, after her mother had stopped chastising her for feeling sorry for herself. Her mother gave her a smack on her bottom to get her motivated, and she smiled at the gesture.

"Oh Ellyria, I know what you could do. You could keep your mind busy, and begin your spell work," her mother suggested, before leaving the room.

Princess Ellyria walked over to the large, white, vanity and sat down in front of the big mirror. She began to work out the knots that had taken up residence in her hair and pondered what her mother had said. There was not anything she could do now about Lord Brom, except to get over him. He was gone again, and she had to face the facts that he may not return this time. She had achieved what she had sent out to do by rescuing him and her brother, from Liza and the wizard. She was the hero this time, and it was her brother, and Lord Brom, that were the damsels in distress. She rescued them all on her own.

Princess Ellyria Rose looked into the mirror and watched it reveal to her something it had never shown to her before. She was curious because it had never revealed anything, but the past before. Until now...

CHAPTER 27

The little cottage in the woods was currently being ransacked. The men that Liza had sent to seek out the amulet, were turning over furniture, and pulling everything out from the cabinets. They were searching every room, and to their surprise, Raul appeared out of nowhere.

"Listen closely, for it will be the last opportunity that I give you this offer. Your current benefactor has met an unfortunate accident. I know that you followed and obeyed her faithfully. Now, I give you the chance to follow me, and those who do not obey... well, how do I put it delicately? It will be the last thing that you will ever do. Do I make myself clear?" the wizard advised.

The few men that were there nodded their heads in agreement.

"Now who is in charge here other than myself?"

A surly guard stepped forward. "I am, sire," he answered quickly.

The wizard motioned for the others to carry on.

"Have you found what you were sent here to find?" he inquired.

The guard shook his head, and then bowed before his master. "No, sire."

The wizard turned and began walking through the cottage, kicking fallen objects out of his way. After a few moments, he abruptly turned to face the younger man.

"I do not believe it is here. Gather your men, head back to the castle. Find me a page, and then bring him back to me in the forests of Narruc. You have two days," he ordered.

Before the men could nod their heads in obedience, Raul went out the same way he had arrived...

Raul emerged into the forest that was on the furthest end of the kingdom of Narruc. The forest was beautiful, lush green trees hovered over the sweet grass, and it harbored many different kinds of animals. He could hear the songs of the birds, watching them as they flew by, and saw a family of rabbits hop across the path in front of him that bounced right into their burrow.

"Oh, damn, there goes my next meal," he directed towards the rabbits.

With a wave of his hand, and an incantation he quoted from his grimoire, the forest was no more. No longer the lush green trees or sweet grasses he had seen, now the trees were barren, and the grass turned brown. He could no longer hear the birds, or see them flying around in the sky, they now lay dead at his feet. The family of rabbits, who had retreated to the safety of the burrow, were now safely on a spit over a nice roaring fire.

The wizard had made his new home in the once beautiful forest, but it is not really a home until you have a roof over your head. He raised his hands slowly from his side, chanting a most commonly used spell to erect a new cottage. From what seemed as though he conjured the new house from the very ground, it was like watching mountains form and climb towards the sky. The cottage was the exact replica of the one he had, which he had burned to the ground only a few days before.

Here stood his new cottage, in the fresh clearing in its new home, in a new feared forest. Raul entered the cottage, and then with a slight flick of the wrist the door slammed shut behind him. He had almost forgotten his supper, and with a snap of his fingers it appeared at the table before him.

After Raul had finished his meal, he left to retire to his bedroom for a long much needed slumber.

Even an evil wizard has to sleep sometime, and dream of the havoc he plans to wreak...

CHAPTER 28

On the far side of the realm, beyond Southern Toledya, and Western Narruc, was another vast kingdom in the North, called Regnuom, which was on the coast of the North Sea. Its people were great warriors and fisherman, but they were known more as the Vikings who ruled the high seas. Raiding many lands they were often mistaken for thieves, but one is not considered a thief if they take with iron and blood. Dead men have no use for material things like gold, or jewels, which makes it fair game and not thievery.

Captain Jake was on his way home, after a long year at sea to reunite with his family he had left back home. His wife, Nicole had blessed him with a son while he was away and he was excited to see him for the very first time. Communication was very difficult; messages were only relayed by carrier pigeon, or by messengers who could only carry letters by horse to ports inland. When he received the news about his son, it was delivered to him while he was at one of the many ports he often traded at. His wife named him Gabe, and one day he would be known as Gabe The Great, he could not wait to meet him. They were still out at sea, but nearing the port in the kingdom of Regnuom.

"Hoist, the mainsail! I want to make port, before nightfall!" the captain ordered the crew.

All of the men scrambled to set the mainsail that would push up their arrival time at port...

Lord Brom had finally made it back to his father's home in Regnuom, and was incredibly tired from the weeklong journey it took to ride north from Toledya. When he arrived his sister-in-law, Nicole warmly greeted him at the door.

"Oh, Brom. It is so good to see you. How long has it been?" she inquired smiling. Lord Brom set his saddlebag down and gave her a long embrace.

"Is good to see you. Where is my father?" he asked.

"Oh, he went to port to greet your, brother," she answered.

Lord Brom picked up his bag and headed up the stairs to his bedchamber, after the news of his estranged brother's arrival. He had not seen him in a few years, and would usually be gone when his brother came inland. He was looking forward to seeing him again. After washing up from his journey, he decided to go and help Nicole with the preparations that he was sure would be needed. He knew that his father would have planned a grand feast now that both his sons, were back home again under one roof.

"Is there anything I can help you with?" he questioned upon entering the room. Nicole turned and smiled at Lord Brom, while holding her son.

"Well, whom have we got here?" he asked surprised.

"This would be your nephew, Gabe," she answered handing him over to his uncle.

Lord Brom smiled at the boy that was the spitting image of his father.

"My brother could not deny this baby, he looks just like him," he cooed at the infant. He handed back his nephew to his mother.

"How old is he now?"

The boy began to cry, his mother now was rocking him to console him.

"He is almost a year old now, your brother was out at sea and did not get to see him born. Your father has been a blessing to us both, and has graciously helped us out."

He was curious what it must be like, being out at sea, while your life passes on by without you. It must be like being away at war.

Gabe began to cry again.

"I need to be getting him fed, I will come back in a little while," she said as she left the room to take care of her son.

Lord Brom watched her as she left. He turned away to look out to the large field of wheat. It was almost time to harvest, that is why he had decided to come home and help his father. But his father was not always a farmer by trade. When his father was younger, he was a fisherman, but the sea can be dangerous. So his father came inland to raise his family and became a farmer. Still Lord of his lands, he earned his title by iron and blood, not by a rich peacock gifting it to him. His father's people hailed from the farthest of the Northern regions, but his grandfather moved south to grow crops, and fish from warmer waters. His mother's people were from the north as well, that had also moved south. His parents met when they were children at a market, having similar interests together as well as their native tongue; they became the best of friends. Later when they were older, they had come to love one another and married straight away. His brother was the oldest, but by not even quite a year between them. His mother, Dalla had become very ill shortly after his fifth birthday, leaving his father to raise them on his own. His father never chose to remarry, becoming the Lord, and farmer he still is today. Lord Brom was proud of his heritage and his family, even though he decided to not choose the Viking path of his brother, or like his father had when he was younger.

Lord Brom's status was that by birth and not by iron or blood. He did go to war in honor of his family, against the neighboring kingdom of Narruc, who's evil King Harold had tried to conquer their lands in Regnuom. Lord Brom was barely a man at that time and did not know then, that evil King Harold was Liza's father. When Liza began her crusade to avenge her father, all those that had crossed, or defeated her father became a target of her revenge. Unfortunately his father was a target only because he was Lord of the kingdom. King Warrick of Regnuom had died trying to protect the realm, if it were not for King Charles's protection, Regnuom would have became part of Narruc's territory. A treaty was signed by King Warrick of Regnuom, and King Charles of

Toledya, before the attack. Regnuom became its own kingdom, and would be forever protected by its sister kingdom of Toledya. To this day, no one has stepped up to the throne of Regnuom. The former King Warrick's wife was not able to give him any heirs, and King Harold had killed off all his bastards during the war. Without anyone to secure the throne for himself, the kingdom became ruled by King Charles since the treaty tied the two sister kingdoms together. Regnuom has been at peace since.

Lord Brom had decided to finish preparing the great dining hall as a surprise for his sister, it was the least he could do for her since she was alone with the bulk of the chores. His father never believed in having servants, so he and Nicole took care of everything themselves, hiring help only when it was planting and harvesting season. Lord Brom, and his brother assisted when they were home, so their father could have a break from time to time.

Nicole returned downstairs with a well-fed, and happy Gabe, now placing him in the cradle for a much-needed nap. She was surprised to see Brom himself, had completed all the preparations in accordance with the grand feast, that she was preparing for her husband's safe return.

"Thank you, Brom," she said embracing her brother-in-law. He was happy for doing it and simply smiled at her.

"Is there anything else I can help with?"

She smiled and motioned him to follow her to the hearth where some rabbits were on the spit, and walked outside to the pit were a large boar was roasting in the ground covered by long boards.

"I believe we have got the meat covered and the bread is in the oven. You could fetch the potatoes, prepare them for the pot, and then place it over the fire."

Lord Brom got to work with his domestic duties, while they waited for the return of his father, and brother...

Later that evening before the sun began its descent into the horizon, a proud father had come back home with his first-born son. Lord Brom had greeted them at the door with open arms.

"Father, so good to see you." Lord Brom embraced him, and turned to see his brother. "Jake, it has been too long, has it not, dear brother?" he said as he embraced his older brother.

Nicole ran quickly to her husband almost pushing Lord Brom out of her way. Her husband embraced her tightly and began to twirl her in the air. He set her down and kissed her. Jake was happy to be with his wife, and was excited to see his son now.

"Where is my son?" He looked at his wife, and then watched as she went to retrieve him from his cradle.

"May I present to you, your son, Gabe," she introduced lovingly. She handed him over to the proud father, and he eagerly cradled his son, smiling and talking to him sweetly.

"He has my eyes," he announced still smiling.

Lord Brom looked at his brother, and his wife. Maybe one day that could be him, and his Princess, admiring their child one day. He shook the fantasy from his mind.

"Good thing he looks more like your wife. Would not want the poor kid to look like you, Jake," he jested.

Jake grabbed Lord Brom and began to wrestle him to the floor, like they did when they were boys.

"Do you think you are a bit old for such foolery?" Jake's wife chided.

Lord Thomas began to laugh at his sons that were rolling around in the floor.

"All right, my sons get up and go clean up for supper. Jake I heard your wife made a fabulous feast in your honor."

Lord Brom and Jake got up and left to go clean up, leaving Nicole and their father to set the long table in the dining hall.

"So, brother, where did you leave your crew?" Lord Brom questioned.

Jake laughed. "I let them take leave to do whatever they wished. So long as they did not plunder in our homeland," he informed him.

Lord Brom raised a brow and smiled. "You left a bunch of rowdy pirates to go and pillage somewhere else then? You are not sane brother," he said chuckling.

Jake was laughing at his brother so hard, that tears came to his eyes.

"Yes, I know, but it is better to let them have a break now, then let them go crazy at sea. I have to deal with them then."

The two brothers continued their jesting when their father came looking for them.

"Are you two going to join us for supper? Or stay up here all night?" their father questioned.

"We are coming, father," Lord Brom answered.

"Yes, father, we just got caught up in jest, we will be right down," Jake added.

Lord Thomas went on downstairs, leaving his sons slowly trailing behind.

"So how long are you staying this time, brother?" Lord Brom inquired.

Jake gave him a look, and then shrugged his shoulders.

"A week, give or take. Depends on what mischief the crew gets themselves into. If it is not too bad, I'll have to depart hastily to keep them from being arrested," he answered laughing again.

Lord Brom shook his head and laughed at his brother.

The brothers finally made it downstairs to the dining area to join their family for the grand feast, and they reminisced about the times they had missed while apart.

CHAPTER 29

Princess Ellyria had been diligently studying her spell work. It had been primarily bookwork, lots of reading and tests, but now she was ready for the next phase, potion making. Her brother, Prince Dakota is the master potion maker, due to his impeccable skills in alchemy. Who better to learn potion making from? Princess Ellyria entered his special wing of the castle, that was primarily built to prevent any accidental explosions or fires from spreading to the rest of the castle. Prince Dakota looked up from the book he was reading, to find his sister standing in the doorway.

"I see you are ready for the next phase of your studies. Are you ready, dear sister, to learn about the various herbs, and chemicals that can be made into different kinds of potions?"

She smiled at her brother. She was much indeed ready to finally have a break from all of the bookwork she'd been doing of late.

"Yes, I am very excited, all the bookwork and studying was getting rather boring," she replied enthusiastically.

Prince Dakota laughed. "Well, I am sorry to say there is going to be more bookwork, and even more studying," he informed her.

She scoffed and rolled her eyes at her big brother, and stuck out her tongue at him.

"It is not going to be all that bad. There are a few lessons on what not to put together, so you do not do something dangerous and blow us up."

She nodded her head that she understood.

"You are right. I am sorry, brother. I just really want to hurry and learn all this, so I can go after, oops," she almost slipped. She quickly covered her mouth with her hand.

"Ellyria. What are you not telling me?" he questioned her raising an eyebrow and sitting back in his chair.

She removed her hand from her mouth and had a sheepish expression about her face.

"Well, I had this premonition about this Amulet of Elements, and I need to go and find it before Liza, and the wizard does."

Prince Dakota got up and walked over to the bookcase where he pulled a very old book from, then blew off the dust. He opened the book and looked through the worn pages, it had been in the family for several generations, so he had to take extra care not to rip them. Finally, he found what he was searching for and read the text out loud for his sister's benefit.

"The Amulet of Elements was originally conceived as a myth, created by an ancient wizard to wield ultimate powers. When the amulet was actually seen by others, by the display of its powers, then many began to covet it. The amulet also has the power to turn anything into the four elements, Earth, Air, Fire, and Water, or to conjure anything from one's own imagination. So, if you imagine a unicorn to appear, a unicorn appears. According to this, it has not been seen in centuries, but this book is really old and has never been updated. I need to go to the library, I think I remember seeing another book about it, a more updated version, if you will." He was almost talking to himself it seemed, since his sister did not appear to be paying attention to anything he had just read. He found her looking through some of his potion vials that he always kept stocked in his cabinet.

"What are all these?"

He walked over to the cabinet and began to point them out. He specifically color-coded them instead of using labels to prevent someone from just grabbing them randomly, and using them for inappropriate reasons.

"This red one is used to make fire, black is for explosions, blue is for creating water; like say for instance you throw it and say rain, or flood. Green is to create vines that will ensnare your enemies, purple is to make someone turn to stone, which I do not use unless I absolutely have to, because it is permanent. Lastly the clear vial is to make oneself become invisible, but it only lasts for a short period of time; it depends on the size of the person. I myself am roughly a little over six feet tall, give or take an inch or two, so it would only work for me maybe an hour. Someone small such as you are perhaps could last up to two hours at the most. Now I have to go and get that book from the library. Stay here and do not touch anything. I will be right back," he instructed.

Princess Ellyria watched her brother exit the room. She walked over to his desk and sat in the large chair that almost engulfed her. She flipped through the old book on his desk and continued reading the myth surrounding the amulet. The Amulet of Elements was forged from the four elements and fused together with unicorn blood. She crinkled up her nose at the idea of how it must have been acquired, and it gave her a shudder. As she read further, she learned that it also gave protection to non-magical people, just the power of blocking unwanted magic. That made her curious. Is that why she never got a premonition from Lord Brom, until after they left Liza's cottage? Thinking back to when he coaxed her into leaving the night of her ball, she tried to get a vision, but could not. Then in the woods she had not even tried, and had one about his father, Lord Thomas instead. She looked to the cabinet, as she sat there for a moment and tapped her finger on the desk. Princess Ellyria began tapping her foot on the floor, looked at the book, and then again to the cabinet.

"Nah, should I? No, I should not. My parents will kill me if I disobey them again," she said out loud. Then she recalled the vision of the amulet, and the images that was shown to her by the mirror. The Universe is trying to tell her something. What? In her vision the amulet was said to be at the cottage. Perhaps if she went there and could find it before Liza or the wizard does, then her parents would be too proud to kill her. Quickly she walked to the cabinet and started to grab the potion vials but had nothing to put them in. She looked around and found a medicine bag that had a shoulder strap. Perfect! She quickly placed all the vials carefully in the bag and left the room before her brother came back. He would be sure to stop her from going on this crazy quest, and she could not have that. Sneaking out the backset of stairs that went in the direction of the stables, she ran down them as fast as she could. She would definitely need Belle's help for this one...

Prince Dakota returned to see the door was left wide open. He entered the room to discover that not only his sister was missing, but all of the potions from his cabinet were missing as well. He did not know how long she had been gone, since he had been in the library for quite a long time reading the information about the amulet. After discovering what he had found about the mystical stone, he was almost positive she went after it. Unfortunately, he had to be the one to inform his father of what she had done.

"He will probably kill me for giving her all this information," he said out loud, "not only about the amulet, but of the potions as well," he had to hurry.

Especially after what he had just learned about the amulet...

CHAPTER 30

Ellyria was well away from home, by the time her brother discovered her missing. She was riding Belle at a fast pace and was constantly looking behind her to see if she was being followed. The cottage Liza kept was not far from where she was now and she hoped to reach it before nightfall. Ellyria urged her horse to run faster to get there sooner. Unaware that she was not alone in her search for the amulet...

Raul's newly appointed men had already ransacked the little cottage in the woods. When they were given leave to return to Liza's former castle to find their new Lordship a page, they decided to stop at a tavern on the way. That tavern, was the exact same one that Lord Brom had visited, where he had become totally intoxicated, seduced the toothless whore, started a bar fight, and then had gotten himself arrested in. While the wizard's men were getting quite drunk themselves they became quite loud in their private conversation about their search for the amulet.

At the same time, at a nearby table, Captain Jake's men were getting quite inebriated as well, but they overheard the guard's conversation and carefully listened to what they were saying. They decided that a bauble like that would fetch a fair price with the gypsies at the market. So with their plan set in motion they laid coin on the table for the ale that had been consumed, and casually left the bar. The guards had not paid any attention to them at all, and had left their horses tied out front. The pirates decided that it was awfully nice of them to leave the horses to borrow. They quickly mounted the horses, and then rode off in the direction they had overheard the cottage was in.

Later the heavily intoxicated guards were ready to leave, they stumbled outside and were too drunk to even notice their horses were missing...

Ellyria had stopped to rest Belle, since the mare had become quite winded. They still had a few more miles to go. She miscalculated the distance that she had believed it to be shorter than it had actually turned out to be.

"Ah, Belle, it is all right girl. We will stay here for at least a little while," she said to her horse. She looked to the sun that was already high in the center of the sky. She knew for sure that her brother would alert their father after he had found her missing. She could not worry about that now. She must continue her quest and retrieve the amulet.

"Ok Belle, we have rested long enough, let us head out," she said. Belle would not move. Ellyria patted her friend and pulled the reins.

Belle walked forward slowly but stopped, and tossed her head back pulling the Princess with her.

"What is the matter, girl?" Belle began to paw the ground. They were in the woods and the road had ended a few miles back. Ellyria heard a hissing sound.

Belle ran in front of Ellyria, reared up and came down hard, and stomped something on the ground. She could not see what her horse was having a fit over. She had never seen her react that way before. Belle neighed softly and turned to Ellyria. She walked over to the place that her horse was stomping. It was a giant snake. Perhaps it was poisonous, but she did not care. It was dead and Belle had just saved her life. She hugged Belle's neck tight, and then hoisted herself up onto her back.

"Come on girl, let us go," she added as they rode off. She needed to be more careful, since she was deep the woods with wild animals. It was not just people that she had to worry about.

Captain Jake's men arrived to the cottage first. They observed by its appearance that it obviously had been searched before, but they were professionals, and they always checked thoroughly before deciding that said object was no longer there.

"Search all the rooms, leave nothing unturned that is already turned over," the leader ordered. Rob the Red was the Captain's first mate, and was in charge of the four men that had decided to accompany him to the tavern. Some of the others stayed with the ship, and the rest he had no clue as to where they had drifted off after he had left them at the brothel.

The men followed his orders and left nothing unscathed as they continued their hunt for the amulet.

"Sir, there is a barn out back. Should we start looking out there?" one of the men questioned. He nodded his head and two of the men went to search the barn.

Ellyria finally made it to the cottage. After seeing four horses that wore the insignia of Liza's colors she rode around the back to where the barn was. Unaware that the barn was currently occupied, she walked Belle right in there. Before she knew it, she was dragged off her horse. Kicking and screaming was no use. No one that cared or could hear her. Her futile attempts at fighting these giant men, that were the size of trees in comparison, continued to carry her into the cottage like a sack of potatoes.

"Who do we have here?" Rob questioned his men.

"I do not know, sir?" she just appeared out of nowhere. Apparently these men had not seen her ride up to the barn. This gave her an idea.

"Yeah, sir, it is like she came out of nowhere, like a Seither," the other man chimed in. The Vikings were a very superstitious people, and anything involving magic or Seithers frightened them.

"Tie her up, we do not want her to get away. In case you are wrong, she will make a good trade, and fill our pockets with lots of gold," Rob added. He admired her beauty, and knew she would fetch more than a fair price in their homeland in the North. Many women there were fair-haired, or had hair the color of fire. Hair black as night on such a beauty as this one, almost made him want to take her for himself, if the Captain would allow it.

Princess Ellyria scowled at the large man with the fiery red hair that was long, and braided down the length of his back, with a long braided beard to match. She had to come up with a plan to escape, but also needed to see if they had discovered the amulet, or not.

"Did you find the amulet yet?" he questioned, still finding himself bewitched by her intriguing beauty.

""No, we had just started to look for it, when she entered the barn, sir."

"Well, go back and keep looking."

The men left the cottage to go back in the barn, leaving Ellyria all alone with the first mate.

Princess Ellyria was still inexperienced with the art of seduction. She believed the day in the barn with Lord Brom was an exception. It did not really count since she was wet and her dress was completely see-through. Knowing that the fiery haired man was attracted to her helped in her present circumstances. Well, she at least hoped so.

"You are so big and strong. What province do you hail from?" She lowered her head, tilted it, and then smiled.

He looked at her strangely.

"I come from the far North, above Regnuom," he replied

walking closer to the enchanting girl. He leaned in close and removed the pins that kept her hair coiled upon her head.

As it came down, Princess Ellyria took advantage of it and shook it all out wildly. Her long black hair cascaded down into deep waves all around her.

Rob took it in his hands letting her hair slide through his fingers, and then before he released the rest of it, he could smell the sweet fragrance of roses. He was in disbelief, that she could be a Seither. Princess Ellyria was too beautiful, wore a nice dress of spun silk, and she smelled too sweet to be one of those wretched creatures. She would indeed fetch a fair price worth more than mere gold, perhaps even rubies. He slowly ran his hand down the side of her face tracing his fingers over her plump rosy lips. Her skin was the color of fine porcelain and was as soft as a newborn babe's bum. Now he was feeling quite aroused by her and could no longer resist her.

Princess Ellyria was helpless as he kissed her viciously, bruising her lips, and then thrusted his tongue in and out of her mouth like a serpent. She thought for just a moment to bite down on his tongue, but if she was going to seduce him into letting her go, she had to play along. She kissed him back to his surprise, equally matching the ferociousness of his kisses. The way he kissed her was completely different than the way Lord Brom had kissed her. Lord Brom had been much gentler, yet passionate. This man kissed her like a wild animal it seemed. He began to get a bit carried away when he started chewing on the side of her neck, but she just kept her head tilted to the side to allow it. She drew the line when he reached up and tried to fondle her breast.

"Oh, please, sire. I have never lain with a man before. Please be gentle," she said innocently.

He immediately stopped and stepped back from her. He had mistakenly taken her for a local whore since she was without escort. He should have known better by the way of her dress, and perfectly sweet smelling hair. If she were a virgin she would be worth even more. Then it seemed all the more enticing to keep her all to himself.

"Are you saying, girl, that you are a virgin?"

She lowered her gaze, and smiled. "Yes, I am afraid so," she answered.

He became excited for the idea of taking her right now, but knew he had to be careful. The Captain would be furious if he damaged the goods before the chance of selling her.

Princess Ellyria was not sure what to do now. He made no more advances, even though the look in his eyes suggested otherwise. So she decided to raise a leg up and over the other to expose a naked thigh. She watched his gaze settle on her leg.

He could not stand it anymore. He would just have a sample. A quick taste of that precious virgin womanhood and still leave her chaste. Before Ellyria could protest, he fell to his knees, lifted her dress, and tried to place his face between her thighs.

She immediately kicked him to the floor.

"What is it that you think you are doing?"

He was not expecting she would resist. No woman resists her cunt being kissed, but he lost his head in the moment, and did not think of her inexperience to such a carnal pleasure.

"Please forgive me, but if you would allow me to kiss you there, I promise that you will like it, and I will not go any further."

She gave him a blank look. Women can get kissed there too? Well even if they did, she was not going to let him do it. She cringed at the thought of him doing it, but now was curious about what it would be like if Lord Brom was to kiss her there.

"No. I do not think so," she stated firmly.

He almost seemed offended, because his face now was an equal shade of red as his hair. Rob went over to her, leaned her back in her chair, and then began to rub her between her legs. She tried to fight him, but she was tilted backwards in the chair. He kissed her again, but this time she bit his tongue.

"Owe, you little, bitch!" he shouted as he slapped her across the face. He did not do it hard enough to bring blood, but her face was red and starting to swell.

"Why did you bite me? I was trying to show you that you could experience pleasure from my touch," he explained.

She was so confused.

"Well, I did inform you that I was not interested, yet you still continued your brutal assault upon me. How is that fair?"

Just then the rest of the crew came running in…

"Sir, we think we got it. We think we found the amulet!" one of the men shouted. He handed Rob the beautiful gold necklace, its chain was woven intricately together, and on the end the amulet itself was wrapped in a gold casing. The bauble itself was almost egg shaped. Its color was that of many, upon tilting it, the amulet seemed to change color as the light struck. Such a fine piece indeed and it will go for enough gold to share with the entire crew.

"Good job, men!" he praised.

Princess Ellyria looked at the amulet, it was breathtaking to look at, but more powerful than they could imagine.

Rob carefully wrapped the amulet in cheesecloth and placed it in his pocket, it would be safer there.

"All right men, let us head out. We got what we came for, you may gather what you can carry that will fetch a fair price at the market," Rob instructed, and then patted his pocket smiling.

The other man looked at him and motioned towards the girl.

"What do we do with her, sir? There are only four horses, and we are already doubled on one?"

"She came in on a horse, did she not? Go fetch her, she is riding with me," he answered the not very bright young man.

Ellyria knew this would be a sight to see, especially since Belle will not allow anyone else to ride her but her. How long would it be before they figured that out?

After the worthy objects were retrieved and secured to the horses, a few of the men were arguing who was going to ride the beautiful white mare with the long cascading waves of mane, and equally long wavy-haired tail. A larger man won by pushing the smaller man out of the way.

Princess Ellyria was not going to miss this. Belle behaved and let the man climb on her back. After he settled himself in, he kicked Belle to get her to go. She went all right, she bolted, gave a quick turn unseating the man, and left him sitting in the dirt. Great laughter rose up, as the furious and embarrassed man tried again.

Once again Belle unseated him, this time rearing up then coming down, followed by a quick buck, and then to the dirt he returned swearing something in his native tongue. It must have been very amusing from the extended amount of laughter that had continued, after the initial outburst. The man was more than determined, but this time grabbed a whip from one of the other horses saddle.

"No! Please do not hurt her. She will only allow me to ride her," she pleaded with the man.

He threw up his hands and walked off after Rob motioned him away.

"Come, I will place you in front, then I will ride behind you. If your horse even tries to throw me off, I will kill her, so you had better make sure she behaves," he threatened.

Princess Ellyria was placed astride Belle, she leaned over to her ear, and asked her to be a good girl. Rob mounted Belle right behind her, turning to his men, and raised a fist in the air.

"Let us move out! To the gypsies, let us ride!" he shouted.

All the riders moved out now heading east to Inamor, land of the gypsies, as the sun was beginning to set in the distant horizon.

This time, there would be no one that knew her, or could save her. The Princess was all on her own...

CHAPTER 31

Prince Dakota had alerted his parents to his sister's actions. Explaining to them it was not entirely her fault, he gave her the ammunition, which probably caused her to go on this dangerous quest alone. King Jason immediately dispatched some of his best knights to follow her trail and tried to console his frantic wife. How could his daughter keep doing this to her mother and himself? Prince Dakota had brought the old books into his father's study with him. He had yet the chance to tell him what he had learned from the ancient texts that was originally thought to have been a myth.

"Father, if I could have but a moment to tell you what I have learned, that Ellyria did not stick around long enough to find out."

His father motioned him to show him the text. Prince Dakota set them down on the table in front of him, with the pages already turned.

"I had told Ellyria only about what the amulet could do, I am guessing she read on her own what it could do in the hands of the wrong person," he explained.

Queen Anna stood up abruptly.

"Like the wizard from her premonition," she interrupted.

Prince Dakota, and her husband gave her a bewildered look.

"Did she mention the premonition to you, about Liza, and the wizard?"

Prince Dakota shook his head still puzzled, and then it dawned on him why she went before he returned. She knew he would have stopped her.

"This is terrible," his mother sighed sitting back down in her chair, placing a hand over her mouth.

"Well, what is this new information you learned that she does not yet know?" his father inquired.

Prince Dakota grabbed the smaller book finding the text and read it out loud.

"The Amulet of Elements, has only the power of protection from one that is free of magic. A person who holds the natural gift of magic can use the power of the amulet for creation. They would have the ability to create anything from one's imagination, and the ability to control the elements," he said.

Queen Anna looked at her son.

"What else does it say?" she asked.

Prince Dakota turned the page to see if there was anything else.

"Not in this one."

"Check the other one."

Prince Dakota turned the page after the initial last page that he had read to his sister.

"The Chosen One is said to be the true master of this enchanted necklace, only they and they alone, can utilize its power without becoming controlled by its magic. The amulet was created for the Chosen One, five hundred years ago. That does not sound right," he said now confused.

"Is there a separate text?" his mother asked.

Prince Dakota read it again to himself, on the off chance he read the ancient text incorrectly to himself.

"Yes, I did read it wrong, it says here that it was created for the Chosen One, which is not mentioned anymore in this text in accordance with the amulet," he informed.

Queen Anna had a strange feeling there was a connection with the prophecy, the amulet, and her daughter.

"See if you can find more on this, Chosen One," she urged.

Prince Dakota searched through the many pages of the ancient text, cross-referencing anything that had the prophecy as well.

"Yes, I may have found something, it is about the prophecy. The ancient prophecy foretells of a female child that will be born from magic, and will harness The Power of Litha during the Summer Solstice, and only during a full blood moon's eclipse. It says it only occurs once every five hundred years. The Chosen One will then have the power to destroy an evil wizard that can only be killed by her hand alone, and must also possess the Amulet of Element in order to destroy him. The Chosen One will then reunite the kingdoms once and for all, bringing absolute peace to the realm," as he finished reading his parents looked like they were in shock.

"What does it say about the wizard?" his father asked.

Prince Dakota looked through the worn pages once more, skimming the text until he found the information on the wizard.

"The wizard was originally born over five hundred years ago, from the belly of a dragon," he laughed, that could not be right? He read the words more slowly. "He was born under the sign of the dragon, he was called the bringer of light. He was seduced by a powerful Seither, who turned him to the dark arts of the most powerful of magic. He killed the Seither, and then took all of her ancient power into him. When the Power of Litha was foretold, he patiently waited for its power to be drawn down into him, and not to the original Chosen One. The Chosen One was never to be found. It says he searched for her, but never found her. She was said to be a powerful gypsy, who had the power of The Evil Eye. Not only protected by it, but it also gave her the gift of immortality. She could then make sure when the new Chosen One was born she could protect her, and teach her how to draw down the Power of Litha into her."

Prince Dakota finished reading and both his parents looked like they had seen a ghost.

Queen Anna looked at her husband. He could only shake his head. She knew what that meant. This made perfect sense to her now. The old woman from the market, and the amount of secrecy and protection needed that was placed on her birth, her daughter's visions, the wizard, the amulet, and the upcoming Summer Solstice. Queen Anna was beginning to piece it all together now.

Ellyria is the Chosen One!

CHAPTER 32

The kingdom of Inamor was the home of the gypsies. They were a peaceful people, living off the land, famous for their trade markets, and their magic. They were a jack-of-all-trades, farmers, fishermen, jewelry makers, seamstresses, blacksmiths, and fortunetellers. Many people came from all corners of the realms for their wares, the knowledge for ancient relics, and the written word.

Princess Ellyria was still being held by Rob the Red, and was nearing the gypsy market in Inamor. They had been traveling nonstop since they left Narruc, and Belle was becoming weaker by the minute. The small horse was not used to many miles of nonstop travel with more than Princess Ellyria on her back, and carrying the huge man as well was becoming too much for her. Princess Ellyria could sense something was wrong with her.

"Could we stop, please? We have been riding for two days now without much rest, my horse is not used to going such great distances," she begged.

The Viking said nothing, and then kicked the mare into a hard gallop. Belle only ran a few feet before she collapsed. Princess Ellyria went tumbling down, as did her red-haired captor. He got up and kicked the horse, and then Ellyria ran in front of him.

"No! What do you think you are doing? It was not her fault, you pushed her after I told you she needed to rest!" she shouted at him frantically.

Rob pushed the girl out of his way, and knelt down by the

barely breathing horse.

"She has gone lame, she is no more use to us." He pulled a long hunting knife from the leg holster.

"What are you going to do?" she inquired as panic took over.

The man took Belle's head in his hand, lifted it up, and then in one fluid motion slit the horse's throat.

"No!" screamed Princess Ellyria. She ran over and began to hit him as hard as she could, even with her hands bound together in front of her.

He rose to his feet, picked her up by the waist, hoisted her over another horse's back, and then climbed on behind her.

"No!" She kicked and tried to wriggle herself of the back of the horse, but it was no use. She lay over the horse's back helpless, and began to sob for the loss of her friend. She watched as everything was stripped from her back, as she lay on the ground in the pool of her own blood.

Rob motioned for the other men to double up as best as they could. Ellyria's medicine bag was tucked away now in the Vikings saddlebag, if only she could get to one of those potions.

"It was the only thing I could have done for your horse. She was going to die anyway. I was not being as barbaric as you might think," Rob confessed.

She did not answer, only cried in silence.

When they reached the market it was incredibly packed with people, horses, and traders of all kinds from all over the realm. Princess Ellyria had been pulled up to sit upright on the horse, she had never seen so many people, and this market was far more vast than the one at home. With this many people around it would be quite easy to get lost in the crowd. If she could only get away from the Vikings long enough, then she could disappear.

After looking around for the right trader, Rob finally found whom he was trying to find. This particular gypsy made hand crafted jewelry, and would always trade for a well-made bauble.

"Look what I have for you today, my friend," the red-haired said. He pulled the amulet from his pocket and set it down on the merchantman's table and carefully removed the cheesecloth. The morning sun caused such a beautiful glimmer on the amulet making it look all the more enticing.

The gypsy gently picked up the magnificent necklace, examining it carefully.

"I'll give you twenty gold coin for this. Fair no?" he questioned.

The Viking thought it might have been worth more so he bartered with the man.

"I want fifty gold coin, and I will throw in all of this other merchandise as well."

The merchantman came around and looked through some of the other wares he offered. He shook his head in agreement, paid the Viking his coins, and then spotted Princess Ellyria.

"What do you want for her?" he inquired motioning to the Princess.

"I am not for sale!" She was not going to be bartered like chattel.

Rob made a gesture for her to keep silent. Ellyria crossed her arms, her green eyes narrowed.

"I will take no less than forty gold coin," he answered.

What? She could not believe she was worth less to him than the amulet and the other trinkets. She started to open her mouth to protest, but was interrupted with a hand gesture to hold her tongue.

"I will give you thirty gold coin, but no more. She looks as though I would get more trouble from her than she is worth," the gypsy said.

Rob smiled at Princess Ellyria.

"Looks like you are mine now, I am not going to just settle for what he thinks you are worth," he chuckled.

She was not for sure if she felt relieved or not.

"Well, let us go buy another horse, and more provisions, it is time to go back to the ship," Rob ordered.

This could not be happening, she could not go back to their ship!

"Wait, can we not talk about this? What do you mean to do

with me?" she questioned.

He looked at her puzzled.

"We are Vikings, we are only docked to trade, we will go back to our homeland now," he answered.

She let out a sigh. She waited patiently for him to return, he went to go and speak to the gypsy about another horse. To her surprise he walked back to her with a beautiful, solid black, Jennet mare.

"You like? I know she does not compare to the one you lost, but she will give you some comfort, no?"

She was speechless.

"Thank you," was all she could come up with.

He bought himself a larger black Gypsy Vanner stallion, and stocked both saddlebags full with the provisions needed for the long journey north, back to Regnuom where their ship was waiting at port. They needed to be back before the Captain returned.

Princess Ellyria was set on her own horse, her hands were untied so she could ride, but her mare was tied to Rob's stallion, so there was no way for her to ride off and get away.

The Princess could only think of home as they rode out away from the market, and briefly looked behind her as if someone was going to rescue her, but there was no one there…

CHAPTER 33

ord Brom was patiently waiting for his brother to bid his wife and son goodbye. He had decided to leave with him, and take in an adventure on the high seas. The more distance he could put between himself and the Princess, would be for the better. He had to forget about her, something he could not seem to do while remaining on land.

Captain Jake finally emerged from his bedchamber smiling.

Lord Brom looked at him in confusion.

"Are you not supposed to be unhappy about leaving?"

Jake just laughed.

"Of course I am upset, but I did just receive a good reason to be happy, dear brother."

Lord Brom got it, he supposed there were in fact some good farewells.

Nicole came out of the room, and blushed, not expecting the men to be standing right outside the door.

"What are you telling him, dear husband?"

Jake just chuckled.

"Nothing my, darling, just business," he reassured her. He took her hand into his and kissed it. "Let us go and find father and see where he has gone with Gabe. I want to hold him a few moments one last time before I leave."

They all left the hall upstairs to search for Lord Thomas, and his grandson. He was sitting in the old rocking chair in front of the fireplace just like he used to do when Jake, and Brom were his age.

"Father, I will take him now," Jake said. He held his first-born to his heart, and hated having to leave him. He would be walking and talking by the time he returned. It was almost unfair, but he had to make sacrifices to see to it that his family were well taken care of. Jake kissed his son and handed him back to his mother.

Nicole watched her husband say his goodbyes to his father. She passed Gabe back to his grandfather so she could say goodbye as well. Jake and his wife walked with arms linked to the door, they both looked deep into one another's eyes, and he leaned in to kiss his wife passionately one last time. When they finally released each other from the tender embrace, he looked at his wife, and wiped the tears from her eyes.

"I will be back before you know it, I promise," he said.

She tried to wipe the tears that would not stop flowing.

"Goodbye, father," Lord Brom said, as he patted his nephew on the head. He walked over to his sister-in-law, and gave her a farewell embrace.

"You had better take care of him," she told him.

Lord Brom smiled at her.

"I will, I promise."

Nicole, and Lord Thomas as well as Gabe, watched as Lord Brom and Captain Jake walked out the door.

Lord Brom and Jake mounted the horses, and took off to port where the ship and crew were waiting.

"I can not wait for you to meet, Abby," Jake mentioned.

Lord Brom looked confused.

"You will see, I think you will like her."

Lord Brom just laughed at his brother, and shook his head.

The port was only a few hours ride from here, so the two brothers made the most of it and swapped tales of their past adventures. Lord Brom was all the more excited for the new adventures to come…

Back on the ship, Rob the Red and the remainder of the crew had finally arrived, with their bounty full of gold, jewels, and one new passenger.

The Amulet of Elements

Princess Ellyria gave up any notions of escaping now, or seeing her family again. She had cried so much the tears no longer came, and was positive that no one would ever know to look for her on a ship out at sea. They had to leave the horses behind since they were no use to them on the ship, and they were resold to the highest bidder on the docks. Princess Ellyria said goodbye to her new friend that she had made, of the beautiful black Jennet mare. That mare had been a small comfort to her on this long journey together. She watched as her horse was sold to a man with foul manners and a whip, before she had her hands tied together once again. Where was she going to escape?

After being led onto the ship, Rob made a serious announcement that she was not to be touched, and whomever did would lose their hand for the crime. Princess Ellyria felt at least a little better knowing she was not about to be the entertainment for the crew. Rob led her downstairs to the holding quarters where they kept prisoners, and he made sure her accommodations were comfortable. He promised to bring her some food, a washbasin with fresh water to clean up, and fresh clothes to put on. She was not going to complain about the incredibly small cabin, that had not a tub to bathe in, the tiny cot to sleep on, or even the small hole in the floor to relieve her bodily functions. She was in fact grateful that he would not be sharing the room with her, but worried that he would expect her to share the bed with him on occasion. Without anywhere else to go, it will be quite difficult to avoid his advances towards her. What was she going to do?

As promised he brought a basin of water, fresh clothes, and a plate of food. She was not very hungry, but thanked him anyway. He had asked if she needed anything else and after telling him no, he promised to check on her later after they had set sail. Then she heard the door being locked, before he walked away. There was no window in the door, and only a small porthole in the wall that she definitely would not fit through if she tried. She proceeded to remove her dirty clothing, throwing them into a heap on the floor, and washed her pale naked flesh with the small amount of water, soap, and sponge that was provided to her. As she finished with her grand whore bath, she slipped into the cream-colored cotton gown that was also provided to her. She did not really want to eat, but she did not need to let herself become weak. She needed all the strength she had to fight off that Viking later. It was a small piece of meat, boiled potatoes, and a small loaf of crusty bread. She felt sleepy after she ate, so she decided to take a little nap. She was exhausted and had not really slept much, only when she nodded off periodically as they traveled. So she turned over the small mattress on the cot, put on the linens that were in a small cabinet on the wall, and placed the thin blanket on as she crawled underneath it.

It did not take long for the Princess to drift off to sleep, and it would be well after they had set sail before she would awaken...

CHAPTER 34

King Jason had sent out his scouts days ago. They had returned with no information regarding his daughter's whereabouts. He felt it was time for a more evasive approach.

"Anthony, gather the rest of your brothers, it will take all of you to search for your sister. I pray to the Gods that you will be able to find her."

Prince Anthony quickly left the room to gather his brothers but was worried for his father. How much more of his sisters disappearances can he take?

Anna went to the window that overlooked the fountain where her husband was standing.

"I keep thinking I am going to look down and see her playing in the fountain with Isis."

She embraced her husband. This was harder on him than she was aware of. He tried to give her even a partial smile, but could not.

"She has proven that she can take care of herself. After all, she is the Chosen One," she said trying to console him.

King Jason worried that he had somehow disappointed his daughter, as a father. Why could he not accept her destiny? Just then Prince Anthony returned with, Prince Dakota, Prince Ian, and Prince Rowan, and they all stood ready to be handed out their mission.

"You all know why I have called you all here together. Your sister has gone missing once again. My personal scouts have found no trace of her whereabouts within the kingdom. With that said, I believe her to have left the kingdom to possibly go to Narruc, in search of the Amulet of Elements. This will be a dangerous undertaking. Liza is still at large and the evil wizard Raul, who may still abide in the Dark Forest of Woe, and possibly searching for the Amulet of Elements as well. Please use caution, for you must split up to cover more ground. Of course, Rowan and Dakota will cover the sky with Gaia and Luna. Anthony, you and Ian will cover the ground with Migata and Odin. If you must, pair off, just be weary of anyone or anything suspicious."

Queen Anna embraced her sons bidding them a safe return, with their sister included. King Jason also embraced his sons and sent well wishes for their safe return with his daughter. The young men bid their parents farewell and left to go call upon their much-needed allies.

They arrived outside to the courtyard, Prince Anthony's steed Odin was already saddled, and made ready for the journey. The giant lion, Migata was saddled as well and waiting for Prince Ian. Prince Rowan played his flute to call to his giant dragon friend Gaia, who had not been too far away, and as she touched down and allowed for Prince Rowan to climb on. Prince Dakota used his talisman to reflect into the sunlight to signal to the giant white owl Luna, as she gracefully flew down from a nearby tree, and Prince Dakota climbed onto her back as well. This was the first quest for the brothers to be going together, at the same time, since they were kids. The journey was not going to be easy, it would be challenging, but if they were lucky they would return with their sister.

The brothers nodded at one another and gave the signal that they were in fact ready to embark on an incredible quest to save their sister once again…

CHAPTER 35

Raul was waiting not so patiently for his men to return from the quest he had sent them on, more than the two days that he had allowed for. He needed a page to clean up around the cottage, and run light errands, so he could not without being spotted. Just when he grew tired of waiting and planning what he would do with the bones of the guards, he heard a knock at the door.

"About time, you idiots! How much time does it really take to round up a page?" The guard pushed the young boy about the age of ten into the cottage.

"Here is your new master, take heed and listen to what he tells you," the man advised.

The young boy started to weep.

Raul looked at him in confusion.

"Where did you get this little wretch from?" he questioned.

The man bowed to one knee before him.

"Oh, get up. What is wrong with this boy?"

The boy tried to hide behind the large man's legs.

"Well, sire, we took him from his father, so I am assuming he is upset about that," he answered hesitantly.

Raul walked over to the man, and slapped him across the top of his head.

"I thought I had instructed to get the one from the castle?"

The man rubbed his sore head.

"Well, sire, we did not make it to the castle," he answered waiting to be struck again.

Raul looked at the quivering man.

"I am almost afraid to ask this. Why the shite did you not make it to the castle?"

The man was surprised he was not struck again, and began to relax.

"Well, sire, our horses were stolen."

Raul looked at the man and rotated his hand, gesturing for him to continue.

"Well, sire, we had been at the tavern and accidentally got inebriated, when we walked out, our horses had been stolen," he recalled.

Raul just stood there for a minute, and then smacked the man again.

"So, if you did not get him from the castle, then where did you find him?"

"Well, sire, from the blacksmith. He did not want to cooperate at first, but we convinced him otherwise. Told him that he would be a page for a great and powerful wizard," he informed him.

Raul's eyes grew wide as he raised his eyebrows at the idiot in front of him.

"Are you seriously that stupid! Or is this an act you are putting on, because you are sure fooling me. I gave you a direct and simple order and you fumbled that up!" The man grew scared, so did the blacksmith's son, but the boy moved away from the man he was standing behind.

"I apologize, sire, it will not happen again, sire," he said fearfully.

Raul felt his head begin to ache. Why did idiots constantly surround him? What in this lifetime did he do to deserve such incompetent minions? He pulled himself together.

"Leave my sight, I do not want to contract your stupidity disease," he ordered as he waved them away.

The boy started to turn and sneak away, but it was too late.

"No, not you. Come here boy and let me get a closer look at you. Well, you seem healthy anyway. What is your name?"

The boy looked him in the eye, as he did not want to show

that he feared him.

"I am Toby, sire."

Raul almost felt sorry for the boy now. What were his parents thinking?

"Well now, uh, Toby, I need to leave for a while. I need you to clean up around here and watch the place for me. I expect you to remain here. We are far from your father's keep, so your safer staying here with me. There is no telling what sort of monsters are lurking around out there in the woods. Do I have your word, boy?"

The boy nodded his head that he would do as instructed. Then before he could blink, the wizard vanished before his eyes...

Raul reappeared in Inamor, to search for a special ingredient that he needed for his new potion. He planned to draw down the Power of Litha, during the full moon that will commence sooner than he would like. He did not have much time if he was to succeed in having not only ultimate powers, to become an immortal, and unable to be killed, by even the hand of the Chosen One.

After searching an endless amount of tables, he finally found the one he was searching for. The spice table not only held various exotic spices for cooking, but it had many special herbs that were used for magical purposes. Mandrake root was sometimes rare to come by and was dependent on the season. Mandrake was a finicky plant indeed, requiring the just amount of climate, water, and thrived only in the richest of soils.

"Pardon me miss, do you have any fresh mandrake root?" he questioned the pretty, young gypsy.

She turned around to face him.

"Yes, I do. How will you be traveling, it will dry out rather quickly if you do not keep it moist," she informed him.

He just gave her a sadistic grin.

"I will be home in no time. I can assure you that it will not go dry," he stated slyly. He dropped more than the required amount on her table, she looked up to thank him, but he was already gone.

Before he was to leave the market, he decided he would look around for just a few moments longer and enjoy his outing. He was not much one to have interest in petty trinkets, but he stopped anyway to see if there was anything of interest to him.

"What can I help you with today, sire?"

Raul looked around the table, nothing but jewelry and semiprecious stones, some necklaces, but not much else that suit his fancy. Just then the man's wife appeared, and asked her husband if he needed any help before she went home. He told her just to wait that he would be ready to leave, after he waited on the gentleman, as he motioned to Raul. Without paying any attention to the chatter between them, Raul looked up for a brief moment when he overheard they were referring to him. Much to his surprise the man's wife was wearing the Amulet of Elements! The Gods did not hate him! Quickly he grabbed the woman, surprising her husband.

"Where did you get this?" he questioned snatching the amulet from her neck. Raul really did not care how they came by it, because he had it now.

"I paid good money for that bauble!" the man shouted at Raul.

The wizard grabbed the gypsy by his throat.

"This was stolen from me. I have been searching for this for weeks now," he lied.

The man began choking, his wife was crying, Raul let him go so he could speak.

"I got it a few days ago," he informed him.

Raul still wanted to know from whom.

"Who was the man? Did you know him?" he interrogated.

The gypsy looked at Raul, trying to decide what curse he would plague the man with.

"He was a Viking, there were five of them, and they had a beautiful slave girl that they had tried to trade also. I would not give him what he wanted for her, because she was too feisty. What about my compensation for the necklace?"

Raul raised his hand lifting the merchant off his feet, the man reached for his throat gasping for air, when he dropped his arm, the gypsy fell to the ground at his feet.

The wizard stood over the man.

"How is that for your bloody compensation? I let you live," he responded with a scowl.

The man held up his talisman and spoke a curse in his native tongue.

Raul laughed at the man, and then vanished before his eyes.

The gypsy man and his wife now knew who he may have been and went straightaway to their bandolier for counsel...

Raul arrived back home to his cottage and surprised the young boy who was scrubbing the floors. He quickly went to the mirror, and put on the amulet. He finally had what he had been seeking for the last several weeks. It practically fell in his lap, without having killed anyone for it. He was sure he would get to kill someone soon enough. Right now he would prepare for the Summer Solstice. Not only did the wizard have the Amulet of Elements, but soon he would have the Power of Litha as well...

CHAPTER 36

Captain Jake had returned to his ship with his brother, Lord Brom. The Captain went straight to his post and took command. He gave the orders to hoist anchor, and signaled to the oarsmen to begin rowing out of port.

"We will set the sail once we are out of the harbor," he said to his brother.

Lord Brom watched as the dock became further out of sight.

"This ship is huge, brother," he observed.

Jake smiled and motioned him to follow.

"Come, let me be your guide. Welcome to Draki, this of course is the main deck, the first of three. The second is for the crew, passengers, mostly slaves, the third is for livestock, and the many treasures of fine goods that we collect, or trade," he said as they walked below deck. "I had separate cabins constructed to give more privacy, so none of the men would grow tired of looking at the other and try to kill one another. The slaves we come by are kept on the opposite end of the ship, it separates cabins as well, with locks of course on the doors and no windows. We do not do much slave trading, mostly fish, and wares."

"So, what happens if you are attacked? This ship does not look like it is built for war?" Jake smiled.

"This is not, but in the event we are, we have an ample supply of weapons," he showed him opening a storage cabin stocked with swords, knives, axes, and barrels of black powder.

"I am impressed, brother," Lord Brom said smiling.

They continued to the third deck where there were a multitude of everything from ancient artifacts, to the large chests of gold and jewels.

"This of course does not all belong to me, although a good chunk of it is," he laughed.

They returned to the passenger deck and Jake showed him the cabin that could be his, and opened his door to the Captain's quarters.

"Well now, this is nice," Lord Brom, said in amazement. There was a large oak, four-poster canopy bed, an oak wardrobe, a desk in the far corner, and the cabin was impressively well off in size no doubt.

"So, what do you think?"

Just then Lord Brom heard a strange noise coming from the other side of the room. Curious, he walked over to a large covered crate to inspect it further. He pulled off the cover, and there in a metal cage was a large parrot that had multiple colors of purple, green, and red. The parrot looked at Lord Brom then tucked its head under its wing.

"Brom, meet Abby. She is an Imperial Parrot, I found her in a cage, at a market across the ocean. She is very smart, and can speak her mind," he said admiringly.

Jake opened the cage and extended his hand so the bird could climb on. She scaled up his arm and perched herself on his shoulder, then what appeared to be her kissing his cheek.

"Abby, this is my brother, Lord Brom," he introduced.

Abby extended her foot to Lord Brom. He laughed and shook her foot. She became quite excited gave a whistle and nodded her head up and down.

"I think she likes you," Jake replied.

Both men chuckled and decided to go above deck to see how far out at sea they had gotten.

When they arrived back on deck, there was a fight that had ensued. The two men were in a very serious fight, and their knives were drawn. Once Jake, and Lord Brom were able to get a closer look, upon arriving to break up the fight, it was Jake's first mate

Rob, and a newcomer to the crew. Both men were equally matched in size and skill, as Rob, and the other man showed no sign of backing down.

"Oh, no! Throw them overboard! Keelhaul, keelhaul!" Abby declared.

Lord Brom could not keep his laughter to himself, which now had the two fighting men's attention.

"Enough! What is going on here?" Jake ordered. He motioned for a few of the other crewmembers to grab the fighting men. "Can someone please, tell me what all of this is about?"

Rob was too angry to speak, so his closest companion answered for him.

"Captain, sir, Rob caught the other man trying to meddle with his goods, sir," the man answered.

Jake walked between the two men and addressed the newcomer first.

"Is what he says is true? Did you try to meddle with his property?" Jake questioned the surly man.

The man lowered his head in shame.

"Yes, but I did not know she was his? I thought she was just a slave girl, to be traded, sir."

Jake turned to Rob with a stern look about his face.

"What girl is he talking about, Rob? You know the rules. If you bring a female aboard this ship to trade, she is fair game, unless you plan to take her for a wife. Then as you know, has to be cleared by me. Is that understood?"

Rob nodded his head. He had not thought until now the idea of taken the raven-haired beauty for a bride, but if Captain would allow it he would. Since she was a captive there was no waiting around to see if an arrangement could be made, but the Captain may give her a choice in the matter.

"Yes, Captain, I do plan on taking her as my wife. She is untouched and pure, and very beautiful," he announced.

Jake looked at his brother, then at Rob.

"Let us go see what all the fighting is about, shall we?"

Lord Brom, Jake, and Rob went down to the prisoner's

quarters, and Rob motioned to the one the girl was in. Jake motioned for Rob to unlock the door. The door was pulled open to reveal the beautiful girl looking out the window, with her long black hair caressing the small of her back.

Rob cleared his throat to announce his presence, when she turned around she only could see her captor at first, then another tall blonde haired man that favored Lord Brom in a way.

After Jake examined the girl, he motioned for his brother.

"Well, now I see what all the fuss was about, come brother, take a look for yourself," he motioned for Lord Brom.

When he entered the small cabin his brother noticed the shocked look upon his face.

"Do you know her?" Jake questioned.

Lord Brom could not believe his luck. He went on the voyage to avoid her, and here she is of all places, and the red-haired man's captive.

"Yes, brother, that's the Princess Ellyria," he announced

Jake turned to look at his brother, and then looked back at the girl who was smiling at his brother.

Princess Ellyria never felt more relieved as she did right now, seeing Lord Brom on this ship with her was a blessing from the Goddess herself.

"You mean, the Princess, the one you have been telling me about?" he whispered in Lord Brom's ear.

Lord Brom just nodded in agreement.

Rob was very confused right now, and worried he was going to be severely punished for kidnapping a Princess.

"Captain, a word, if I may," Rob motioned to leave the cabin to speak privately. "I swear I did not know who she was, she never stated she was a princess. I never even got her name," he confessed.

"Did you not think to ask her who she was?" the Captain questioned.

Rob shook his head no.

"Well therein lies the current state of the circumstances you are in now, does it not?"

"Does this mean I can no longer take her as my wife?"

The Amulet of Elements

Jake rubbed his temples and looked at his first mate that he did not hire strictly for his prowess, or for the lack of intelligence.

Rob understood and left to go back above deck.

While the Captain, and the first mate were in the hall having their private discussion, Princess Ellyria, and Lord Brom were in the midst of their own.

"How did you manage to get yourself abducted by Vikings?" he asked, almost not wanting to know the answer.

She looked at him with those sapphire blue eyes of hers.

"Well, I went looking for an amulet."

Lord Brom shook his head.

"You mean to tell me, you left the comfort of that big castle you live in to search for a simple amulet, you could have had one of your servants retrieve for you?" He tried to understand.

Princess Ellyria went to him and embraced him.

He held up his hand to pause her. She stood there confused, and slightly tilted her head to one side, giving him a blank stare.

"It was not just any ordinary amulet, it is the Amulet of Elements the wizard is after," she informed him.

Lord Brom raised his hand to his face, and then sat down on the cot.

"Oh, that amulet. So you not only left home, but risked your safety as well?"

Princess Ellyria fell to her knees in front of him.

"Please, I knew the risks, but I just felt compelled by something I can not explain, because I do not understand it myself," she said.

Lord Brom looked at the girl kneeling before him and watched as her eyes swelled with tears. He pulled her to her feet and stood up to embrace her.

Just then his brother entered the cabin.

"Am I interrupting something?" Jake questioned.

Lord Brom followed his brother out in the hall, after he made motion to do so.

"What is between you two? Are you together? Is she yours? What? I need to tell my crew something, or she will end up becoming any man's choice," he informed his brother.

Lord Brom looked in on Princess Ellyria, he could not just throw her to the wolves, but he was not going to declare her his either.

"Well, she is not mine, but I do not want her to be a plaything for your crew either." Jake was Captain, so he supposed he could just say she's off limits due to her royal title until they figure out a way to return her to her family.

Jake turned to lean in the doorway.

"Are your accommodations fair, or would you like a better cabin?" he asked the Princess.

She looked up at him from the cot she had seated herself at and shook her head. "Although these are fine accommodations for any prisoner, I would like something slightly larger if possible. With a bath."

Lord Brom shook his head upon hearing her requirements. We are on a ship. Where does she think she will get a bath?

"At your service, your Highness," Jake bowed to her.

Lord Brom had seen it all, now his brother was smitten with her charms too.

After the Captain gave orders to make accommodations for two of the cabins to be made into one large one, the crew carried up a white porcelain bath, with gold claw feet, and set it on the far side of the cabin. They also carried another bed similar to the Captains, and brought in a writing desk, as well as a wardrobe full of gowns to choose from. Also an additional large chest filled with gowns, corsets, and fine silk women's undergarments arrived shortly after.

Once the room was properly made fitting for the Princess, they filled the tub with hot water that was especially boiled for her bath. Lord Brom could not believe the effort that was placed for her comforts. The Captain not only made sure she was comfortable, but also informed his crew that no man was to touch her without facing punishment. He was at least at ease with the Princess being kept safe from the crew.

Princess Ellyria had never felt freer in her entire life. She had walked out on the main deck and stood at the bow of the ship. She looked out into the open ocean, the wind blew her hair back, as well as her red satin gown she put on after her luxurious bath she had. Lord Brom was watching from afar, leaning up against the single mast and the giant wool spun sail that had caught the wind propelling the grand merchant ship forward. He watched as the Princess outstretched her arms as if she was flying, while the wind blew through her long shiny black hair. The sleeve of her gown had been blown off her right shoulder, exposing it, and the hemline had been carried up just enough to expose a pale thigh. Her beauty that was enhanced by the sunlight captivated Lord Brom, and he was unaware of his brother that now stood beside him.

"She is quite enchanting, I will agree with you there. I can understand why you are so in love with her," his brother observed.

Lord Brom's gaze never wavered.

"I am not in love with her."

Jake began to laugh.

"You can not even take your eyes off of her. I saw the look in your eye when you saw her in the cabin, it is the same look you have in your eyes right now. Why can you not just admit it? You know one day you are going to wake up and wish you never let her get away," Jake advised.

Lord Brom turned to face his brother.

"I do love her. I had even asked her to marry me, but she rejected my proposal," he confessed.

Jake placed a hand onto his younger brother's shoulder.

"I am so sorry, brother. What was her reason? Did she give you one at least?"

Lord Brom looked back at the Princess who was still basking in the sun, but no longer looked like she was trying to fly.

"She said she was not ready. She had just turned of marital age when I met her, but she is practically still a child. I am almost ten years older than her, and I have experienced a lot more out of life, than she has."

Jake stood beside his brother silent for a moment, watching him watch the fair maiden that had ensnared his heart.

"You should go to her, Brom. Tell her how you feel, make her see that it will be the last time you make this offer. If she tells you no again, then you have to forget about her." That was the last advice he gave his brother on the matter before he walked away.

Lord Brom stood there, absorbing what his brother had said. He kept thinking about what he advised, and that he should not let the opportunity pass him by. Why did fate step in several times, after they had said goodbye the first time? Many of these opportunities have come and gone. How many more chances would he be allowed?

Throwing caution into the wind, as he went to her, he would not let her slip through his fingers again. He loved her and was not going to risk losing her forever. Before he was able to make it to her side, he spied a warship heading right towards them off the starboard bough. He had to be the one to alert his brother, he saw no one else on deck.

He quickly ran below deck.

"We have got company!"

The Captain and crew hurried above deck, Lord Brom pointed to the ship.

"She is coming in fast, alert the rest of the crew. Sound the alarm!"

The cabin boy rang the bell, all hands on deck, the call made.

Princess Ellyria turned to the sound of all the chaos on the other side of the ship and ran down to see what was going on. She could not see Lord Brom, or his brother. Men were bringing out the oars to try and change course, but the big ship could not turn as fast as she was needed to now.

"Captain, she is right on our arse, and we can not turn fast enough to outrun their warship," Rob informed.

Jake had to make a decision fast, his merchant ship was too big and heavy to outrun them, even if her bay was emptied of the cargo she carried.

"Sound the alarm, have the men get to their battle stations, get all the weapons you can!"

Lord Brom ran over to his brother.

"I can not find the Princess," he announced.

This was the last thing Jake needed right now was to worry

over a woman, even if it was his brother's. The ship was under attack, and they would more than likely try to tie themselves on and board her with the intent to pillage mercilessly.

"Take a few men with you, she can not be far, maybe she has finally gotten herself below deck."

Lord Brom led a few of the crewmembers to the front of the ship, where he had seen her earlier. She was not there. The men ran back to the steps to go below deck. As they began their descent, the ship was hit, causing the men to go rolling down the stairs. Much to his relief stood the Princess in the entryway of the passenger area.

"Are you alright?" she questioned while helping him to his feet. There was no more time the ship had been hit, and the marauders would soon board them.

"You need to go to your cabin, lock the door, and barricade it if you can, and stay in there. Do not come out no matter what you hear. Understand?"

Princess Ellyria nodded her head, but before she turned away, he pulled her to him, and kissed her passionately before letting her go. She ran as fast as she could to her cabin, heard the fighting that had ensued above deck, and she feared for Lord Brom's safety as she finally made it to her cabin, locking the door behind her.

Lord Brom grabbed a sword from the supply cabin before he returned above deck. Another viking clan invaded the ship, and they had set out gangplanks to enable them to climb aboard. They attacked without mercy, killing every man they could, but Captain Jake's men were no strangers to battle, and had been training since they could hold a sword or axe in hand. Lord Brom joined the battle, fighting fearlessly for his brother's ship, and for his Princess. He saw Jake trying to fight off two surly men, so he ran towards him, slashing through the enemy to help him. By the time Lord Brom made it to his brother, he had already run one through with his sword, but the larger man was wearing him down. Lord Brom pushed the other man off his brother, and now he was clashing blades with him. He fought hard, matching every strike, and when he backed him up against the rail of the ship Lord Brom ducked, and then grabbed the man's feet throwing him overboard. Before he was able to turn around, another man had come at him from behind cutting Lord Brom's arm. Lord Brom then unleashed his fury on the man and stabbed him right through the chest. Out of breath, he looked about trying to find his brother, but he was now lost in the clashing of swords and axes flying through the air. Lord Brom ran towards the battle at the stern of the ship, slashing each man down in pursuit of finding his brother. When he finally saw him, he had fallen to his knees, and was about to receive a fatal blow. Lord Brom raced to his brother, paying heed to no other man that tried to cut him down on the way. When he reached his brother, he jumped on the man, knocking him down, and then plunged his sword deep into his chest. He turned to check on his brother, while everyone else was battling overhead.

"Are you alright? Can you get up?" Lord Brom questioned.

Jake nodded, he had only been stabbed in the right shoulder, and he would live.

"Let us get you to your cabin," he insisted.

He shook his head no.

"I will not leave my crew, now hand me a sword," his brother said courageously.

Lord Brom tossed him his sword and watched his older brother jumped in to attack the enemy. Before Lord Brom joined him, he saw several of the men from the other ship go down below deck. He grabbed a sword from one of the fallen men, since he was no longer using it, and ran below deck after them. The men had a head start on him, and as soon as he entered the passenger deck, he could not see where they had gone. He quietly walked through the corridor to surprise attack them from behind.

Princess Ellyria sat on the bed, her pulse racing as she heard men outside her room, kicking in the doors of the neighboring cabins. They had arrived at hers, but it proved more difficult to kick it in since it was locked. When she had believed they had passed hers by, she got up from the bed to try and find a weapon of sorts, that she could use. Just then she remembered the medicine bag she had the potions in, but that was in that red-headed Viking's bag still. She needed to go find it, as it may be their only hope in ridding the ship of these marauders.

She put her head close to the door, and could not hear anyone, so she took her chance to leave the cabin. She unlocked the door, opened it, and then peered out on either side, seeing that the coast was clear, and then began looking for the first mates' cabin. Without knowing exactly where it was, she had to search through all the crewmember's cabins with the hope that she would not get caught. The first room she went in was a wreck, they had already looted this room. She searched through the room quickly to find the familiar saddlebag, but it was not there, so on to the next one she went. The next room was in the same disarray, but still no saddlebag. She darted in and out of the cabins, with still no luck in finding it. What if it had already be taken? She still had one more cabin to go through. She entered the room that strangely had not yet been touched, and started to look about the room. In the corner on the other side of the wardrobe, a brown strap was sticking out from the far corner. As she ran over to the other side of the room beaming with excitement, she had a feeling she finally found it. She bent down to pick it up, it was the saddlebag she was searching for. Before she could turn around and flee, two of the men that had tried to get in her room, were right in front of her. Remembering the Northman were a superstitious lot, she had to use one of the potions and fast. She could not remember which one, and before she could reach into the bag to grab one of the vials, one of the giant men grabbed her.

Lord Brom heard her scream and instantly ran to find where she was, frantically looking in all the cabins. When finally he saw one of the men on top of her and the other holding her down. The men had pulled up her gown and were ripping away her undergarments, paying no attention to Lord Brom running into the room. Princess Ellyria was screaming and trying to fight the man off, when all the sudden his head fell from his shoulders. She screamed again scrambling to her feet since the other man let her go to fight Lord Brom. He was no match for Lord Brom's bloodlust as he landed on the floor beside the headless body. Lord Brom went to

Princess Ellyria and embraced her tight.

"I thought I had told you to stay in your room!" he chided.

She held up the bag pulling her medicine pouch from it.

"What is that?" he questioned.

"You will see."

Grabbing him by the hand, they quickly ran up the stairs to the upper deck. The men were unrelenting as they fought over the dead.

"Here, throw this," she said handing him the blue vial.

He threw it straight into the middle of the fighting mob. It crashed onto the deck and a puddle of water appeared, the men began to slip and slide into one another.

He looked at her.

"Now what!"

She could not remember which color did what, so she pulled out the next vial.

"Throw it!" he shouted.

She looked down at the vial it was red. She threw it hard to the men, whom had gotten up and continued fighting. This time when the vial hit the deck it burst into flames. Men quickly tried to run from the flames. Captain Jake's men continued to fight their enemies, sending some of them back to their ship, while others were either killed or thrown overboard. They were frantically trying to cut away the ties connecting the ships, so as their own ship did not catch fire as well. Princess Ellyria stayed out of the way and watched Lord Brom run off to join the last of the battle. As the last of the crew had finally jumped back over to their ship, they began to sail away quickly. A few of the stragglers that had not made it to climb across the long boards, before they were pulled away, were now jumping from this ship to theirs. Some did not make it and fell into the ocean.

The crew cheered and hurried to put out the fire before the sail was engulfed in flames. Buckets were filled with water from the ocean and thrown onto the fire. Men worked in teams, to fill the buckets, then were passed down to the men on the end, that threw it onto the fire. Finally, the disaster was averted, and the mast and sail were saved. The ship had minor repairs, and would have to find a port to dock the ship soon, before they became too severe.

Lord Brom found his brother standing over his crewmen that had fallen. They would have a warrior's funeral when they docked the ship. Until then they would be carefully wrapped, and placed below deck. He went to Jake, and placed his hand on his shoulder, and just stood by his side as they mourned their northern brothers…

Princess Ellyria watched as the men removed the dead bodies and the cabin boys scrubbing the blood from the deck. The ship's course had been changed, since they were still too far from home, so they decided to dock in the kingdom of Inamor. The Vikings traded with the gypsies often and did not fear them, and their port was now the closest. Lord Brom had gone to take his brother to mend his shoulder, while some of the others were tending to their wounds as well.

Princess Ellyria walked out to the front of the ship. The wind blew against her face, as she closed her eyes, stretched out her arms, and imagined herself flying…

CHAPTER 37

After a week of searching land, sky, far and wide; Prince Anthony, Prince Dakota, Prince Ian, and Prince Rowan had found no sign of their sister anywhere. They were cautious in their travels, not talking to anyone about the quest at hand, and were especially careful while they were in Narruc. To them Liza was still at large, so was the wizard, and they could be anywhere. The men decided to look for clues in the Dark Forest of Woe. Even with their reservations of entering the evil forest, they knew they were no match against the wizard, if they came across him.

Prince Anthony looked all around him. This was not like the forest he came through before.

"This can not be right, none of this was green before?" He was confused.

They continued walking through the now lush forest as birds flew overhead, and various other woodland creatures scurried about.

"Maybe it is an illusion," Prince Dakota suggested.

Prince Dakota was on foot, as well as Prince Rowan. They had left Luna and Gaia at the entrance of the forest, since they would make too many loud noises simply by walking through the woods. Migata was the tracker and she had her nose to the ground trying to get the scent of the Princess. Prince Ian was walking alongside her, looking for any clues left behind by his sister.

"Wait look, I think Migata is onto something," Prince Ian said.

Migata picked up the scent and was now running further into the woods. The men on foot were having difficulty keeping up with the giant strides made by the oversized kitty. When the big cat stopped, it was at the clearing in the woods, where the remains of the wizard's cottage had stood.

"Well, this is the cottage," Prince Anthony observed. "What is left of it?" He dismounted from Odin's back, as his brothers followed him, to the half standing remains of the cottage.

"I wonder what happened here?" Prince Rowan questioned as he carefully entered the house behind his brothers.

They all looked around, watching their steps as they walked on the unstable floors.

"This was not an accidental fire. I do not even think it was set by hand either," Prince Dakota observed. He leaned down to the floor to look for any scientific signs of scorch marks, or black powder residue. He went to the shutters that felt as though they had been locked from the outside, but that was impossible, most shutters and doors are locked from the inside not the outside.

"Well, what do you think, brother?" Prince Anthony inquired.

Prince Dakota turned back to face him.

"This fire was magically set. There is no evidence to prove otherwise. This fire was not set by torch, black powder; flint and stone, not one of those items had been used." Not to mention it was the wizard's cottage Prince Dakota analyzed.

"So, what you are saying is that the wizard purposely burned down his own house with magic. Have I gotten this strait so far?" Prince Rowan asked sarcastically.

Prince Ian, and Prince Anthony laughed.

"Yes, that is exactly right. Good of you to pay attention, dear brother," Prince Dakota teased.

Prince Rowan just gave him a smirk.

"So, if we know now the wizard set his own house on fire. Why did he do it?" Prince Ian inquired.

The men continued searching for clues, deciding to split up to look in the adjoining rooms.

"Hey, I think I may have found something!" Prince Anthony

called out.

The men followed the sound of his voice to what appeared to have been the wizard's privy room. The room was covered in black soot, but seemed to have been pretty well in tact. The wizard's bed frame was still pretty well preserved, but the goose down mattress had not survived the fire. Underneath the remnants of the mattress was a trap door. The men shoved the bed out of the way, and pulled open the door that led down into what appeared to be a tunnel.

"Shall we?" Prince Anthony asked.

"We shall," said Prince Rowan smiling.

Prince Dakota, and Prince Ian just looked at one another, they were always the ones to think things through before doing anything rash, like jumping straight into tunnels, without a clue as to where it leads. Unlike their other two adventuresome brothers who go recklessly jumping in feet first into unknown tunnels.

"Come on Ian, let us make sure they do not get into any more trouble," Prince Dakota said. They followed their brothers into the tunnel, which was surprisingly now large enough for them to stand upright in, even for Prince Ian, the tallest of the four brothers, who stood at six foot three. After a short period of time, they spied a ladder that led a few feet up to another trapdoor. They climbed the ladder, and slowly opened the door, peering out around them. Seeing that no one was around, they climbed on out of the tunnel and found themselves at the opposite end of the forest.

"Well, was that not handy for whomever managed to escape from a burning house," Prince Anthony said matter-of-factly.

Prince Dakota began to ponder what Prince Anthony just said.

"What are you cooking up in that genius head of yours, brother?" Prince Ian asked.

"Anthony, did you not say when you were held hostage here, that Liza was working with the wizard?" Prince Dakota questioned.

Prince Anthony nodded his head.

"What does that have anything to do with it?" Prince Rowan questioned.

It started to make sense to him, but he still was not sure.

"What if Liza angered the wizard somehow? Then he decided he no longer needed her, locked her up in the cottage, and then set the fire," Prince Dakota said putting the pieces together.

"Well, that does make sense," Prince Rowan agreed.

"Let us not stand here in the woods all day. We are not even sure if all this is true or not," Prince Anthony suggested.

"He is right, let us go back to the cottage and look for more clues," Prince Ian said, leading them back to the cottage.

After they had arrived back at the cottage, they hurried to finish looking for any other clues, to see if Liza was the one trapped in the fire, or if she managed to get away.

"I may have found something in here," Prince Rowan said.

They gathered in the other bedroom, it looked as though Liza had stayed in here. There were female items left on the table, a hairbrush, a hand mirror, and the remnants of some woman's burnt clothes, but not destroyed wardrobe.

"Do you think Liza, and the wizard, were uh, you know?" Prince Anthony implied.

Prince Dakota gave him a slap to the head.

"One, that is disturbingly gross, and two, is that all you ever think about?" Prince Dakota questioned.

Prince Rowan, and Prince Ian both laughed at their oldest brothers.

"This is no time for silliness. We need to figure out if Liza's dead, or not so we can report back to father. We need to bring back some sort of good news since we have found nothing on our sister," Prince Dakota chided.

"He is right. Keep looking," Prince Rowan agreed.

The four brothers continued searching the cottage. So far, they had not turned up any evidence to suggest whether Liza had survived or not.

"I think you should come and look at this," Prince Ian said.

The men followed him over to the large black cauldron, that had been turned upside down in the floor. After picking it up together and setting it upright, they gasped.

"What or who was that?" Prince Anthony questioned covering his face with his hand.

The foul stench of burnt human was invading their nostrils.

"Who do you suppose it was, Dakota?" Prince Rowan inquired.

His brother leaned down to examine the body that was so badly burned that they were unrecognizable.

"It is so hard to tell, the clothes are burned away so bad that you can not tell if they were a male or female. The hair has been singed away, and the flesh is so far gone that not much remains. I know this will be rather disgusting, but if I could see the genitals, I could better tell if this had been a woman, or not," he examined.

They all turned away; they did not want to see the body displayed in that manner.

Prince Dakota was having difficulty moving the body's legs from the position it was in.

"Someone come give me a hand to turn the body over to see underneath its legs," he asked.

The brothers all looked to see who was going to assist him. No one made a move. Suddenly Prince Anthony set his foot in front of Prince Rowan's and gave him a shove. Prince Rowan fell to his knees beside Prince Dakota.

"Oh, thanks brother. You get the upper part, yes, that is right, grab underneath the arms, and good, careful now. You would not want it to break and fall to pieces all over you," Prince Dakota advised.

Prince Rowan gave Prince Anthony a look that would kill if he had Medusa's powers.

They were finally able to turn over the body, and Prince Rowan was helping to hold it up for his brother.

"Anthony, hand me your knife please," he said.

He handed him the knife, and if he had only known what he was going to use it for, he would have declined.

Prince Dakota cut away the material from the victim's arse, and gently pulled it away.

"Well, what do you see?" Prince Ian asked.

Prince Dakota motioned for Prince Rowan that he could lay the body back down.

"Well, from what I could tell there were no signs of a manhood. The skin was so badly burned that it was hard to tell, but there should have been the remains of the manhood for sure.

"So is it safe to say that Liza died in the fire?" Prince Anthony questioned.

Prince Dakota nodded his head.

"Well, I suggest since we have enough evidence of Liza's death, then let us just head on home then," Prince Rowan said.

"All right, I agree. We will decide where to look next for our sister, and get father's advice," Prince Anthony said.

The brothers left the little cottage in the woods and started back on their journey home, to convey the good news about Liza, and the bad news about their sister...

The journey home was only a couple days ride; it seemed to the brothers that it was taking forever. Their hearts were heavy. They were not returning with their sister as they had hoped to, and their parents would not be pleased.

"Look! Here they come!" Queen Anna shouted to her husband. She had been looking out the window obsessively since her son's departure; with such anticipation of them bringing home her daughter safe and sound. King Jason got up from his seat at his desk and walked over to the large window in the study that overlooked the courtyard.

Upon hearing the men's entry into the foyer; Isis came running from out of nowhere it seemed, wagging her tail with excitement that her mistress had returned. When she approached the men, she could not see her lady. She sniffed the brothers, but no scent of her was on them. Isis then slinked off with her tail tucked between her legs.

"What has gotten into her?" Prince Anthony asked. His mother greeted him at the door with open arms and a sad look upon her face.

"She was hoping like I was that Ellyria was with you," she said with a sigh.

King Jason was right behind his wife.

"The poor girl has not eaten since Ellyria went missing, and refuses to do so," he relayed. "What happened out there?"

Once the greetings were finished they all gathered in the study.

"We could not find her, father, we looked everywhere in Narruc, and in between with no sign of her," Prince Anthony confessed.

Queen Anna began to cry, her husband reached over and held her hand under the table.

"We did find something of interest though," Prince Rowan announced.

His father looked at his sons who were standing in front of him.

"We have reason to believe Liza is dead. We found the remains of what appeared to be her body that was severely burned unrecognizably," Prince Dakota informed.

His mother looked over at him.

"What do you mean? How are you sure it was her?" she questioned.

"Dakota examined the body," Prince Ian added.

Queen Anna smiled, she felt relieved that there was one less person that wanted to harm her daughter.

"So, if Liza is dead, where is the wizard?"

"That we do not know. The cottage was destroyed, and the forest was like he was never there," Prince Anthony informed them.

King Jason stood up and walked to the window, then turned back around to face his sons.

"Is there any chance the wizard has her?"

The brothers all shook their heads.

"I do not think so, father. Why would the wizard want to be around Ellyria if he knows she can kill him?" Prince Dakota suggested.

"He is right, Raul will know that she is the Chosen One, and want to avoid her," Queen Anna interrupted.

The King shook his head. He was not sure where she could be.

"Stay here, you need to rest. We will come up with another plan first thing in the morning," King Jason said.

As his sons left the room, Queen Anna got up and joined her husband.

"What are you thinking?"

He looked her in the eyes and tried to smile.

"I am not sure what to think. I can not keep risking our son's lives to go on a wild goose chase. We have searched all of Toledya and Narruc. The only two kingdoms that had not been searched are Inamor and Regnuom. Those are the Viking and Gypsy kingdoms, and she would have no business going there. If she was after the amulet, or even the wizard, they are both in Narruc. So I am at a loss," he answered.

Queen Anna embraced her husband. He had so much burden placed on him right now, and she could not blame him, if he was out of sorts right now.

"We will find her. We have to."

The King and Queen would not give up on their daughter now...

CHAPTER 38

The great merchant ship Draki arrived in the port of Inamor, docking for much needed repairs, after the viking warship had made its attack upon her. Captain Jake needed to stay back with the ship and the crew. He could not accompany his brother, or the Princess on their quest to find the gypsy merchantman, that had bought the amulet from Rob the Red.

"I will be docked here, brother, for at least two weeks. So take care of what you need to do. I do hope I will not be seeing you, if all goes well with you and the Princess. If it does not, then you are more than welcome to join me. Like I said, a few weeks are all I shall need before I set sail. Good luck."

Lord Brom embraced his brother.

"Thank you, brother."

Princess Ellyria stopped and gave Jake a farewell embrace.

"It was a pleasure to have met you, even under these circumstances," she said.

He gallantly bowed before her, and smiled.

"The pleasure was all mine, your Highness."

Princess Ellyria smiled as Lord Brom escorted her from the pier, to the marketplace.

After several hours of walking around in the crowded marketplace, trying to find the same merchantman's table, Princess Ellyria was nearly ready to give up when she finally spotted him.

"That is him."

Lord Brom looked at her.

"Are you sure this time? That is what you have said at every jewelry table we have come to," Lord Brom asked.

Princess Ellyria grabbed him by the hand, yanking him along with her and hurried over to the table.

"Ah, it is you. I see they finally sold you, to one that will put up with you," replied the gypsy.

Lord Brom looked confused but assumed that this was the merchantman she was looking for, seeing how he has already had the pleasantry of meeting her before.

"I am not a slave now, nor have I ever been. I had been abducted by that barbaric man," she told the gypsy.

"Oh, the truth comes out. You think my people are barbaric, do you?" Lord Brom asked feeling quite insulted by her.

The gypsy just watched the two of them argue.

"Are you two married?"

Both Lord Brom, and Princess Ellyria looked at the man, and said "No!" rather quickly at the same time.

"You could have fooled me," the gypsy replied, laughing at the two of them.

Princess Ellyria was becoming frustrated with this man. She slapped the table and leaned over it, looking the man in the eyes.

"I am not a slave, and I am definitely not married to him. I am the Princess of Toledya, and I am searching for the amulet that has been stolen from me, that the Viking sold to you. I demand you give me back my property!"

A woman possibly the man's wife went up to him, and whispered something in his ear.

"The amulet you seek, I do not have anymore," he said.

Princess Ellyria looked at Lord Brom.

"What do you mean? What happened to it?" Lord Brom asked.

The merchant's wife took the Princess by the hand.

"Come, you must follow me, your Highness."

Princess Ellyria, and Lord Brom followed the woman into to an empty tent.

"The amulet was taken by a wizard of dark magic. He threatened to kill my husband, if he did not give it back to him. He claimed that it had been stolen from him, but I know it is you who are the rightful owner," she informed.

Lord Brom looked at Princess Ellyria, they both knew she meant Raul. What did she mean by Princess Ellyria was the rightful owner?

"How long ago was this? Do you know where he was going?" Lord Brom questioned. The gypsy woman just shook her head.

"I do not know, he just vanished into thin air," she answered.

The wizard was more powerful than either of them had predicted.

"What makes you think, she is the rightful owner of the amulet?"

The woman peered out of the tent, then looked back at Princess Ellyria.

"You must come with me and speak with my bandolier, she is the one that can answer all your questions, and she has been expecting you," she answered as she led them to the secret encampment.

Princess Ellyria was amazed by all of the gypsies, in her observations walking through their camp. They appeared to be a very peaceful, family-oriented people.

"They look like a bunch of vagabonds to me. They do not even live in houses, just in tents and wagons," Lord Brom criticized as he looked around.

The gypsy woman turned to Lord Brom.

"Our people are nomads, we travel to many places in accordance with the seasons. Right now it is almost summer and we will remain north by the ocean so we can fish and grow crops here to store for the winter. When we begin our journey south in the fall, we will remain there until spring. We do not build homes because we do not need them. The great Mother Earth provides us with food and shelter in the forests," she explained.

Princess Ellyria turned to Lord Brom and gave him her glare.

"You are being very rude," she whispered to him.

Lord Brom felt like a horse's arse now.

"I apologize for my ignorance of your people. My people have only traded with you, and I have not been taught of your people's ways," he confessed. He looked at Princess Ellyria, who was smiling with approval.

"My mother was a gypsy from birth, but I do not know where she was from," she informed.

Lord Brom looked at the Princess, now he understood why she was so wild and carefree.

"That explains a lot," he teased.

She glared at him.

"I knew you to have gypsy blood. I could see it in your eyes," the woman said smiling.

They finally arrived to the bandolier's elaborate tent, which was constructed by various materials in a patchwork pattern. Before they had even had the chance to open the tent, the old woman called out for them to come in. Once the came inside, the guests were in awe by all the beautiful scarves in various textures and the colorful beads that were draped across, in several different directions.

"I have been expecting you, my dear, since before you were born actually," the old woman smiled.

Princess Ellyria was confused.

"Please, come and sit down," she motioned them to sit on large brightly beaded pillows, that were positioned in a circle on the floor, and matched the scarves and beads above them.

Lord Brom, the gypsy woman, and Princess Ellyria sat down. The Princess was seated next to the white haired older woman.

"My name is, Vadoma, and I know who you are, Princess Ellyria Rose. I also knew your grandmother, she was my phral, or as you call it now pal, like your best friend Isis, no?" Princess Ellyria was taken aback, from the personal knowledge this woman had of her.

"How did you know that?" she questioned the woman.

Vadoma smiled at the girl, and took her hand into hers.

"The same way that I knew your mother was carrying you, before she did," she smiled again.

Lord Brom sat in silence. He was too confused for words.

"I am the awenyddion, the shaman. I have lived for centuries now waiting for you my child. It is my duty to pass down my knowledge to you, as you are the Chosen One.

Lord Brom now could no longer hold his tongue.

"She is what?"

Princess Ellyria was even more confused than before. How could she be the Chosen One?

"It is ok to feel confused, as was I. But unfortunately, I had no one to prepare me for what was to come. I know you have many questions, and I can answer all of them for you," she added.

This was a lot for Princess Ellyria to absorb.

"What do you mean by, I am the Chosen One, why me? How is it that you have been around for centuries?"

The woman reached to the other side of her, and produced an object with a black silk material covering it. After removing the cover, she revealed a clear, glass ball cradled atop a small curved wooden pedestal.

"This is a crystal ball, and the wood it sits upon is made from a beech tree. The special wood aids the crystal and allows for us to see into the past, present, and future. Your vanity is made from the same wood, and your mirror was created from the same crystal. I know this because my family made it for your grandmother as a wedding gift. You can see things in it, no?"

Princess Ellyria nodded her head.

"Let me show you in this crystal the answers you seek," she waved her hand over the ball and images appeared like magic before Princess Ellyria's eyes. A younger woman appeared. It was the past image of the old woman as a young girl. The girl appeared to be glowing, but a man was now trying to kill her, using magic it seemed.

"What is this you are showing me?" Princess Ellyria inquired.

The woman waved her hand again. The image was now of the wizard, the image of the man before him was a reflection of himself, but he had changed.

"This wizard came to my village and tried to take the Power of Litha that was coming down to me during the Quickening. I had no knowledge of this powerful magic that was meant for me. He was taught by a powerful Seither. That trained him in the dark arts and had foresaw the coming of this power, during the blood moon's eclipse and the Summer Solstice. That only happens once every five hundred years. I was the Chosen One of that time. Chosen to rid the kingdom of the Seither, and her apprentice Raul. I was already a seer by birth, along with our mothers and yourself, all sharing the gift of premonition. The wizard pushed me out of the way during the Quickening, stepped into my place taking in the power unto him, and rendering him more powerful than his maker. He killed the Seither with his bare hands, ripped out her heart, ate it, and consumed all of her powers. He then became the most powerful wizard that he is today. Now that he has the Amulet of Elements, he will stop at nothing to take in the Power of Litha again and become an immortal. Even you will not be able to kill him, once he takes in the power. He may even try to self proclaim himself to be a God, which will start an epic war, with the Gods themselves. You must do as I say, so you can receive the true power, and retrieve the necklace that was forged for you and you alone. You will be the only one that can control the amulet, without becoming controlled by its limitless powers. Right now the wizard has it, you must get it back from him, do what you must take in the Power of Litha, and learn to master your powers. Our fate is in your hands," Vadoma said.

Lord Brom could not believe that his Princess was the savior of all the kingdoms.

"What can I do to help her?" Lord Brom asked.

The old woman looked at Lord Brom, and smiled.

"You have already done your part by bringing her here. Although your journey does not end here. You must stay with her, as she will need your protection, until she returns home to complete her transition. It will take time for her to master her knew abilities. They will not come to her all at once. There are three powers that she will be blessed with and her power of premonition will be enhanced. Each power will come when she is ready to accept and learn them, when the need arises, is when she will need them the most. They will not be easy to master, and they will be tied to her emotions, so be careful when she becomes angry, or upset," she informed.

Princess Ellyria looked at the woman.

"What are these three powers?" Lord Brom asked.

The woman smiled.

"The first is the ability of telekinesis, to move things with your mind, objects, and people. You will later be able to use your hand as well, after you can control the power in your mind. The second power is empathy, you will be able to feel others happiness and pain. The ability once mastered also lets you utilize those powers to channel others' powers as well, and to send back what they have sent out. The third ability is to be able to summon animals and speak to them. Animals can be called when you have need of them, and will be able to communicate with them using your empathic capabilities, once you have mastered them. Understand now, that this is not an easy task, and will be difficult, but I can help to prepare you," she advised.

"When is she to receive these powers? When is the blood moon eclipse you keep talking about going to occur?" Lord Brom asked.

Princess Ellyria was curious as well.

"It is in three days, we do not have much time," she answered.

Princess Ellyria was still trying to absorb all the information that she had just received. It was a bit much to swallow all at once.

"Tell me what I have to do then," she said.

The old woman nodded her head and smiled.

Princess Ellyria Rose was ready to accept her new destiny...

CHAPTER 39

Meanwhile, in the deep forests of Narruc, Raul was preparing the newly formulated potion. For the spell he would use, to call down the Power of Litha into him. He now needed the heart from an innocent to complete it.

After racking his brain, to what constituted such a being, he decided to try cross-reference the information in the grimoire. He quickly read through the text and nodded his head.

"A virgin! Really?" he laughed out loud. That should be easy enough. The book did not say as to whether it needed to be a male or female virgin. Which one do I choose? It was not a decision to be made lightly. An innocent is usually considered that of a female, or a child. He needed to decide soon, the full blood moon's eclipse was in three days time. Without much time left, he needed to send his men out to find him a virgin, or a child, or a virgin child, it did not really matter to which they brought back.

"I need you three to find me a virgin, or a virgin child, it does not matter which. I need it before nightfall tomorrow, no later, or my potion will not be complete in time for the Quickening," he ordered.

The men nodded their heads they understood, and left on the quest to seek out a virgin for their master.

"I really hope those idiots do not muddle things up this time," he said to his page that was preparing his supper.

The boy just looked up at his master, he paid little mind to what he said unless he was barking orders at him. His life was meaningless now, that he was a slave to a madman. Toby had wished many a night that he could be reunited with his father, leaving this wretched forest for good. He had tried to come up with a plan to run away, but the wizard knew things, and he was afraid of what he would do to him if he were caught. Such actions would be punishable by death, but he did not think the wizard would be that merciful.

"Come here boy, I have an errand for you," the wizard called.

Toby set the wooden spoon down on the table sitting beside the large pot, above the fire in the heath.

"Yes, sire," he said, as he stood in front of the wizard obediently.

Raul looked at the waif of a child.

"I need you to go to market and fetch me a new atheme, I seemed to have lost mine in a fire," he instructed.

The boy nodded his head, fetched his satchel, and the wizard gave him coin for purchase. He left the cottage thinking this could be his chance to flee, but he was afraid.

"Oh, and boy. If you should choose to not return, I would have to kill your confounded father. Carry on now," the wizard said with an evil grin.

The boy had no choice now, but to return.

While Raul prepared for the upcoming Quickening someone else was preparing for it as well…

CHAPTER 40

King Jason had ordered his scouts to search for his daughter one last time. He had also sent his personal messenger earlier in the week to send for Lord Brom. If anyone could help him find his daughter, he could. Now it was just a matter of time before he expected the courier to return with news.

Queen Anna had been trying to get Isis to eat, but she still refused. Her daughter's best friend had grown very weak. She sent for her son Prince Dakota, to see if there was anything he could do.

"Yes, mother, I heard you needed me. What is the matter? Is there more news of Ellyria?"

She shook her head.

"No, it is Isis. I still cannot get her to eat, and now I fear she is trying to will herself to death over Ellyria's absence," she said. "I am so worried about her. Is there anything you can do to help her?"

Prince Dakota examined the big wolf. Her black coat had lost its luster, her body had become thin, and her eyes no longer held her spirit.

"I am not sure what to do, mother? She may certainly will herself to die if my sister does not return home soon," he said. He had thought about the new potion he was working on that could manipulate time, almost freeze it in fact. Perhaps he could put her in a type of suspended life.

"I have an idea, but it is risky. Let me run a few tests and I will get back to you before nightfall," he said as he hurried to his loft, to test his theory.

Queen Anna stayed with Isis, to keep her spirits up.

"It will be ok girl, I promise your mistress will be home soon," she said for her own benefit as well.

Prince Dakota had returned to his loft and began to test his formula. His first to experiment on would be a horsefly that he had caught in a jar. He had just a few tiny holes, large enough to place drops of the potion on the fly with, poked through the top. As the fly was flying around in the jar, he placed the drops directly on it. To his amazement the fly was beginning to move slower, but was still going. If he adds a little more to the formula to make it stronger, it should cause the fly to freeze, and be suspended in the jar.

The messenger had finally returned to relay the news to King Jason. He was in his study when the currier announced his presence.

"Your, Highness, I come bringing news from Regnuom, Sire," he said.

The King looked up at him.

"Well, what is it?"

"Lord Brom was not with his father, at Lord Thomas's province, Sire. He had left with his brother, Captain Jake to work on his merchant ship. No one there had seen or heard from the Princess there either, Sire," he informed.

King Jason was completely at a loss. What was he going to do now? If Lord Brom could not be acquired to assist him, then who could? He dismissed the messenger and prayed to the Gods that his scouts could find her. They were his only hope in finding her now.

After balancing his formula and strengthening its power, Prince Dakota tried it once again on the fly that had now regained normal movement. He applied a few drops on the fly once again. Stupendous! It worked! The fly was completely frozen! Quickly he put some of the potion in a vial and took it and the jar with him as he went running out of the tower.

"Mother, I did it!"

Queen Anna looked at her son in confusion.

"What did you do, my son?"

Prince Dakota handed her the jar with the fly suspended inside it. She looked at it in fascination.

"How?"

Prince Dakota began to explain his formula and how it worked, telling his mother that they could use it on Isis.

"You want to put this on Isis?" she inquired.

He nodded his head.

"Yes, it may be the only way to keep her alive until Ellyria returns,' he answered.

Queen Anna was worried, she was not sure if suspended time, as her son put it, was the solution.

"What if she does not wake up?"

He had not thought that far ahead. Although the fly did come out of the initial slower suspension, he decided to see if it would come out of the frozen time.

"Ok, we will see if the fly resumes its normal functions first," he said.

She would feel better knowing that Isis was not going to be harmed but felt it will be better to do something before she gives up her will to live.

Moments later the fly resumed its continuous pursuit to find a way out of the jar. Prince Dakota was very pleased with the results. He and his mother both agreed it should be safe for Isis. They carried her to Dakota's tower, so he could keep an eye on her. Queen Anna watched as he placed her in a comfortable position, and then placed several drops of the potion all over her. He would see how much led to how long the potion would work, applying more if needed. This was the only way. It had to work.

Queen Anna left to check on her husband in his study, now that she was no longer worried for Isis. She was now in Dakota's care.

"Has there been any news from the currier?" she asked her

husband.

King Jason shook his head.

"No, my love, I am afraid not," he said. "Not good news anyway. Lord Brom has joined his brother on the high seas, and no one in Regnuom has heard anything about Ellyria either."

Queen Anna was worried that her husband has fallen into a state of despair. She wished she could help him, but she was not quite sure what to do either. Where was their daughter?

CHAPTER 41

Princess Ellyria was preparing for the nights Summer Solstice Festival that was celebrated every year to welcome the new season. She was also making herself ready to embrace her new destiny as the Chosen One. Vadoma had been instructing her in how to draw down the Power of Litha, and Lord Brom on how to protect her. In case the wizard comes, as he did to her all those years ago. Princess Ellyria was also learning various ways that her powers will work and how to control them. Mostly by breathing exercises, and channeling energy; all of which included learning to control her emotions will be equally as important as the magic itself.

Tonight, her life would change forever…

A big celebration was soon underway. There would be a great feast, dancing, music, and then the ritual, that would guarantee Princess Ellyria would be the only one to receive the ancient power. Vadoma had gathered her most skillful women in her village, to create a protective circle around the Princess, and to block any magic that may come to harm her. They understood that if the wizard comes, that some or all of them might in fact be killed tonight. Lord Brom was prepared as well. He was gifted with the talisman of the Evil

Eye, the village's sacred magic. He would be a decoy to lure the wizard away from the sacred circle, to protect the Princess…

Raul was waiting patiently for his men to bring the virgin, and his page had already returned from the market with the finest athame his coin would buy. The cauldron was ready for the final ingredient, without it the spell would not work and he would have to take the power the hard way. Just then his guards came back with a young woman, who was kicking and screaming on the way in the door.

"Let go of me!" she screamed.

Raul had instructed for her to be bound to the table.

"Do not worry my pretty. You have been brought here to do a great service. Before too long you will have given me your heart," he said then smiled at the woman.

She lay there frightened on the table, and had worked herself into such a frenzy, that she passed out.

"Oh, it is so much better when the victims are sleeping. I can hardly think from all that screaming she was doing," he complained. As he was preparing the last phase of his spell, he began to sharpen his new athame. He motioned for the guards to stand outside and the page to his room. He must have total concentration if this was to work…

Meanwhile, in Toledya, King Jason and Queen Anna both knew in a few short hours the eclipse would begin. The full moon was glowing brightly in the night sky, and they worried for their daughter.

"I do hope she is all right. I wish I could be with her during the Quickening," Queen Anna said, looking out into the night sky.

"I am sure she will be fine. The Gods will definitely be watching out for her, as they bless her with their gift of Litha," her husband said, holding her in his arms. They continued to look up at the night sky together in anticipation for their daughter's safe return…

The Amulet of Elements

Prince Dakota was in his tower waiting for the eclipse to begin as well while he kept a watchful eye on Isis, who was frozen in time. He wished he would have had been able to finish the lesson in potion. So his sister could better protect herself, and perhaps the vials she had taken had served her well…

Lord Brom and Princess Ellyria were enjoying the great festivities. They ate their fill and were now joined with the entire village in dancing to the music, that was skillfully played by several of the villagers.

"The gypsies sure now how to celebrate, they almost put my people to shame," he jested. Princess Ellyria laughed as Lord Brom continued to twirl her around in circles, in time to the beating drums. When she saw Vadoma, she knew it was time.

"It is time, I must go now," she said.

Lord Brom kissed her gently.

"I will be watching over you, I will not let that wizard harm you. I promise," he said, before he kissed her one last time. He watched her join the woman, and went to his post with a few of the other men to stand guard over the ritual.

Vadoma gathered the women together to sit in a circle around Princess Ellyria who was seated in the middle. As the eclipse began in the sky, they began to chant the protection spell. They swayed in time with the beating of their hearts, creating the cone of power. Princess Ellyria was to concentrate on the sound of her own heartbeat and to allow herself to be completely open during the Quickening. So she could receive the Power of Litha.

Raul watched as the moon was just about to begin the eclipse. It would only be a matter of moments before the full moon turned to the color of blood. He plunged the athame into the woman's chest and pulled out her still beating heart. He recited the ancient words then threw the heart into the cauldron. Nothing happened. There should have been an explosion or at least a small poof of smoke even. What went wrong? Raul was furious. This was no virgin! He called the guards inside.

"What the shite!" Where did you find this girl? Because she was no virgin!"

The men shrugged their shoulders, with a surprised look on their faces.

"We picked her up in a tavern. When she asked us what we would like, we told her we wanted a virgin. She told us she could be anything we wanted her to be, a virgin too," he answered for them all.

Raul could not believe what he just heard.

"Are you that incompetent? You can not tell a virgin from a common whore! Idiots!" Raul has grown tired of them, and almost out of time. He would deal with them later. And then he was gone...

The Quickening had nearly begun. Princess Ellyria was in total concentration. The gypsies continued to chant, while Lord Brom and the others were standing guard.

All of the sudden, Raul came out of nowhere and the gypsy men were powerless against him. He was flinging bodies away like rag dolls, as he was walking straight towards Princess Ellyria. Lord Brom attacked him from behind with his sword, plunging it straight through his back. Raul turned around to face Lord Brom.

"Have we not met before? Oh yes, I killed your horse did I not? I should have killed you when I had the chance. I will not make the same mistake twice," he promised.

With the flick of his wrist, he sent Lord Brom flying into a large oak tree, knocking him out. Raul pushed the sword back out of his body, and then the wound sealed itself. He saw the circle of gypsies. No doubt that old bitch must still be alive, well he would fix that this time. The women saw him coming but did not stop chanting. They must protect the Princess, it was now only moments before she would be blessed with the Power of Litha.

Raul stood before the circle of women and laughed. This was going to be too easy. One by one, he sent the women soaring through the air. Princess Ellyria was unaware of the wizard's presence. Light was beginning to descend from the blood moon to the center of the circle. It would be only moments before it surrounded Princess Ellyria, to be taken into her. Vadoma was waiting for Raul, she called to the power of her ancestors, to aid her and protect the Princess. As long as she lived, the power would protect her until she received her powers. She continued to chant, the cone of power still surrounding her. She raised her hands to the sky, pushing the power out into the wizard and back far away from the circle.

"Is that all you have, wench?" he said quickly rising to his feet. "I thought you were once the Chosen One? Oh yes, now I remember, I deprived you of that, did I not?" he laughed maniacally.

He crossed his hands, and quickly made a swift striking motion, and broke the energy flow. Vadoma was hurled away from the protective circle and was trying to get up. Raul moved to her side and leaned down, grabbing her by the throat.

"You are too late, Raul. You will never take her powers now," she gasped.

Raul dropped her to the ground and turned to look at Princess Ellyria. He was too late. Princess Ellyria was encased in the light of the moon that was circling all around her. Her eyes remained closed. She could feel the light entering her and filling her with great warmth, as she welcomed it inside her.

Raul tried to run to her and try to channel the power into him, but the gypsies trapped him. They had joined Vadoma and began to recite a trapping spell, it would not hold him long, but they only needed a few moments. Raul then broke their spell using the power from the amulet to block their powers and continued to go after the Princess. Vadoma ran after Raul and jumped on his back, knocking him to the ground. He flung the old woman off, then grabbed her by the neck choking her.

"I am going to at least enjoy this, since I can not get the power. I will end you, and your pretty Princess too," he promised. "Goodbye, crone!"

Princess Ellyria stood up, but was too late to do anything to help Vadoma. Raul reached into the old woman's chest, and ripped out her heart.

"No!"

Raul let go of the lifeless body in his hands, tossing her heart away after he took a bite out of it, and then turned towards the Princess.

"Oh, I see you have gotten your powers. Well I will be taking them from you, just as fast as you received them," he said wiping the blood from his mouth. Raul lunged for her, but she quickly moved out of his way.

"What is the matter? Am I too fast for you, wizard?"

He was tired of playing games. Raul held out his hand as she was slowly being drawn to him. She could not move, it felt like she was trapped. She tried to focus like Vadoma said, yet nothing happened. She waved her hand, nothing happened. She began to panic, when she found herself in his hands.

Lord Brom had gotten up and saw that Raul had her, he ran as fast as he could to attack the wizard. By the time he reached the wizard, Raul held out his hand and raised Lord Brom into the air. Princess Ellyria's green eyes narrowed and Raul went flying backwards. Lord Brom fell to the ground, as Princess Ellyria rushed to his side.

"Are you alright?"

Lord Brom shook his head and motioned that the wizard was getting up and walking towards them. Princess Ellyria stood her ground and placed her hands to her temples, sending Raul back to the ground. He got up again, and then vanished. He had finally backed down, but she had a feeling he was going to be back, and the next time she would be ready…

The gypsies paid great homage to their dead. Their bandolier had been taken from this world, but she would not be forgotten. Her vardo was no longer needed. Vadoma's possessions, along with her body, would be burned upon the pyre. Many came from miles around to honor their loved one, and to say farewell.

Princess Ellyria placed the flowers beside the body, that had been carefully wrapped in the special white cotton fabric and said her goodbyes. She was never able to thank her for all she had done for her. She wished she could have saved her. She stepped back, as Vadoma's body was now being placed in the wagon along with the personal belongings, then it would be set on fire. Vadoma will be missed.

Lord Brom had made ready the horses, that were given for the journey back to Toledya. Princess Ellyria said her farewells, to the new friends that she had made and promised to return someday. Lord Brom helped her onto the horse, then mounted his. It was still light out, they would ride through the night and then rest when the sun came up.

Together, Lord Brom, and Princess Ellyria would ride east to south, so they could avoid riding through Narruc. This was just the beginning to the journey home...

CHAPTER 42

The road home is oftentimes the longest journey. At least it was for Princess Ellyria. She only had one thing on her mind, the wizard. Even though she had been able to drive him away, he had yet to be defeated. What made matters worse is that he had the Amulet of Elements. She, and Lord Brom still had many miles of traveling to do, but she no longer wanted to go home. It was early morning and they had traveled now nearly two days. There was still time to head west to Narruc. That is if she could convince Lord Brom into coming with her.

"Do you think we could rest for a while?"

Lord Brom nodded and slowed his horse.

"Look there," he pointed, "We can rest under that huge oak tree."

As they approached the great tree, they saw the most amazing view looking out over a beautiful lake. This gave Lord Brom an idea.

"Care for a swim, Princess?"

He motioned to the lake and smiled. She thought that was a marvelous idea. The midday sun was beginning to beat down on them, and she had not been able to bath since she was back at the gypsy camp.

"I think that is a wonderful idea," she smiled, and got a wild look in her eyes, "I shall race you."

Before Lord Brom had a chance to reply, she already had taken off towards the lake. The lake was not very far from the tree, maybe just a few feet, so it took Princess Ellyria no time to beat Lord Brom. Lord Brom was out of breath, and she laughed at him.

"Are you too tired for swimming now?"

Lord Brom went to her, grabbed her in his arms, and began kissing her passionately. She returned his kisses only for a moment, before she pushed him away and giggled. The beauty of the lake distracted her. It was so crystal clear that she could see all the way to the very bottom. Lord Brom joined her in peering into the lake. Water lilies were growing all around the edges, and the forest almost encircled it, creating a secret oasis. The fragrance of the lilies was most exquisite and heightened their senses, creating pleasure for the mind. Lord Brom turned to Princess Ellyria. He lovingly gazed into her eyes, taking her hands into his, and leaned down to kiss her ever so softly. There was no going back now. To his surprise, before he could confess his love to her, she began to remove her white linen dress and the comb from her head, as her long black hair cascaded down. She was now standing naked before him, with hair that cascading down the length of her body, she pulled him to her to kiss him, and her beautiful supple breasts, pressed into his body. Then quick as a rabbit, she turned away and dove into the lake. Lord Brom was in shock, he was not certain of what to do next.

"The water is wonderful. Are you not coming in?"

Lord Brom wasted not a moment longer, as he quickly disrobed and joined her in the lake.

"You are so beautiful, Princess," he said swimming to her in the middle of the lake.

She swam part of the distance to him.

"You are not so bad yourself, handsome," she teased. She giggled and splashed him a few times, before he caught her.

They peered deep into each other's eyes. Lord Brom's were the color of the bright blue sky, and Princess Ellyria's were the color of sapphires. Lord Brom pulled her to him, kissed her gently at first, but as his passion inflamed, so did the ardency of his kiss. She returned his kisses feeling her own passion igniting within. She pushed Lord Brom away and laughed as she quickly swam to the other side of the lake. Lord Brom was an excellent swimmer, learning from an early age from his father. He was able to catch up with her in no time. He grabbed her, and pulled her to him.

The edge of the lake was surrounded not only by lilies, but was also covered with thick beds of soft clovers. The couple began to kiss once more. Princess Ellyria had her back pressed up against the embankment, and Lord Brom was able to stand up on this shallow end. His body was still halfway out of the water since he stood well over six foot four. Princess Ellyria was barely over five foot, and the water still covered well over her breasts that were floating to the surface.

They searched each other's mouths with each thrust of their tongues, and he began to explore her body with his hands. She flinched a little from the gentle caress along the sides of her ribs, but relaxed when his hands slide underneath her to grab onto her buttocks, pulling him into her. She could feel the swell of his huge manhood, as it bounced around in the water and pressed into her stomach. Her hands explored his perfectly sculptured body, as each muscle flexed beneath her touch.

His broad chest was so chiseled that it could not be replicated in stone. No man could carve enough detail into even the finest marble. She reached around to let her hands enjoy the pleasure of feeling his broad back that was strong and hard. Lord Brom let his hands further in their exploration of her petite body. He glided his hands from the small indention of her back that was right above her buttocks, and around again to the sides of her tiny waist, which fit perfectly in his hands. He glided his fingers up her stomach to cup the bountiful breasts in his hands. He stopped kissing her long enough to suckle each one of those strawberry hued nipples in his mouth. Princess Ellyria leaned over backwards onto the bank for a moment, while he continued his attack on her senses.

Lord Brom rose up from her breasts to look upon the vision before him. She was almost like a mermaid being halfway in and halfway out of the water, her long black hair clung to her body, as she enchanted him to join her. He grabbed her by the waist and hoisted her up onto the edge of the bank, spreading apart her supple thighs. He could no longer wait to taste her. She lay down on the embankment and arched her back in pleasure she had never known before. He could feel her womanhood swell with pleasure, as he parted its lips to kiss them fully, plunging his tongue deep within her. She grabbed his wet hair in her hands, arching her pelvis into his face.

She could no longer take anymore of this torturous pleasure and pulled him by the hair of his head to her. He came up out of the water, locked his arm around her waist from underneath her, and pulled her up off the embankment into a thick patch of the soft clover. He kissed her passionately, as the water from his body dripped onto her skin as he was hovering over her. She pulled him to rest on top of her. He was gently nestled between her legs, his manhood was swelled with the anticipation of having her. He wanted to wait until she gave the signal that she was ready for him to enter her.

They kissed and explored each other's bodies with great vigor as the sun warmed their bodies. He needed to entice her more, found the spot where he planted the seed of pleasure, and caressed it gently to ensure it would be ripe for the harvest. She arched her body into his fingers that he slowly pushed inside her. Was she as ready as he was? And then he was certain when he felt her soft hand wrap around his hard member. She explored it with great fascination, and traced every bulging vein with her fingertips. He ached for release, and his urgency to have her was causing great pain in his loins. He kissed her again, she release him, and allowed him the freedom to enter her. She arched herself into his body, wanting him to take her now, and was so swept in the wave of pleasure she was beside herself, pulling him to her.

He received her message with eagerness and withdrew his fingers from inside her to replace with his manhood. The heat from his body matched her own, and she waited for a fire to ignite between them. And just as he prepared to enter her, they suddenly realized they were not alone.

Lord Brom looked up and saw riders by the tree, and was checking out their horses. They quickly got up to dress, and ran to hide. Lord Brom could not believe his luck, nor could he believe it was her father's men. The banner they carried was unmistakably the crest of the King. Princess Ellyria started to run towards them, but Lord Brom grabbed her and pulled her back behind the hedges.

"Do you really want to be caught out in the middle of nowhere alone with me? We are both soaking wet, and your dress is not tied the rest of the way, and my trousers are not even done up. Do you want your father to have me hanged?"

She looked at him and shook her head. She had not considered how all this looked, without her father here to just simply explain how she felt for Lord Brom, so there was no way to get out of the state of her appearance with the castle guards. The riders moved on, leaving their horses behind.

"That was a close call. Now where were we?" he stated.

She pushed him over onto the ground and leaned over him.

"There is no time for that now. If we hurry we can get to Narruc before nightfall," she said.

Lord Brom gave her a strange look.

"I thought you wanted to go home?"

She leaned in to kiss him, and then he pushed her upright.

"You are avoiding my question," he said.

She lowered her eyes and smiled sheepishly.

"I changed my mind. I want to surprise the wizard," she announced.

Lord Brom sat up on his elbows.

"We do not even know where he is?"

She raised her hand to her face, rubbing her chin.

"What if we lured him out?"

Lord Brom sat and pondered for a few moments, before he answered her.

"How do you plan to flush out a powerful wizard?"

She stood up and helped him to his feet, while looking him in his eyes, and she knew he would not like her idea.

"We will use me as bait," she stated.

He shook his head and grabbed her. He was not going to allow her to use herself as a way to entice the wizard from out of the shadows.

"No. That is not going to happen. I will not allow you to do that," he scolded.

She knew he would say that. Now she had to do it the hard way.

"I am going with, or without you, Brom. It is my responsibility to these people to get rid of this evil man." She stood up and walked up the hill without him.

Lord Brom understood that it was her destiny, but she was not able to control her powers yet.

"Wait, Princess, I will go with you," he said shaking his head. He could not believe she talked him into it. Actually, he was bewitched by her, so yes he could believe it.

She stopped where she stood and waited patiently for him to catch up. She thought he would see things her way and smiled in his direction.

They walked up the hill to prepare the horses, filled their pouches with the fresh water from the lake, and picked some of the sweet grasses and clover for the horses for later. This was going to be a long journey to Narruc…

CHAPTER 43

Raul searched through his grimoire, trying to find a spell he could use to extract the Princess's powers from her. He had taken powers before, like he did with the Seither, but he did not want to have to kill her to do it. He had other plans for her. He just was not for certain what they were quite yet. Never in five hundred years had his desire for a woman been awakened like the Princess had, during their fight in the gypsy camp. He saw a fire in her eyes and her beauty was burned into his memory. She was a rare creature indeed, that he must possess. How would he capture her? He must find a way to entice her, lure her to him, and then seduce her. His Seither taught him more than just magic alone. She taught him the way into a woman's heart. She also instructed him in the art of lovemaking as well. That is it! He would seduce the Princess and extract her powers. His own genius, astounded even him. Now to find the perfect spell to take away her power, he thought as he continued his search through the grimoire...

Lord Brom, and Princess Ellyria had finally reached the border of Narruc. They had been traveling for an additional two days in their reroute west. They were both exhausted, having only rested once during their long journey.

Lord Brom pulled up on the reins to stop his horse.

"Have you a plan of action yet?"

Princess Ellyria had stopped her horse alongside Lord Brom's.

"No. Not yet," she confessed.

He just looked at her. How could she have come so far, without a plan in mind?

"Anything remotely close to a plan? Or at least an idea of what you are going to do?" he questioned her again.

Princess Ellyria had only one idea, and she was not certain it would even work.

"I thought we could go to Liza's castle, they will capture us, alerting the wizard, and then we will have him where we want him," she said matter-of-factly.

Lord Brom was dumbfounded.

"You mean to let us be taken prisoner? Then how do you propose to attack him from behind bars?" He was beginning to think she had taken leave of her senses.

She just smiled at him.

"It will work, you will see. Do you trust me?"

Lord Brom let out a sigh and smiled. Now he knew she was crazy.

"Yes, of course I trust you. I just think you have lost your mind," he teased.

They both rode off in the direction of the castle to get themselves purposely arrested by Liza's guards, and to entice the wizard to them. It may prove to be the their most courageous plan yet…

Raul had found the perfect spell to use to remove her powers. There was a catch though. He had to get her to drink the potion for the power-stripping spell to work. He would have to somehow trick her into drinking it. Just as he was trying to come up with a solution to his current dilemma, the guards rushed inside, and interrupted his chain of thought.

"This had better be bloody well good," he said.

Raul turned to the guard waiting patiently for a good excuse to kill him. He was in a foul mood.

"Sire pardon the interruption, but the Princess and Lord Brom were just arrested, and placed in the castle dungeon as we currently speak," he announced.

Raul could not kill him now. This news was too good to be true.

"Make sure they are guarded well, I do not want any mishaps," he said. "I shall be there shortly." Raul could not have come up with a better opportunity than that, as he hurried to place the potion in a vial and leave for the castle...

Lord Brom, and Princess Ellyria were locked in separate cells deep in the castle's dungeon. The first part of the plan succeeded. They walked onto the castle grounds, when the guardsmen spotted them, they were taken into custody immediately. Now here they are waiting for the second part of their plan to unfold...

Raul entered the dungeon. He had ordered that Lord Brom be left in his cell and asked that the Princess be brought upstairs to one of the empty rooms. Princess Ellyria was not thinking that they would be separated from each other, as she was then forced to accompany the guard.

The wizard was now waiting for her arrival in the huge bedchamber, as he was pacing back and forth in the room.

The big double doors opened and Princess Ellyria was escorted inside.

"Leave us and lock the doors. I do not want her trying to escape," he ordered.

Princess Ellyria stood at the entryway.

"Come and join me, your Highness," he motioned for her to be seated beside him at the table.

She did not want to, but this was a perfect opportunity to get close enough to try and kill him. He stood up and graciously pulled her chair out for her to be seated.

"Thank you," she humbly replied.

Raul took his seat next to hers.

"Care for a drink?" he said offering her a glass of wine.

She looked at the fine chalice filled with wine, then pushed it aside.

"No, thank you, I am not permitted to drink, I am too young," she stated.

Raul had not taken her age into consideration. He was unaware of the fact that she was still practically a child. He would have to put the potion in something else that she would drink.

"Excuse me, I had no idea. Let me offer you something else. I could make you some tea if that would better please you?"

The last time someone offered her tea, she woke up finding herself locked in a crystal cage.

"That is quite all right, you do not have to go through all that trouble just for me," she answered coyly.

Raul took a deep breath. This was beginning to become an awkward situation.

"I will cut right to the chase then. I am here to offer you a deal. I will release Lord Brom in exchange for your hand in marriage," he offered.

Princess Ellyria had not expected this at all. She could not even fathom the idea of him being closer to her, than the distance between them already. He was so vile to look at, that he made even Rumpelstilzchen look attractive. She could not think she had it in her to even pretend to find him attractive.

"Do you promise to let him go free, if I agree to marry you?"

His eyes widened with excitement.

"Oh, yes. You have my word," he said smiling. He always kept his word. He himself would not kill him, but he did not promise that his men would not kill him. He took Princess Ellyria's hand into his. "Will you marry me then?"

She could not believe she was going to say it.

"Yes, I will marry you," she answered.

Raul surprised her, and pulled her into him for a kiss. It took every ounce of her being not to throw up in his mouth. His breath was foul, and his tongue darted in and out of her mouth like that of an angry serpent. He released her, as tears stung her eyes.

"Are you upset, my dear?" he asked wiping the tears that had fallen onto her cheeks.

"No, those are tears of joy, milord," she lied.

Raul kissed her on the cheek before he got up from the table.

"I must prepare for our wedding. It will be hard pressed to find a High Priest to wed us so late in the day, but I am sure I will find one," he said with a smile exposing his blackened crooked teeth.

As he left the room Princess Ellyria tried to open the door, but they were locked. She went to the windows, and they were locked as well. She had to think.

Raul returned to the dungeon to see Lord Brom one last time before he had him executed. He was sure going to miss that one.

Lord Brom grabbed the bars of his cell upon seeing the wizard.

"What have you done with the Princess, Raul? I swear if you have harmed her in any way, I will cut off all off your limbs and scatter them across the four corners of the realm, so you can never piece yourself back together!"

Raul laughed, that would be a challenge for him indeed.

"I have done no such thing. Have not even harm a hair on that beautiful head of hers," he assured him.

Lord Brom looked at him confused.

"Then what are you going to do with her?"

Raul smiled, he could not wait for his reaction on this one.

"I plan to take her as my bride. I am sorry you are not invited to the wedding, due to the fact that you will be dead. Oh, but maybe I should keep you alive just until after our wedding night. So, you can watch me deflower your Princess!" he declared laughing maniacally before leaving Lord Brom. He still heard his screams as he walked out of the dungeon.

Lord Brom had to get out of here, and fast. He was not about to let that madman marry his Princess!

Princess Ellyria was waiting patiently for the wizard to return. She devised a plan that she would seduce him before the wedding. If she were able to somehow trick him into getting ready for lovemaking, once he leaves to fetch a bath, she would tell him what she required of him, and then slip something into the door preventing it from locking. Allowing for her to escape. The plan had to work, so she could then rescue Lord Brom from the dungeon. She did not trust the wizard to keep his word that he would not harm him.

Just then she heard a knock on her door.

"Princess Ellyria are you in there?" the voice whispered.

It sounded like, Lord Brom. She went to the door.

"Yes, Brom, I am in here get me out," she answered.

Lord Brom opened the door and grabbed the Princess, twirling her around.

"How did you escape?"

"When the guards were moving me to be executed I knocked one of them out and shoved the other one into my cell. I came looking for you as soon as I could," he said.

"I am so glad that you are here, but the wizard is going to return any moment, with a Priest in fact. We must hurry and leave before he comes back," she urged.

Lord Brom took her in his arms and kissed her fiercely, he had never been so rough before, but she still returned his kisses with equal passion. He picked her up and carried her to the large canopy bed, laying her on her back. He removed his shirt and continued to kiss her.

She stopped him for a moment.

"Do you seriously want to do this here and now?" she

questioned as he vigorously kissed the side of her neck.

"Oh, yes, I want to make love to you Ellyria, I love you. I cannot wait a minute longer to have you," he confessed making his way to her breasts.

She lay there while he groped her breasts. He was a little rougher than last time. Perhaps he was feeling vigorous? He uncovered her breasts, taking a nipple in his mouth, and then bit her.

"Ouch, you are hurting me. What has gotten into you?"

Lord Brom looked up at her, her eyes were a brilliant emerald. He looked confused for a moment.

"I am sorry, my love. I will try to be gentler," he said.

He continued to seduce her, but she pushed him away.

"I just do not feel comfortable doing this now," she said.

Lord Brom pulled her up to massage her shoulders, placing lighter kisses upon her neck.

"You just need to relax, have some wine," he suggested.

Princess Ellyria knew now, that this was not Lord Brom, but she did not want to let on that she was aware of Raul's deception.

"No, I like what you are doing right now. Oh, yeah, just a little lower," she said.

He stopped rubbing her back, when she turned to climb on top of him. He was surprised by her wild streak, but he liked it and was now even more aroused. He grabbed her breasts, as she was the one seducing him now. She kissed him with ardent fervor and he matched her kisses more roughly than before. He could not wait a moment longer, and he flipped her over on her back, grabbed her dress, and then pulled it up over her thighs, trying to position himself between her legs. She had not expected this to get that far, and tried to fight him.

"I like a challenge," he said.

He held her hands with his one hand and tried to grip his manhood with the other. Just before he plunged himself inside her Lord Brom kicked open the doors. Princess Ellyria was relieved. When she turned back to look at his double the wizard was back in his true form.

Raul grabbed her by the hair and dragged her off the bed, and pulled out his athame placing it to her throat.

"Take one step closer and I will slit the maiden from her twat to her face, and there will not be anything left to desire," he threatened.

She nodded at Lord Brom to do as he said. Lord Brom stepped back and raised his hands over his head.

"Please do not hurt her, Raul. I will do as you ask just do not hurt her," he pleaded.

Raul stepped back with the Princess.

"Come now my pretty, we have a Priest to find," he announced.

Princess Ellyria focused on the athame. She envisioned it flying out of his hands. To everyone's surprise the knife came out of the wizard's hands and was sent flying across the room, barely missing Lord Brom, as it became wedged into the wall. Princess Ellyria quickly got away from Raul before he could grab her again. She ran to Lord Brom who handed her one of the vials. Then she turned and threw it at the wizard. It smashed into the floor, as vines began to grow all over him. They did not wait a moment longer and ran out of the room. Lord Brom had to fight the guard at the end of the hall before they could continue to run down the stairs as fast as they could go.

Once they had made it to the foot of the stairs, Raul appeared in front of them.

"Did you think those vines could really bind me?"

They stepped back on the stairs behind them. The medicine pouch was on the left side of Lord Brom, while Princess Ellyria was on his left side. She reached into the pouch slowly with her right hand.

Raul saw what she was doing. He locked the doors with a wave of his hand. "You are not going anywhere, my love," he said.

The wizard raised his hand in the air, then with a motion to the right sent Lord Brom sliding across the floor. The vial had fallen to the floor, when she made a move to reach it, he stopped her.

"Your powers are still weak Princess, but you are very clever. No wonder you were able to escape from Liza so many times," he said laughing.

"What happened to your accomplice anyway?" Lord Brom inquired, not that he really cared.

"Oh, she met an unfortunate accident in a house fire. It was so very tragic," he answered. "I never liked the old crone anyway."

Lord Brom tried to get up, but was still pinned down, and he could not move. Princess Ellyria tried to reach the vial, but she saw the wizard shake his head.

"I would not move if I were you. I have enough pressure on your man there to crush him in an instant," he said.

Princess Ellyria just stood there at the bottom of the stairs. Seeing Lord Brom in pain like that angered her. She needed to get to the vial.

"Please, do not hurt him, and I will leave with you," she pleaded.

Raul was not fooled.

"Walk to me, slowly," he ordered.

She looked at Lord Brom.

"You can do this, I trust you," Lord Brom said.

She focused all her energy on the vial, envisioning it coming off the floor, and smashing into the wizard. But it did not move.

"Come here, Princess," Raul said.

He made a squeezing gesture with his hands. Lord Brom screamed in pain.

"No!" Without thinking she waved her hand at the vial and sent in crashing into the wizard.

"No! How did you?" he said as the stone crept up his body.

Princess Ellyria ran over to Lord Brom and helped him to his feet.

"Come on, let us go! I do not know how long that will hold him," she said.

They went for the door, and managed to get it open. Princess Ellyria turned to make sure the wizard was still trapped, as they made a run for the stables. They were surprised that the barn was not guarded and found their horses. They wasted no time, and rode away from the castle.

After they had put several miles between them and the city, they stopped to rest their heavy winded horses. Lord Brom helped Princess Ellyria down from her horse and held her in his arms.

He raised her chin up to meet his gentle kisses, that she had known before. How could she have been so duped by the wizard's trickery? Lord Brom pulled away for a moment.

"How long were you aware that it was the wizard, and not me that was about to make love to you?"

She looked at him. If she did not know any better, she would think he was jealous.

"I knew after he told me, that he loved me. Because you had not said so, since the night in the gardens when you proposed to me," she answered.

Lord Brom looked her in the eye.

"I do love you. I always have and I always will," he confessed, before he kissed her again.

She returned his kisses, before she stopped him again. She could not bring herself to tell him how she felt just yet.

"Let us go home," she said and kissed him again before he assisted her onto the horse.

He mounted his own steed, and then they both kicked their horses into a steady gallop. They never looked back.

The journey home is sometimes a long one, but it is worth the ride when the ones you love are there waiting on your return...

CHAPTER 44

"Argh!" Raul screamed, as he broke free from his stone prison with the power of the amulet.

His men had tried to break him free with axes, but they were not strong enough for the magic that had encased him in stone. He sent the men soaring out of his way, before he vanished from the castle.

Raul reappeared in his cottage, startling the boy. He needed to think. He paced back and forth frantically. *Her powers are growing stronger. He must get her back somehow.* Then he went back to the grimoire. *If he could somehow create a potion, such as the ones she had used on him, then he could simply throw the power stripping potion on her instead of making her drink it. That may work. The formula of course would have to be completely remade, but it will be well worth it. He must get her powers. He refused to wait another five hundred years for the next blood moon eclipse.*

"Boy, come here. I need you to go to market for me. Make haste and bring me what is on this list."

Raul handed the parchment to the boy. Toby stood there for a moment.

"Is there a problem?"

Toby began to cry.

"I can not read, sire," he confessed.

Raul covered his face with his hands. He took the parchment from the child and drew pictures of the ingredients he needed for the potion.

"There, that should do it. Do you understand the pictures?"

Toby nodded his head.

Raul called to the guard outside his door.

"Go with him, make sure he gets what is on the list, and find him a tutor as well. Now go," he ordered.

Raul could not have any more idiots around him. He would see too it the boy did not grow up to be uneducated. If he is to work for him, he needed to know how to read. He would train him as his apprentice if he took to his lessons easily...

Toby, and his escort made it to town, and the man said they were to look for a tutor. He did not know where one could be found, and he hoped for the man's sake that he did. They arrived at the market and the man helped to retrieve the items from his list, that he paid with the wizard's coins, and then placed them in his pouch.

As they were leaving, they stopped, and the guard asked where they could find a good tutor. They were sent to a tent that was at the very end of the tables past the posts that the horses were tethered to. When they arrived at the tent, the young boy opened it, and there sat an older lady, with her face halfway covered.

"Are you a tutor ma'am?" he asked timidly.

The woman smiled under her scarf.

"Yes, I am, dearie," she replied.

The boy became excited that wizard would be pleased and that he would not be punished now.

"Would you become my tutor?"

The old woman nodded her head.

"Come here this time tomorrow, and we shall begin your first lesson," she told the boy.

Toby left the tent and told the man that she agreed to be his tutor. Then he and the guard began the journey home, to bring the wizard the items he required and to tell him about the tutor he had found...

Raul was patiently waiting for the boy to return when he finally arrived with the items he requested. Toby told him about the old woman in the market that agreed to be his tutor, and to return the next day, at the same time. The wizard nodded his head and sent the boy to fetch some more firewood.

While the young page Toby was gathering the firewood, he was unaware that someone had followed him home, and was watching him right now...

CHAPTER 45

The scouts that the King had sent searching in the other kingdoms had finally returned with news of Princess Ellyria.

"Your, Highness, we searched the kingdoms, and we had reported to us of two sightings of the Princess. One was in Regnuom, and the other in Inamor, both kingdoms held no current whereabouts of the Princess, Sire," one of the scouts said as they entered the King's study.

King Jason felt better, that he at least knew she was alive. Where was she now?

The Queen was in the parlor when her husband came in and sat down beside her. Queen Anna saw the worried look on his face. This could not be good news that he was about to share.

"The scouts have returned. Princess Ellyria was seen in Regnuom, and Inamor. No one they had spoken to knew where she was, or where she was heading," he informed.

Queen Anna began to cry. She was grateful for her to be alive, but she wanted her back home where she belonged with her family.

"It is all right, my love," he said before he embraced his wife.

She continued to cry on her husband's shoulder.

After a few moments had passed Queen Anna sat up and King Jason helped her to wipe the tears from her cheeks.

"There was nothing else? Not even about whom she was traveling with?"

Her husband just shook his head.

"No, I am afraid. The only thing they said was that they

had seen a girl fitting Ellyria's description," he said still trying to comfort his wife.

Prince Dakota entered the parlor. He saw his mother crying again. He wished he could alleviate her pain, but only his sister's return would mend her broken heart. King Jason, and Queen Anna turned to see their son, and they both tried to smile.

"How is Isis doing?" his mother asked.

Prince Dakota joined his parents at the table.

"She is doing well. The potion lasts in her case, for several hours, before it begins to wear off," he replied. "Is there any news of my sister?" he questioned.

"Yes, she was spotted in Regnuom, and in Inamor. There is nothing else on her current whereabouts," his father replied.

Just then Prince Anthony, Prince Rowan, and Prince Ian came to join them. Their father filled them in on the latest news that he had of their sister.

"Father, is there anything I can do to help find her?" Prince Anthony asked.

"I think we all should still be out there looking for her," replied Prince Ian.

Prince Rowan, and Prince Dakota also chimed in that they would help as well. The King just looked as his sons. He was so very proud of them. As a father he could not ask for more, with the exception of the return of his daughter.

Suddenly, the tower guard came running into the parlor out of breath.

"Your, Majesties, riders are approaching the gate! It appears to be the Princess, and Lord Brom!" he shouted excitedly.

Queen Anna stood up and ran for the window.

"Oh, Jason! It is, Ellyria!"

She turned for a moment to see if anyone was going to follow her to the courtyard to greet her daughter. King Jason, and his sons were right behind the Queen.

Princess Ellyria, and Lord Brom rode into the courtyard where everyone had gathered to meet them. When Lord Brom assisted Princess Ellyria from her horse, her mother was the first in line to embrace her daughter.

"Oh, my darling, daughter. You had us all worried sick over your disappearance," she said as tears of joy escaped her eyes.

Her father was right beside her, and embraced her next.

"I am so happy that you are finally home safe. What made you decide to go out on your own like that, again? Do you not know that it almost sent your mother into worried fits and almost put Isis in the grave?" He did not think he could be so happy and angry with his daughter at the same time.

Princess Ellyria's brothers were in line as well and each of them embraced their sister. When Prince Dakota managed to get in his turn, he decided to mention Isis now, since his father blurted it out.

"Isis is going to be fine. She ended up becoming lethargic in your absence. I will go let her know that you are here," he said.

The entire various greetings she had received was welcome, but she had not wanted to leave Lord Brom out of the picture, it overwhelmed Princess Ellyria. Lord Brom was cooling down the horses, removed the saddlebags, and their blankets when Princess Ellyria's father approached him.

"Thank you again, for bringing her home safe. I think it is time that you and I have a talk, after you settle in the horses, and have some time to rest yourself," he said.

Lord Brom smiled and nodded his head.

"Yes, your Highness," he answered and left to put the horses in the stable, before he went on to the guest quarters.

Queen Anna went with her daughter to her chambers to get cleaned up, and rest for a while. She was glad to see that she was in a much better condition, than the last time she had returned home, after weeks of being absent. They made it to her chambers and her mother ordered her a nice hot bath, and some food. While they waited for the rest of the hot water to be brought upstairs, her mother was curious as to what had happened.

"Did you get what you went searching for?" her mother inquired.

Princess Ellyria shook her head.

"No. I just knew if I would have asked, you would not have approved," she answered. She began fidgeting with a string that was loose on her gown that had started to unravel.

Her mother placed her hand over her daughter's.

"What happened?" she questioned her daughter.

She smiled at her mother.

"I had quite the adventure, that is for sure," she began to tell her tale.

"I can not wait to hear what prompted this little adventure this time," her mother teased.

Princess Ellyria smiled at her mother and for the next few hours they shared as much laughter as they shed tears together. She worried that her mother would have been entirely way too upset over what she had done but the mother daughter bond between them was stronger than ever before. If only she had the courage to share all of the intimate details with her mother.

After she had finished telling her story, Queen Anna looked at her. She felt there were some things missing from her story, but she would probe her some other time about them. While they were talking, the rest of the water for her bath had been brought in, as well as the rose oil that Queen Anna always put in Princess Ellyria's bath.

"I will let you soak in the tub and rest, I shall be back later to check in on you," her mother said before she left the room.

Princess Ellyria let the linen dress fall to the floor, before stepping into the tub. The water was perfect, not too hot, not too cold, the scent of roses filling her nostrils, with the memory of the arousing scent of lilies, from that afternoon she had spent with Lord Brom. She became excited just thinking about all of the sensations he caused her body to have. Her body ached to feel his touch again. The way he used his hands down there made her curious if she could do the same. Visions of Lord Brom entered her mind, the way he kissed her, from her mouth to her neck, the way he suckled her nipples, placing kisses down her stomach, and then to the inside of her thighs. She slid down into the tub further, arching her back, some of the water splashed out into the floor, as she recalled how he kissed her soft lips. When he kissed the length of the inside of her thighs it sent chills down her body, and the inside of her core felt as if it were on fire. She remembered what Rob the Red had said when he tried to do that to her. He had said that all women liked to be kissed down there. He was right about that.

The more Princess Ellyria imagined Lord Brom parting her, like the soft petals of a flower, when the bees enter in search of that sweet nectar. More water splashed into the floor as Princess Ellyria lay her head back into the water for a moment, to contain the sound of her moans. She rose up out of the water, as the tendrils of her long black hair now clung to her body. She was nearly out of breath. She had no idea that she could accomplish the same wondrous sensation, that Lord Brom was able to create, and give so much pleasure to her body. She smiled and closed her eyes, drifting off to sleep and dreamt of Lord Brom…

King Jason had called Lord Brom to the study. When he arrived he was not surprised to see all of Princess Ellyria's brothers were there as well.

"Lord Brom please come inside, I think you remember my sons. Come, sit down, it is time we had a talk," he said.

Lord Brom wrung his hands together and waited for the interrogation to begin.

"Yes, your Majesty," he answered before he took a seat between Prince Anthony and Prince Dakota.

"There is no need for such formality. Please, you may call me Jason, in private. I want to thank you again for saving my daughter."

"Your welcome, Sire. I only watched out for her. She was amazing, after she received her powers, she actually saved me." Lord Brom smiled, recalling certain events, but he was sitting in a room with her father, and four older brothers. He should not be thinking about his daughter and their sister, in that manner while he was sitting in a room alone with them.

"So, how long were you with my sister, before you returned

with her?" Prince Anthony questioned.

Lord Brom rubbed his hands on his trousers.

"I first saw her on my brothers ship. She had been mistaken for a slave. I quickly remedied that problem, and then she was treated in accordance to her station," he answered. How many more questions would he have to answer, he thought to himself?

"Why did you not dock immediately, or send word home that she was safe?" Prince Rowan asked.

"Soon after I was aware that she was on board, we were attacked by a warship full of another clan of Vikings. There was no time to send word. We did dock soon after, for the ship to be repaired," he said. He was starting to feel uncomfortable.

"What happened after you docked? Where were you? Why did you not send word then?" Prince Ian questioned.

"Ellyria wanted to go back to the gypsy market since we docked in Inamor. The gypsies took us in and told her that she was the Chosen One, and began to prepare her for the Quickening. Everything happened so fast. The wizard attacked us, she got her powers, and fought him off. We started to head back home after that," he said.

"So what took you so long to come back, after you left Inamor?" Prince Dakota asked.

"Ellyria decided she wanted to go after the wizard, and surprise him. We left soon as we were able to get away," he said leaving out the details.

King Jason stood up.

"Leave us please," he said to his sons.

The young men left the room, shutting the door, but they could not resist eavesdropping through the closed door. They could barely hear what was being said, when their mother caught them. like when they were little, and sent them on their way. She watched for them to leave and stood next to the door herself, just in case they came back.

"After listening to the relay of questions and answers between you and my sons. I feel that there were some details that you perhaps left out. Am I correct on this assumption?" he questioned.

Lord Brom looked the King in the eyes.

"Yes Sire, I did," he replied. Lord Brom was going to stay firm.

"What exactly did you leave out?" King Jason inquired leaning in towards Lord Brom.

"Well Sire, for one, the wizard shape shifted into appearing as me, trying to deceive your daughter. He was delusional thinking he was going to marry her," he answered still leaving out the details.

"In your opinion do you feel the wizard will try to come after, Ellyria again?"

"Yes, I do not think he will give up until he has her powers. I think the marriage thing was a ruse to get her to drink his wine. She stated that he kept trying to ply her with it," he said. King Jason found this news rather interesting, he would have to see if Prince Dakota would know anything that the wizard could be trying to use, to take his daughters powers.

"I know you have spent a lot of time with my daughter. Just how much time have the two of you spent alone?"

Lord Brom had a feeling the conversation was going to go this route.

"I have been a gentleman if that is what you are asking," he answered. "Yes, there have been times I have been completely alone with your daughter, but nothing has happened. Sire, I can assure you," he lied.

King Jason searched the young man's face. He believed he was telling most of the truth.

"So, tell me then, Lord Brom. What is your intentions with my daughter?" he asked. Just then, Queen Anna interrupted, as she entered the room. She felt Lord Brom was in need of rescue from her husband. She was right, and Lord Brom gave her a smile of gratitude.

"What have I missed?" she questioned her husband.

He knew his wife had come in just in the nick of time too. Tricky woman.

"Not much dear. Lord Brom was just about to answer a question I had just asked him, before you rode in on your white horse," he teased.

Lord Brom looked at Princess Ellyria's mother, to bail him out of this somehow. It was not that he did not want to answer the question, he just did not know how.

"Can you not see the young man is tired from his long journey? He brought our daughter home safe, that is all that matters to me," she said as she gave Lord Brom a wink.

King Jason lost this battle for now, but it will be him that wins the war.

"All right my, dear, you are right. Go rest yourself for a while Lord Brom, we will finish our discussion later," the King said.

Lord Brom left the room.

Queen Anna turned towards her husband.

"What was that about? Have you gone mad? Can you not see that man is in love with your daughter? Are you trying to send him away?" she interrogated her husband.

King Jason knew his wife was right, as she always is when it comes to these matters. What did he know? He was just being the concerned father.

"You are right, my love," he just nodded his head in defeat, and smiled lovingly at his wife. "How about we celebrate. A ball to celebrate love?" he suggested.

"Well, we did not celebrate the Summer Solstice," Queen Anna suggested. "This time let us not do it so hastily," she teased.

He smiled.

"Whatever do you mean?" he said coyly.

She just gave him a wicked smile.

"You know very well what I mean, dear husband," she chided.

He laughed out loud.

"I know, it was just but a jest," he teased. "We will hold it tomorrow night, I will have my messenger send out the invitations today," he said smiling.

"That is a little better, we have at least an entire day to plan, instead of only just a few hours," she teased.

He laughed at her, took her into his arms and kissed her passionately.

"I love you, my dear."
"As I love you, my husband."

They stayed in the study for a good part of the afternoon, planning the ball in celebration of the Summer Solstice...

CHAPTER 46

The Summer Solstice celebration was held outside in the courtyard. Both gardens were decorated with paper lanterns and an abundance of several different types of flowers. The dancing would still be in the grand ballroom, with the large double glass doors left open to the courtyard. Two sets of minstrels were summoned to play, one to play inside for the dancing and the second for soft music for the gardens. With more time allotted to plan for the event, the King was slightly overzealous with all of the elaborate decorations, musicians, stage performers, and a feast that was fit for the entire kingdom, which he had practically invited. The guests had come from miles around for this joyous occasion to celebrate the summer with the promise of a bountiful harvest by fall.

King Jason made his way through the crowd, to the stage that had been temporarily built for the entertainment later. He now stood on the stage and tried to get everyone's attention.

"May I have your attention please? Good people of Toledya. I want to thank you all for your attendance here tonight. On behalf of my beautiful wife, Queen Anna Marie, and I both welcome you to our home, and to celebrate with us tonight the Summer Solstice. Blessed be!" he announced.

"Blessed be!" joined the crowd.

The dancing and dining commenced and everyone one was having a splendid time, except for Lord Brom. He had not had a chance to see the Princess all day. He had wanted to speak to her well before the party ever began, but he had not had the chance…

Princess Ellyria had just finished getting ready for the ball, when Isis blocked her from leaving the room. After she had finished with her bath yesterday, she quickly dressed to check on Isis, whom was overjoyed to see her return. She had finally begun to eat and act like herself again. Now she was obviously worried, that she was going to leave her once again.

"Isis, it is alright, girl. I am just going down to the party. You can come too if you like, you will just have to be on your best behavior. Do not get underfoot, or steal any food. Ok, girl?" Isis wagged her tail excitedly.

Princess Ellyria opened the door and Isis followed her down the grand staircase. Her brothers were there waiting at the bottom of the steps. They had the look of mischief about them, like they did when they were children.

"What is it you are plotting?" she asked of them, when she reached the last step. They took her by the hand and led her into the parlor. There were several objects aligned on the table, a book, a chalice, a candle, and a bell.

"What is all this?"

Prince Dakota moved to the table and pointed to each object stating what they were. The brothers laughed in unison at the look on their sister's face.

"I know what the objects are, thank you very much. What are they doing like this, on the table?" she questioned, her eye color quickly turning green.

They stopped laughing for the moment, so Prince Dakota could answer her.

"We were wondering if you could make these objects move for us," he asked.

She glared at him, placing her hands in her hips.

"I am not a performing monkey. I am also not supposed to use my powers for personal gain," she chided.

Prince Dakota looked at one of his other brothers to chime in and say something to help him out.

Prince Rowan walked over to his sister.

"It is not for personal gain if we want you to use your magic. Right, Dakota?" Prince Rowan added.

They all nodded in agreement. Princess Ellyria was now blushing.

She was not sure she could do this.

"I do not know. I do not think I should," she said.

Prince Anthony took her by the hand and pulled her to the side.

"If you do not want to do this you do not have to. Are you not supposed to be practicing your powers anyway? This is a good time to do so and a much safer way to do this, instead of going all out to try and fight the wizard without experience. Do you understand where we are coming from?"

She knew they were right, and she did need to get a handle on her powers.

"Alright, I will do it," she agreed and walked over to the table, but kept a few feet away.

"Now focus on the book first. Try to see if you can open it and flip the pages," Prince Dakota instructed.

Princess Ellyria tried hard to focus on the book. She waved her hand, as if she were turning the pages herself. That was her intent, but the book flew off the table barely missing her brother Prince Ian, that was standing a little too close. He was able to dodge it, then he and her other brothers moved out of the way, just in case.

"Now, this time focus. The chalice is filled with wine, so try to raise it up off the table, and then gently set it back down," Prince Dakota said.

Princess Ellyria again focused on the chalice, imaging it lifting up from the table. Raising her hand palm side up in a slow upward motion, the chalice slowly came off the table and was suspended in the air.

She was so excited.

"Look, I did it!" And quickly she turned to Prince Dakota.

When she made the motion to Prince Dakota, she accidentally threw the cup right into him, covering him in wine. Everyone else could not help but to laugh.

"Oh, I am so sorry, brother. I did not mean for that to happen," she apologized with a giggle.

Prince Dakota just shook his head. let out a sigh and wiped the wine off his face with his cravat.

"This time try not to hurl it at one of us. Once you raise something do not turn anywhere or move your hands until you know where you are sending the object. Do not get overzealous," he advised. "Next I want you to move the candle to the small table over there," he said motioning to the small table in the far corner of the room.

Princess Ellyria closed her eyes, as she focused her energy. She opened her eyes, pointed at the candle, then directed her hand up, and the candle rose from the table. Without losing focus, she slowly traced a path in the air, with her hand guiding the floating candle to the table. Isis barked, she lost her focus, and the candle fell to the floor.

"At least it did not hit anyone this time," Prince Ian scoffed.

Princess Ellyria looked at Isis and instructed her to go lay down somewhere. Isis did not understand what she had done wrong, but she obeyed and now lay in the far corner.

"Ellyria, listen. There are going to be a lot of distractions when it comes down to it. You will have to not let your focus waver, concentrate. Now I want you to ring the bell," Prince Dakota instructed.

The Princess closed her eyes, heard the sound of the music in the distance, the crowd's laughter, Isis panting in the corner, and then she blocked out all the sounds; except for the sound of her own heartbeat, until she could no longer hear that as well. Slowly she opened her eyes, and with her hand outstretched in front of her, she made the motion of picking up the bell. The bell rose in the air off of the table and with a few short motions of her hand, the bell began to ring.

"Now slowly set it back down on the table," Prince Dakota said.

She lowered her hand and the bell returned to the table. She turned to her brother smiling and embraced him.

"I did it that time!" she said with pride.

"Now you must learn to focus in other ways, do not close your eyes, you must have your abilities in unison with your will. Or, it could pose as a grave danger to you," he chided.

Just then, their mother entered the parlor.

"There you all are. I have been searching for you everywhere. I only happened to hear the ringing of the bell, that alerted me to come in here. Why did I hear a bell? What is everyone doing in here anyway?"

"Mother, I was just practicing my powers. My brothers felt that I should practice more to prepare for my next altercation with the wizard," she stated.

Queen Anna understood it was her daughter's destiny to destroy the wizard, but it did not mean she had to like it.

"Well, now is not the appropriate time, or place to do so. You have several guests that are here, and one in particular that has been waiting for you all day," she said before she left the room.

"Was it something I said?" She did not want to risk upsetting her mother, for the sake of her destiny. Her family was more important to her than being the Chosen One.

"No, I would not think so. Do not worry about mother, she is just not handling your new destiny very well," Prince Anthony said.

Tears began to well up in Ellyria's emerald colored eyes.

"I did not ask for this. It just happened, all of the sudden. My own family did not even tell me, that I was the Chosen One. I had to hear it from complete strangers!" she shouted, before she ran out of the room crying.

"Should we go after her?" Prince Rowan asked.

"No, leave her be. She has to deal with this on her own," Prince Dakota answered.

"Well, this can not be easy for her. She has a lot to deal with right now, learning to control her new powers, and her destiny to defeat the wizard. That is a lot for any one. We could only imagine having to deal with this, or how she must feel." Prince Anthony stated.

"I agree brother, but she needs her space right now, to think about everything," Prince Ian said.

The men left the parlor to join the party. They felt bad for their sister and wished somehow, that they were able to guide her, so she did not have to go on this journey alone...

Princess Ellyria ran out to the large fountain, her favorite place to think, but already too many people were standing around it. She tried the summerhouse, yet again it was also filled with too many guests. She began to feel she had nowhere left to go, to escape. Then she considered the stables, and decided to go for a ride. She was not properly dressed for riding, but she did not care, she was leaving.

The horses were quiet, for all the commotion in the distance. The noise from the music and the crowd, did not seem to bother them. She only put the blanket and a bridle on the pretty Paint mare that the gypsies had gifted her with, and pulled up her satin purple gown, before she mounted. She had left the doors open so she could quickly ride out and no one could stop her. She rode out away from the crowd. In the courtyard, Lord Brom spotted her and ran to the stable to collect his horse. He too covered his horse with a blanket and hurried to put on the stallion's bridle. Princess Ellyria would be already a few miles from the castle by now, but he knew the stallion could catch up to her in no time.

Princess Ellyria could not think straight. She was still too upset. Why did she have to be the Chosen One? Her mind was conflicted with so many things that she felt it would be better for her, if she just left everything: the noise, the people, her parents, and her brothers. She felt horrible for leaving Isis behind, after she had nearly willed herself to death over her absence before, but she was not going to be gone long this time. Lord Brom saw the Princess up ahead, and urged his stallion on faster to catch up. Once he was behind her, he started shouting at her to stop.

Princess Ellyria turned, saw Lord Brom riding behind her, and pulled her horse to a stop.

"What are you doing here?"

Lord Brom grabbed a hold of her horse's reins so she would not ride off.

"I saw you leave. I had been waiting to talk to you all day. When I did not see you at the party, I decided to go looking for you, and there you were leaving, again!" he said.

She looked at him, and smiled.

"I was not trying to avoid you. I have just had a lot on my mind. It seemed to be a bit overwhelming for me," she answered.

Lord Brom dismounted and pulled Princess Ellyria down from her horse.

"I was not going to let you leave without me!" he said, before he pulled her to him, and kissed her deeply.

She returned his kisses, but only for a moment before she pushed him away.

"I can not do this right now, I am sorry," she said trying to walk away.

Lord Brom grabbed her arm and pulled her back to him.

"What do you mean, you can not do this?" he questioned. "I thought you were ready for us to be together?"

He lifted her chin gently with his hand and looked into her big sapphire colored eyes.

"What is really the matter?"

She covered her face with her hands and began to cry.

"I do not think I am ready for all of this," she said.

He embraced her and stood there a moment.

"Ready for what exactly?"

She walked away from him, then turned back around to face him.

"All of it. My destiny, my powers, my having to be the Chosen One, I am just not ready. I can not control my powers, the wizard is so much stronger than I am, and all I can think about is you. I want to be with you, I know that now. I say let us just leave right now, tonight, just the two of us. We will finally be free to be together. I do not want to lose you again. I do not care about being the Chosen One, or my destiny. I only want you, to be my destiny," she confessed.

Lord Brom let out a sigh. He knew the importance that her destiny was not just about her, or her family, or even him. It was about the safety of the entire realm.

"What about the wizard? Do you think he will stop trying to take over the entire realm, just so you can have your storybook ending? What will happen to all of those people? Women, children, and men, who are going to be at his mercy? Are you going to be able to live with yourself knowing that he has done horrible things like torture, kill, and rape, whoever crosses his path and gets in his way? You need to think about that. I was there, I heard Vadoma speak of the horrors that he will inflict on humanity. You are the only one that can stop him. If you want to quit, fine, quit. But he is not going to, and he is not going to stop coming after you, for your powers. Are you willing to give up everything you hold dear, and the people you love just for me? If your answer is yes, than I can no longer be part of this," he said.

"What are you saying? That you do not want to be with me?"

"Not if it means everyone else will suffer, because I said yes, and let you give up on the greater good of the people," he said placing his hand on her shoulder. "I will stand by whatever decision you make, but I will not stand by you if you give up on yourself, or your destiny to save these innocent people." He stepped away from her, and then mounted the stallion. "Let me know what you decide by tomorrow morning. My brother's ship departs in two days, if I leave first thing in the morning I will be able to catch him before he sets sail, so I can go join him," he announced, and then rode off in the direction of the castle.

"Brom wait!" she screamed, but he was already too far away to hear her call. She stood there and wept, before heading back to the castle.

CHAPTER 47

King Jason was in his study bright and early this morning, when he heard a knock at the door.

"You may enter," he said.

Lord Brom walked into the study.

"Ah, Lord Brom, good morning. You are up early. What could I assist you with?" he asked. "Come in, please sit."

Lord Brom sat down.

"I wanted to come to say goodbye, and thank you for your generosity," he announced.

King Jason looked puzzled.

"I had expected that you were going to be staying? Has something changed?"

Lord Brom looked at the King.

"I have decided for the sake of your daughter, that it would be wiser for me to leave, than to stay," he answered.

King Jason was not for certain, whether to be angry, or not.

"What makes you capable of making this decision for her?"

Lord Brom apparently worded his last sentence incorrectly.

"I am not making the decision for her. I am simply saying that she will be able to fulfill her destiny better, without me. She is confused right now. She does not realize that the decision she makes affects us all. Right now she is willing to give up everything to run away with me. So if I remove myself from the situation right now, then she will be able to focus her energies on what needs to be done, for the greater good of the realm. Not just for her selfish reasons," he said.

King Jason understood his reasoning but felt concern for his daughter.

"Have you taken into consideration how Princess Ellyria might feel in all this? Do you even love my daughter?"

"Yes, I do love your daughter, and that is the exact reason I am doing this," he answered. Lord Brom stood up and walked towards the door. "If you ever need me for any reason, please send for me. I will be here at your service. I will be aboard the Draki, with my brother. If you send a message I will receive it," he added before he walked out the door.

"Lord Brom, do not leave without telling my little girl goodbye," King Jason requested.

Lord Brom nodded his head then left the room in search of the Princess.

Princess Ellyria was with Isis, sitting in the summerhouse looking out into the distant horizon that welcomed dawn, with the warm embrace of the sun. She could not sleep and had come out earlier, into the darkness and thought a lot about what Lord Brom had told her last night. Was she really being selfish though? That she wanted a normal life? Yes, she had yearned for her own destiny, and to live her own dreams, but ones of her choosing. She did not ask to be the Chosen One, or to be the only one to kill the wizard. Why does life present us with difficult decisions, that require the absence of one's own desires for the sake of others? She looked at Isis, who lay in her lap, happy and content to be at her side. That is how she felt about Lord Brom. She would be happy and content to just be with him. Princess Ellyria's parents had always taught her the difference, between right and wrong, and to put others first before herself. When will it be her time? Is happiness, not included in her destiny? These were all very important questions, that she already knew the answers to. She just did not want to admit, that the answers are the right ones. Lord Brom was going to be devastated by her decision, but she knew in her heart, that he would understand.

The Amulet of Elements

Princess Ellyria got up from the swing to go find Lord Brom, when she saw him coming towards her.

"I was just coming to find you," she said with a smile.

She tried to embrace him, but he stepped back.

"I have come to speak with you about something, and I need you to listen," he said.

She looked at him.

"I was just coming to say the same thing," she added.

"You first then," he said.

She did not want to have to say it this way, but she had no other choice.

"I have made my decision. You were right. I can not let myself be selfish and forsake the lives of others, just to be with you. I have so much to prepare for, that I can not just run away from. I know that now, and I am ready to embrace my destiny," she confessed.

Lord Brom let out a sigh, he was worried that his words would hurt her and cause her more pain.

"I am glad to hear that. It will be better, you will see. I know that your destiny is of grave importance, and I will not stand in your way of seeing it fulfilled. I have decided that I am going to leave, and set sail with my brother, to become a merchantman such as he. I wish you the best of luck on your quest, I am only an ocean away, if you ever need me. I love you, Princess, and I always will," he said.

He saw her tears falling onto sun kissed cheeks and wiped them away, before he kissed her one last time. He stopped to look at her, wanting to permanently burn her image to memory. He would never forget her, and he would always love her.

When Lord Brom turned and walked away to where his horse was waiting in the courtyard, Princess Ellyria felt herself unable to move. She watched him mount his horse, but she could not find the ability to even say goodbye. She did not want to say goodbye. Lord Brom looked at her one last time, watching her cry made it harder to leave. He wanted to go to her and be there for her every step of the way, but he could not. This would be better for the both of them. He turned the horse and rode out of the courtyard.

Princess Ellyria watched him leave, tears made no effort to stop coming. Why did she not tell him goodbye? She wanted to run after him, but he was already almost out of her sights.

"I love you," she whispered. She did not move from her spot, until he was no longer visible. Isis and she went back to the castle, to return to her chambers. She needed to be alone now…

Queen Anna felt sorry for her daughter. She could not imagine the pain, that she must be going through right now. Her husband had informed her, that Lord Brom was going to leave and his reasons why. She did not blame him, for she actually agreed. Without understanding how the event played out, she was not for certain, what state of emotion her daughter would be in. As she made her way to the top of the grand staircase, she turned in the direction of her daughter's room and could already hear her crying.

Princess Ellyria sat up in her bed, when her mother entered her room. Her eyes were red and swollen, making the emerald color of her eyes stand out more against their bloodshot backdrop.

"I heard what happened with Lord Brom. I am so sorry that I can not take away your pain, my child, but I will be here for you, and I will listen. If you would like to talk about it," she said. Queen Anna sat down on the bed, as Princess Elyria laid her head down on her mother's lap. Her mother stroked the hair from her face, and wiped the tears from her cheeks, as they appeared.

"Why does doing the right thing hurt so bad?" she questioned her mother in between sobs.

Queen Anna looked down at her daughter, curled up in her lap as she used to, as a child. The only thing that has changed over the years was her size.

"If it were easy to do the right thing than we could not learn from it. Life is not just about the journey itself, it is about how we get there. Everything that we do in life is of our own free will, but it is up to us to choose whether it is the right thing to do. What you did is painful to you now, but you will see the greater good that will come from your sacrifice," her mother advised. "Nothing in life comes without its own price."

"Do you think that I will ever see him again?" Princess Ellyria asked.

Queen Anna was not sure if she would ever see Lord Brom again, or not. Who is to say what fate will allow?

"I do not know, my darling, daughter. If you are meant to be together than you shall be in time," she answered.

Princess Ellyria sat up and looked at her mother.

"How do I know if we are meant to be together?" she asked.

She smiled at her daughter.

"There is really no way of knowing for certain, but if you are reunited again, I would definitely take it as a positive sign, you just may be made for one another," she answered.

Her daughter smiled. It was the first one that she had seen in awhile. She really wished for her, that they were meant to be, because she felt that Lord Brom was her match, and that they would find each other again someday.

"Why do you not try to get some sleep? I will see you when you are ready to come down," Queen Anna said, before she arose from the bed and kissed her daughter's cheek.

Princess Ellyria embraced her mother.

"Mother."

"Yes, dear?" Queen Anna was standing in the doorway.

"Thank you." Princess Ellyria was looking up at her mother from the bed and managed to smile.

"You are welcome," she answered and then she walked out of the room.

Princess Ellyria was not sure if her mother was right about her and Lord Brom, but she wished it to be true. She was most assured that her decision was the right thing to do. She just wanted it to not leave such a dull, empty ache in her heart. What if she would never see him again? She knew her destiny is to kill the wizard. Will her destiny allow her to love? She lay in the bed and stared at the sheer material, that covered the top of her canopy bed. She had never noticed before the eloquently woven material, that delicately hung slightly in the center, and over each corner of the bed frame. There were so many things like that she took for granted, simple things to her, but for many it was a luxury. What of the women that spun the material, from the fine threads of the silkworm, or the other women that sewn the material together to be used on this very canopy bed. How about the men that risked their lives at sea to bring the material to market for trade, or others that saw to it that she would have this meaningless piece of cloth, to adorn her bed with. These are real people that hold true meaning of its worth, the ones that sacrificed their blood, sweat, and tears for its creation. Did they even receive enough compensation for such a fine trade of a seamstress, or the real nobility of the merchantmen? What of their children, and their homes? It was up to her to see to it, that these people and others like them throughout the realm, will not have to suffer at the hands of that monster, Raul. She was selfish to hope that her sacrifice would not be in vain.

Princess Ellyria turned over and curled up in the bed. Isis was asleep in her favorite spot on the floor by the heath. That is exactly what she needed, sleep. Without much sleep the night before, she felt herself feeling quite tired. It is easier said than done, because she could not stop thinking of Lord Brom. She had wanted him to stay and help her to decide a battle strategy for dealing with the wizard, and to be by her side during all of this. She knew she had to do it all on her own, but she was scared, and did not know what she feared the most. Did she fear the wizard more, or losing Lord Brom? Princess Ellyria began to cry again and sobbing onto her goose down pillow. She would get through this. She had to, not just for herself, but for others as well. The fate of the kingdoms was now in her hands.

Princess Ellyria cried herself to sleep, from not only the heavy burden that fate placed upon her, but for the love that she had to sacrifice…

CHAPTER 48

Lord Brom had arrived in-the-nick-time in Inamor, where his brother's ship had been docked for much needed repairs, after the battle with the other viking warship. After riding for a few days, with only a few short rests for his horse, he had discovered riding straight up the coastline to the port, proved to be a much faster route. He would have to remember that for future reference. He finally reached the end of the pier and saw his brother Jake, preparing to set sail.

"Look who made it just in time. Good to see you brother. I take it that things did not go so well seeing, that you are standing here," Jake said.

Lord Brom embraced his brother.

"It is good to see you, and no it did not, but it is for the best," he answered.

Jake gave his brother a pat on the back.

"Well, there will be plenty of time to discuss things, once we have been out to sea for a few months," he teased.

Both men boarded the Draki and set sail for the deepest parts of the ocean, to begin the fishing season. They would not come into port, until their nets were full. The crew hoisted up the anchor and rowed the ship out of the harbor. Once they were out at sea, they unfurled the mainsail, that caught the afternoon breeze. It will guide their ship to the middle of the ocean.

Lord Brom returned below deck, so he could clean up after his long journey. His brother had never bothered to change back the cabin, that had been created for comfort for the Princess, so Lord Brom took that cabin for himself. The linens had not been changed, so he was still able to smell the scent of her. Memories of their tryst at the lake came flooding back, as the scent reminded him of the lilies, that grew all around its banks. How lovely she looked, almost like a mermaid, that had tempted him into the water, to seduce him with her wiles. Lord Brom missed the scent of her hair, the softness of her skin, those beautiful large breasts of hers, and the sweet nectar of the flower he was able to sample; yet he was not able to pluck her delicate petals. He wondered if he would ever be able to see her again, to touch her, and feel the caress of her soft hands upon his body. He knew not to worry for her, but he did. What if the wizard is able to trap her again, or worse? He could not think of such things. If anything ever happened to her, he would never forgive himself. He would show no mercy to anyone that ever did any harm to her. It would be the last thing they would ever do. Now that Lord Brom got himself all worked up he was not sure, that he would be able to rest. He rose up, got off the bed, and walked over to the porthole to look out the window. He could no longer see the dock. It had long since faded into the backdrop of the ocean. Turning around away from the window his gaze fell upon the opened wardrobe of gowns. There were so many. He did not recall her wearing any of them, except the one red satin one, that fell off her shoulder as she stood at the bow of the ship. The wind blew through her long black hair, and the slit in her gown, that had been blown from her leg to expose her thigh. On the floor was the cream-colored linen dress that she was wearing, when he first saw her on the ship. He walked over to pick it up, then smelled it, and it too still held onto the lingering scent. Lord Brom draped it over the door of the wardrobe and returned to the bed. He lay back onto the bed and looked up at the ceiling of the cabin.

This was going to be the longest journey ever…

CHAPTER 49

Princess Ellyria had awakened and decided to go downstairs for some breakfast. When she opened her chamber door, it was no longer the hall that led to the stairwell. She shut the door and quickly turned around leaning back against the door. Did she just see a forest? She turned to reopen the door, and there was a forest in the hallway.

Princess Ellyria stepped out of her bedroom, into the dense forest. When she turned back around and tried to open her door again, it was not there. Enormous trees and tall thick grasses now surrounded her. The Princess stepped forward through the heavy branches that lay low to the ground and the tall grass caressed the leaves on the trees. She could barely see in front of her, the woods were so thick, but she continued to walk through, pushing aside the lush greenery. This seemed to her that the forest would never end. After, what felt like miles of woods she had just walked through. It began to become sparser. She was relieved to see a clearing up ahead. Upon her exit from the trees, she was like a wide-eyed doe checking for predators before coming out into the clearing…

Princess Ellyria saw nothing on either side of her, and then her eyes peered to the center of the clearing, and she spied a little cottage. The cottage looked abandoned. As she came closer, she could no longer hear the birds, or the scurrying of squirrels chasing each other up and down the tree branches. When she looked behind her, gnarled dead trees had replaced the lush forest. Brown dead grasses and the dried out vines were all that remained. She stepped onto the doorstep and tried to look in the window, but could not see inside. The door was not locked, so she carefully turned the knob to open it. Instead of what you would think the inside of a cottage would look like, it was now blackened from what had appeared to be a fire. She was cautious, as she stepped inside, since she was not sure of how sturdy the structure was. The horrible stench of burnt furniture barely masked the scent of burnt human flesh, that had invaded her nostrils. She began to look around not quite sure why she was even there, and then saw the remains of a charred body that had roasted into a permanent curled up position. After walking into one of the bedrooms, she saw a trapdoor that was open and stepped down into the hole in the floor.

When she reached the bottom, she had found herself in a tunnel that was large enough for her to stand upright in. The tunnel only went in one direction and she followed it to the very end, where she saw a ladder fixed to the wall that led upwards. When she reached the top, she carefully opened the door and peered all around her outside. After seeing that the coast was clear, she climbed her way out of the tunnel. She stood up only to find herself in strange scenery...

Princess Ellyria walked out, to examine the perfectly trimmed hedge, that scaled up over her head nearly ten feet. She followed the length of it and it seemed to go on and on in either direction. Then she saw an opening and walked through, in between the hedge line, only to see more of the wall of shrubbery. The path she was taking, leads her to more green walls, that seemed never ending, and getting her absolutely nowhere. Every turn she made, led to yet another turn, that ended with more of the giant brush. New openings only led to dead ends. She had found herself in a labyrinth of sorts. Just when she had thought she had gotten one step closer to finding her way out, she found herself to be lost all over again. That was enough, she now grew tired of this maze and was going to see to it that she made her way out. Princess

The Amulet of Elements

Ellyria stood in the middle of one of the green walls and with her hands placed with the backs together. She made a parting motion with her hands, separating the hedge wall. She continued to go straight through her self-made paths, when she heard a sound in the distance. The sound grew louder the closer she came through the maze, it was the sound of laughter. Recognizing it to be the wizard's voice, she decided to keep a look out for him, just in case he popped out in front of her somewhere.

It seemed as though she had been trying to get through this labyrinth for hours now. She began to feel angry, as the sound of his maniacal laughter grew increasingly louder by the minute. She now used only her right hand in a fluid motion, as a tool for her mind to move the giant green wall out of her way. Princess Ellyria was beginning to tire, and just when she thought she could not go on, she stumbled out of the labyrinth into another clearing in the woods. No longer did the wizard's laughter assail her ears as she walked out into an open field…

After she had regained her bearings, she recognized where she was. She was standing in the cornfield, between the corn mill and Liza's castle. How did she end up here? Suddenly she saw a beautiful doe grazing in the field. She saw it raise its head up and look towards her, she stood perfectly still not wanting to frighten it, and then it began to run right towards her. The deer approached her without any fear.

"Come, you must follow me."

Did she just hear that doe speak to her? She knew the ability to communicate with animals was one of her new powers, but was not expecting it to develop so soon.

The doe stopped running a few feet ahead and looked back at her.

"Are you coming or not?"

She was not sure if she would ever get used to this. The doe, however, could not speak, but Princess Ellyria could hear her telepathically, due to her enhanced empathic ability. She followed the doe through the field, until they came to the edge of the forest.

"I can not lead you any further, good luck."

The doe took off and Princess Ellyria was left alone again. She was dreading the thought of having to trudge through another forest. This forest felt different to her. It felt as if there was an evil presence about it. She kept walking further into the forest. The lush green began to change again into brown decay. As she came upon another clearing in the woods, she saw another cottage. This one looked different. The tiny hairs on her arms stood up, and she tried to rub her forearms with her hands to ward of the sudden chill. There was silence all around her, not a sound of the wind blowing through the trees, or that of the forest animals. She could only hear the sound of her feet crunching dried leaves, twigs, and the sound of her own heartbeat. The closer she came to the cottage, was when she began to feel ill. She kept walking closer, trying to fight off the urge to be sick. It was too late, Princess Ellyria leaned over where she stood and began to vomit.

She wiped her mouth with the back of her hand, as she was not turning back now. Just as she reached the steps of the cottage, she heard a familiar voice, and went to the window to peer inside. It was Raul, she had found his lair. He appeared to be talking with a young boy, who did not seem to be frightened of him. He could be the wizard's apprentice. There it was, the Amulet of Elements, but it was around Raul's neck. How was she going to get the amulet from him? All of the sudden Raul picked the boy up off of the floor and was screaming at him. She could feel the boy's fear, and Raul's anger, it left her feeling almost breathless, and her head began to hurt. She raised her hands to the sides of her head, rubbing her temples. It took every ounce of energy for her to block out the wizard's anger. She began to feel overwhelmed with emotions, she had to do something. When she stood up she became dizzy, and now falling…

When Princess Ellyria awoke, she found herself in a familiar setting. One that she had never suspected that she would once again, be inside of the crystal cage. Only this time it did not look like she was in a barn, it looked more like she was in the dungeon of the castle. She tried to open the cage door, but it would not budge, she tried to focus her energy, and then with a wave of her hands tried to magically open the door, nothing. She was trapped.

Raul suddenly appeared before her, and raked the bars with his athame as he walked to where she was on the other side of the cage.

"How do you like your prison, Princess? I created this myself, so Liza could use it to incarcerate you the first time. She fell for your trickery, but I will not. You had your chance to rule by my side, but you turned me down and went to your lover instead," he said, as he touched her fingers that were wrapped around the bars.

"What do you want from me?"

Raul laughed at her. How could she be that innocent?

"I want what you took from me, and you will give it back," he stated.

Princess Ellyria looked at him puzzled. She did not understand what he meant.

"What are you talking about? I have nothing of yours?"

He became tired of these little games, that she was playing.

"The powers you took from me. Those were meant to be mine, but if it were not for you and those meddling gypsies, ruining that for me, we would not be having this discussion. Would we?"

Princess Ellyria stepped back from the cage door. There was no way out, she may not escape this time she feared. The wizard had her right where he wanted her.

"You can either do this the easy way, or the hard way, it does not make any difference to me which you choose. In the end I always get what I want," he declared. Princess Ellyria had to use common sense, he was not going to be fooled as easily as Liza was, and he may not fall for seduction again either. She had to think fast and choose. That is it!

"I choose the easy way, Raul. Honestly, I did not even want these powers. I really want to be with my lover, as you called him. You can have my powers. What do I need to do to be rid of them once and for all?"

Raul could not believe what he was hearing, but he did not want to be overly excited about it.

"That pleases me. Now it does not have to get messy," he pulled out a vial. "Drink this, and you will be free of your powers forever."

"I am not quite up to speed on how this works, exactly," she said.

The wizard looked surprised, this should be common alchemy practice, had no one taught her anything?

"It is a power stripping potion. You drink it and your powers come out of you, then I stand here and wait for them to enter me, simple," he said matter-of-factly.

Princess Ellyria started to laugh hysterically.

"What is so funny?"

She did not answer him, just kept laughing. When she was finally able to refrain from laughter for a moment, she looked him in the eye.

"You expect me to drink this potion that will release my powers, into this cage you built to keep powers in?" She could not help from laughing once again.

Raul was vexed. She was right, he needed to get her out of the cage.

"Before I release you, know this, any funny business and I will simply kill you, to get your powers," he threatened.

Princess Ellyria nodded her head in agreement.

Raul unlocked the crystal cage door and stepped aside, when the Princess began to walk out, he grabbed her arm.

"Now drink," he said, handing her the clear vial.

She took it in her hand and looked at it. She watched the wizard, as he was standing in front of her, and waiting patiently for her to drink it. Just then one of his guards came running in and distracted the wizard. When he turned away from her, for a split second, it gave her a chance to switch the vials. After he came back to her, he motioned for her to drink it. She opened the vial in front of him and drank it down. He pulled her to him and kissed her to make sure she had swallowed it. She nearly vomited, and then slapped him across the face.

When he turned back to her, she was gone.

"You tricky, little girl! Where in the realm did you go?" he screamed.

Princess Ellyria laughed, and then realized she had the upper hand. She waved her invisible hand and hurled him to the ground.

"Whom are you referring to? It could not be me?" she asked, as she made a motion to pick him up off of the floor and throw him up against the wall.

Raul was now incredibly angry. Utilizing the power of the amulet, he created a protective force field around himself, and then summoned the element of water, to reveal to him where she was.

Princess Ellyria squealed, as she was drenched in the cold water. It still did not reverse her invisibility, but Raul was able to see her wet footprints that she had left behind. Once he was able to see where she was, he conjured a sandstorm. The sand was able to stick to the wet Princess, who was now choking from the sand, and then staggered to the stone floor rubbing her eyes.

Raul laughed, he had her where he wanted her now. He released the storm, and the remainder of the swirling sand fell to the floor. The wizard grabbed Princess Ellyria and calling upon the element of water, again hosed down the sand from her body. She was now visible, he had broken down her invisibility spell, and she stood there dripping wet before him.

Princess Ellyria backed up and sent the energy, from all of the anger she had absorbed from him, and then within her hands it manifested into an energy ball. She hurled it at him, knocking him back into the wall. She tried to make a run for it, but was pulled by him. With the amulet in his possession, she could not defeat him.

"Oh, Princess. When are you going to learn that I am more powerful than you? It is a joke really, that you are even called the Chosen One. Your powers are so weak in comparison to mine. So, give them up or die!" he shouted, as he pulled her closer to him, held up his hand, as he was slowly closing it into a fist.

Princess Ellyria screamed out in pain, as she fell to the floor in despair.

With a quick motion of his hand, he released her and pulled her to her feet, as he neared her.

"You see, my dear, I will always win," he said, before he began reaching into her chest for her heart…

Princess Ellyria sat up screaming, sweat drenched her body, and clutched her chest as though her heart had been ripped from it. She must have blacked out. Was she dead? Or was she alive? She looked around and found herself in a bed, that was not her own. She tried to get up, but discovered she was tied down, and tried to yell for help. Just then, Lord Brom came in.

"Oh, Ellyria, I have been so worried, that you would never awaken," he said, as he embraced her. He started to untie her bonds.

"What do you mean, you thought I would never wake up? Where are we?"

Lord Brom looked at her and placed his hand on hers.

"You had another one of your episodes. You started acting as if you had these powers, that you do not have again, and I had to restrain you. It was only for your protection. I see that you are all right now, so I can take them off," he said.

Her eyes skimmed her surroundings.

"Where are we?" she asked, feeling very confused.

He scrunched his brows and cocked his head to one side.

She could not feel anything from him or read his thoughts.

"Do you not recognize our home? You always talked about that little cottage in the woods, so that is where we are," he said reassuring her.

Princess Ellyria stood up from the bed and began to walk around the cottage. It looked familiar, but she just could not remember anything prior to her waking up. Then as she walked to the main living area, she saw a small boy.

"Brom, who is that boy?" she questioned, going to him, and he looked so familiar to her.

"Do you do not remember him?"

She shook her head no.

"That is our son," he said.

What happened to her? Why could she not remember anything? She started to sway and reached out for Lord Brom.

"Here, why do you not lie back down," he said, as he gently picked her up and carried her back to the bed.

After he laid her down, she looked up at him.

"Why do I not remember anything? I do not recall any of it? We have a house, a child, and I am guessing that we are married then too, right?"

He leaned down to kiss her, deeply, passionately. He closed the door after making sure the boy was occupied. He removed her clothes and began to ravage her body with kisses. She succumbed to his attack on her body, and she was helpless to resist him. His mouth covered every square inch of her body, and she returned his kisses, with a passion all her own. He quickly removed his clothes, from his magnificent body, and stood at the foot of the bed in front of her. He leaned down to crawl up the foot of the bed to hover over her, spreading her legs, as he rested his body between her thighs, and returned to her mouth to kiss her with ardent fervor. She arched her body into his, ready for him to enter her, but stopped and tried to delay him, from taking her right away. He grabbed her breasts and squeezed them in his hands, roughly taking her nipple into his mouth and bit it. She pushed him away and sat up in the bed.

"Are you alright? Do need some water, you look like you should drink something," he urged. He handed her a cup of water that was on a nearby table and tried to get her to drink it, but she waved it away.

"I am not thirsty. Why are you being so rough with me?"

He silenced her with kisses and tried to show her, that he would be gentle now. She laid back down as he nestled himself back between her legs. She could feel his excitement for her pressed up against her thigh, his hand reached between her legs rubbing her now, and probing her with his fingers. She kissed him deeper and arched her body into his, ready for him to take her. He plunged himself deep inside her, the full length of him penetrating her very core. She received him fully and wrapped her legs around his back. She closed her eyes at the pleasure of him inside of her, and wrapped her arms about his neck tighter. He began to thrust harder, and was to the point of release, when he began to laugh. She opened her eyes and it was not Lord Brom!

Princess Ellyria woke up screaming. She frantically looked all about her. This time she was in her bed, in her chambers. She was covered in sweat. Suddenly her door opened and her mother rushed to her side.

"Oh, Ellyria, you are alright," she cried, as she embraced her daughter. "We did not think you would ever wake up." Princess Ellyria wiped the tears from her eyes and tried to figure out what her mother was talking about.

"What do you mean, mother? How long have I been asleep?"

Her mother sat on the edge of her bed, and held her daughter's hand.

"Ellyria, you have been asleep now for two days," she explained.

She could not believe what she was saying. How could she have been asleep for so long? She got up from the bed, turned to say something to her mother, but then she was not there. She left her chamber to go downstairs. When she got to the bottom of the stairs, she fell to her knees. Everyone was dead, her parents, and her brothers. She could not believe it, she was just upstairs talking to her mother. What had happened? She pulled herself up from the floor and went outside to the courtyard. Everything was destroyed, the fountain, the stables, and the nearby field was on fire. She began to cry. What has happened? The doe from the field was now at her side.

"This is what will happen if you let the wizard take your powers. You are the Chosen One, my dear. You must rid yourself of your personal desires. You have not truly accepted who you are. You must embrace your destiny, or this is what the rest of the realm will look like if you do not," she said. Then the doe became Vadoma.

"How are you the doe? I thought you were dead?"

"When you die your spirit becomes one with nature, allowing me to come to you in a form that you can see and understand," she said.

Princess Ellyria had so many questions to ask.

"I do not understand. Why can I not be with Lord Brom? I love him and he loves me. Why can he not be with me through all of this? Why do I have to be the Chosen One?"

"You were the one foretold in the prophecy long before you were born, even before your mother was born. There is no one else that can defeat the wizard. You can not be with Lord Brom because he is a distraction to you and must have total focus in order to defeat the wizard. The wizard will use Lord Brom as a weapon against you, because he knows that he is your weakness. That is why he appears to you and changes his image into that of Lord Brom. I am not saying that you can not love him. Love will be your greatest power against Raul. In time, when you need him the most, he will return to you. Ellyria it will be up to you to defeat him, the fate of the entire realm depends on it," she said, as she began to fade away.

"No, wait! How am I to defeat him? He is so much stronger than I am, since he has the amulet. How do I get it back?" she pleaded.

"You must strengthen your powers, it is the only way. You must wake up now. Ellyria, time is of the essence," she said.

Then Vadoma faded away...

Princess Ellyria sat up in her bed. She felt herself all over, and looked around the room. Isis was in the floor and raised her head up.

"It is about time you woke up."

She looked at Isis strangely. Was she still dreaming?

"You are not asleep, and it is not a dream. You have been asleep for two days now. Your mother has been worried sick and has been checking up on you practically every thirty minutes. She is due to come in soon, so you have to listen."

"Wait, I thought I would not be getting this power yet?"

"You have not, just yet. Vadoma could not remain in your dream long, so she is channeling through me. Raul is going to try and take your powers, no matter what, do not let him. It will be better for you to develop your powers, before you try to go after him. It is the only way. This will be the last time that I can help you. You will be on your own now. I was sent to help you find the path again, to your destiny, now that you know what you must do, there is no turning back. You are the Chosen One, Ellyria, find your strength, and defeat the wizard." Isis rubbed her ears with her paws and rolled over on her back, before she lay back down.

"Vadoma?"

She was gone.

Just then her mother entered her room.

"Oh. I am so glad that you are awake. You had us all scared. You know you were asleep for two days? I even sent for your nanny to try and see what she could do, then I called for your brother, Dakota, and he was helpless to wake you. Now here you are finally awake," she said, as she embraced her.

"I will run down and get you something to eat and be right back."

She watched her mother leave the room.

Princess Ellyria got up from her bed and walked over to the window. She looked out into the grassy field, and looked at the beautiful majestic mountains, they were a natural perfection. She would see to it that they remain as they are, perfect and untouched.

Later on, that day, Princess Ellyria went to enjoy time with Isis at the fountain, to play in the cool, refreshing water…

Chapter 50

Princess Ellyria Rose was dripping wet from playing in the fountain with Isis. As she opened the door from the courtyard, she found a not- so -pleased Nan standing just inside the doorway. Princess Ellyria walked past her nanny, ignoring the disappointed look on her face, as she entered the great hall.

"What have I told you, young lady, about romping in the fountain?" Nan asked, chastising the girl for her unladylike tendencies.

"I do not know exactly. Why do you not tell me again?" she said, with sarcasm in her voice. She was so tired of being chastised by her nanny. It was like the old woman had nothing better to do with her spare time.

"Well you had better start thinking about it, and act like the young lady you are, a Princess in fact," Nan scolded. Nan looked down at the puddle on the floor she had just finished scrubbing, then looked back to the besotted girl before her.

Princess Ellyria just stared back at her with a scowl on her face.

"I am so sorry, it will not happen again, she smirked. I will try to conform to my duty and station." Placing a hand on her hip, she looked down at the help. "Now I order you to clean up this mess. I will be in my chambers, if anyone needs me," she said regally, enjoying the shocked looked upon Nan's face.

"Princess Ellyria Rose!" Nan said, crying. "You dishonor your family as well as yourself, in treating me so. You should be ashamed of yourself. I only say what I do, for your own good. Furthermore, I deserve a little more respect than that. After all, I did help in your upbringing."

Princess Ellyria felt horrible. That had not been her just now. Who was that girl anyway? She had never been so brazen before, but now all that had changed. She was not the same, she left that girl behind. She embraced the woman, who had always been there for her.

"I do apologize, Nan, I do not know, what came over me just then. It must be from all the stress, over the last several weeks, that is making me a little temperamental."

"It is alright, dear. Now go upstairs to your chambers and change out of those wet clothes straight away, before you catch yourself a cold. I am going to have to go change myself now," Nan replied with a smile.

As Princess Ellyria turned around and began to walk away, Nan called out and motioned for her to come back.

"Make haste dear, before your mother finds you in your present appearance, and take heed to not disturb your father. He is in his study working," the nanny warned.

The Princess nodded, waved her hand in understanding, and went on upstairs to her chambers.

After placing her wet dress over her changing screen, so it could be laundered later, Princess Ellyria slipped into her favorite cream-colored silk dress. Now that she was warm and dry, she proceeded to comb out her near waist length black hair.

Princess Ellyria sat in front of the big mirror on her vanity, that she always peered into when she was thinking. The reflection in the mirror changed before her eyes, shifting from her, to visions of a certain handsome young man who had helped save her life, and the frightened young girl she used to be. As her memories came flooding back to her, so did some of the nightmares she had thought she had left behind. Why could her memories not be pleasant ones? She paused for a moment, and then picked up one of her favorite books on her vanity and opened it up to the first page.

"When did someone get the idea that a princess's life was really like a fairytale?" she asked Isis.

Isis looked up at her from her bed by the fire, and laid her head back down closing her eyes.

Looking back to the careworn pages of the book, she read the first sentence out loud as, if Isis were listening.

"Once upon a time," she paused, "who writes this stuff anyway?" She flipped to the back of the book and read the last sentence aloud. "And they lived happily ever after." Even though it was her favorite book, it made no sense to her, and there were not any comparisons to her own life.

Placing her book down on the edge of the vanity, she looked back at the mirror, as visions from the past emerged in the glass...

Princess Ellyria Rose believed that if her story were ever told, it would not have ended with happily ever after...

About the Author

Rose Marie Machario is the creator and hostess of Dream Big. A show all about real people who are making their dreams come true.

When Rose is not inspiring others to follow their dreams, she is a nationally and internationally published pinup model, and a blossoming actress having worked in several featured, or principal roles. She has been seen in various television shows such as Ozark, The Originals, Nashville, Homicide Hunter, Killer Couples, Murder Chose Me, Murder Comes to Town, Snapped, #Murder, Justice by Any Means, Notorious, Fatal Attraction, Murder Mystery, Murder Decoded, and American Nightmare. Her movie credits include Tag, Super Fly, The Road Less Traveled, and The Last Movie Star.

Rose is also a published author of her debut fantasy novel, The Amulet of Elements. She also writes in the romance, and horror genres, and her column called Dream Big.

In her spare time she enjoys a daily routine of yoga, loves to cook, and cuddling up with her fur-babies while watching her favorite television shows, and movies.

www.ingramcontent.com/pod-product-compliance
Lightning Source LLC
Chambersburg PA
CBHW030643020726
47493CB00006B/1849